SHIELD AND VILE SERPENTS

ENERGY OF MAGIC
BOOK FIVE

J.E. NEAL

To those who believed in the magic from the very beginning

CONTENTS

CHAPTER I

SONS OF DIAPOLEY

After spending the weekend moping around the house and trying to stay out of Logan and Adeline's way, Rainer was thankful to fall into his desk chair Monday morning. No one deserved to be privy to his irritated mood.

"Good morning, sunshine," Logan chirped just to annoy him.

"Bite me," Rainer growled.

"Geez, she's only been gone three days. You can't be that stiff yet."

It was so much more than being mildly sexually frustrated. Rainer missed talking to her, seeing her smile, feeling her sleep beside him, and hearing her laugh. Three and a half weeks sounded like a lifetime to him at that moment.

He narrowed his eyes at Logan and threw his hands in the air. "I miss her, okay? I miss everything about her, not just that. So, could you just shut it, please?" He was thankful that no one else was in the office yet.

"Okay, okay, I get it. I'm sorry for trying to get you to quit acting like a prick." Logan rolled his eyes and glanced around his desk for something to do.

"I'm sorry." He knew that the assessment was fair. Logan's scowl let Rainer know it was going to take more than an apology.

Before Rainer could continue his lamentations, Vindico breezed through and ordered them to meet him in his office.

"I'm sorry. I've been an ass." Rainer sighed as they stood and followed Vindico's path.

"Whatever." Logan wasn't letting him off the hook.

Vindico was pacing. He still looked exhausted. His eyes were spinning slightly. He'd come from the weight room, and it appeared he'd been lifting for hours.

"All right," Vindico began as soon as Logan closed the door behind him. "I'm still not certain this is even a problem for Iodex, but it could certainly become a problem for us if I don't come up with a solution."

"What exactly is the problem?" Logan asked.

Rainer noted that Vindico seemed distracted. It was extremely odd. Dan Vindico was never distracted. He was the youngest appointed Chief of Elite Iodex in the history of the American Realm. His sheer size, mass, and determination made him appear immovable. Everything about him was chiseled and hard, but this morning something was different.

Rainer's mind moved back over the events of Friday evening. He supposed that brutally killing your deceased fiancée's rapist would shake anyone.

He edged forward. He wanted to help with whatever was going on. Vindico drew a deep breath. Defeat etched the chiseled features of his face. His overly muscled body seemed to have given up some of its fire.

"Chancellor Wilshire and the Venton governors have been calling me all weekend. It seems Candor Pendergrath's son, Clarence," he spat the name with disdain, "is quite a handful." Vindico rolled his eyes. "He's been accused of several counts of harassment, and the chancellor and the academy governors want to expel him, but he's barely sixteen. He's a minor, and he has no other living relatives, save his *father*. Pendergrath murdered Clarence's mother right after he was born. She knew too much, and he wanted an heir to raise up in his footsteps. After Clarence was born, she was no longer necessary."

Silence loomed for a few seconds before Vindico continued. "Anyway, Wretchkinsides has appealed to the Russian government to release Pendergrath early should his son be expelled. I only managed to get Pendergrath on tax evasion and fraud." He glanced at Rainer. "The Russian government has agreed to rehear Pendergrath's trial should Clarence be forced out of Venton."

"Okay, what can we do?" Logan asked.

Vindico leaned forward and placed his arms on his desk.

"Now that we have a new Crown Governor, and I feel like the security teams I've hired to make certain your parents and younger brothers are always safe, Elite Iodex is going to get back to taking down Wretchkinsides and the Interfeci for good. The rest of the team and I are going to be working to try to find more substantial evidence of Pendergrath's heinous crimes to see if we can't keep him in Diapoley for the rest of his life. It took me two years to prove tax evasion and fraud beyond a shadow of a doubt, so we have our work cut out for us. Nevertheless, Pendergrath's release from Diapoley is exactly what Wretchkinsides has been waiting for. He'll bribe most of the Russian board of governors, I'm certain. So, whatever we find has to be damning."

Diapoley was a Gifted reformatory in Belgorod. The prison was surrounded by heavy deposits of iron ore, just like Felsink, but it sat in a unique field of magnetic energy. Diapoley was known to cause Gifted criminals to go insane if left in the prison too long. Realms around the world had begged Russia to build their prison somewhere else to no avail.

"Wretchkinsides and Pendergrath are an extremely dangerous combination." Vindico shuddered.

"What do you need us to do?" Rainer restated Logan's question.

Vindico grimaced and offered him a sorrowful glance. "What I would like you to do isn't exactly what Iodex typically takes care of. I was hoping you'd agree to spend some time at the academy, keep an eye on Clarence, and maybe scare him a little. Don't touch him. Basically, I just need Clarence to stay in the academy and for Wilshire and Sherman to get off my back. They informed me that if I wanted Clarence to stay at Venton, then I could provide them a little help. I know you spent most of your dad's campaign babysitting, but if you two are willing to keep tabs on Clarence during school, and then come back here and pull a few later hours for the next few weeks, I'll be happy to give you a few days off when Miss Haydenshire returns from Brazil."

"I think I'd better leave that up to my partner. I've kind of been an asshole the past few days," Rainer admitted.

Logan laughed. "Yeah, it's fine. Adeline's got a study group for her oral boards at the end of the month, but maybe I could convince her to go somewhere with me when Em gets back."

Rainer immediately thanked him.

"What kind of crap has the kid been pulling?" Logan quizzed.

"So far, he's stolen Mentor Durtrox's Cadillac. He used his own energy for a joy ride." Vindico was trying not to laugh. Rainer and Logan cracked up.

"Aww, do we really have to scare him? I think he may be my new hero," Logan joked.

Vindico finally chuckled with a knowing nod. "If that were it, I might take the kid out for a beer, but he's been harassing other students. One in particular, a uh…"—he searched through some paperwork on his desk until he located a notepad and flipped to the third page—"Tilly McIntyre? One of the mentor aides has filed several complaints on her behalf, as have a few of the mentors. It's getting out of hand. If we don't do something, they're going to have to expel him."

Logan and Rainer shared a quick, ominous glance. They didn't have to guess which aide had been filing complaints.

Rainer squeezed his eyes shut for a moment. *Fergus, what did you do, you moron?*

The answer seemed obvious. Perhaps Logan and Rainer's idiotic sidekick from the academy hadn't hidden the fact that he was dating a student all that well.

"Clarence has also been accused of attempting to set fire to the female Receivers' dormitories. He's getting more and more violent." Vindico sounded extremely concerned as Logan and Rainer nodded their understanding. "Like I said, we can't touch him. If you catch him in the act of harassment or destruction, you can arrest him, but he's a minor."

"We'll take care of it." Rainer let the annoyance wash through him.

It appeared that he and Logan were going to come to Fergus's rescue yet again.

"Don't forget your dad's swearing-in ceremony. Full uniform, here in the chamber, seven o'clock sharp," Vindico reminded them.

"We'll be here for that too." Logan chuckled at the idea that he would forget his own father's inauguration to officially become the Crown Governor of the American Gifted Realm.

It had been a long, hard-fought battle, but for once, good had triumphed. The Realm had been kept from the clutches of Wretchkinsides. The battle had been won, but no one believed the war was over.

Rainer hated that Emily was going to miss her dad's swearing-in. He hated that he was going to go watch the very process his own father had fought and died for without her. He missed his dad so much more when she wasn't there.

Rainer recalled sitting in the chamber room just after his fourteenth birthday. Peace and contentment settled on him from the memory alone. He'd seated himself on one of the observer benches in the grand courtroom. He would cup his hand and watch as his own shielding energies formed their incandescent green glow.

His shield had become accessible to him as soon as he'd finished puberty, just like all Gifted children. Though he'd been instructed not to, he couldn't help but play with his new abilities.

With the slight movement of his hand, he could cast his shield over his own body or outwards. He and Logan had been playing with them for weeks. They'd used their shields to throw each other to the ground several times.

Governor Haydenshire and Governor Lawson had asked them to find something else to do when Logan had ended up with a black eye, and Rainer had landed against the trunk of a massive oak tree on the Haydenshires' farm. He smiled as he recalled the shock of the air in his lungs escaping in a sharp gasp from the hit.

Since it was summer, their fathers had decided to bring them into work with them to prevent any further injury. Rainer had always suspected that Mrs. Haydenshire requested the reprieve.

They'd been allowed to watch Vindico and the rest of Iodex at work. Both Ioses Predilects, Logan and Rainer longed to be chosen to serve on the Elite task force when they were grown.

That day in the chamber, his father was seated in the center of the governing board. Logan and Emily's dad was to his right. Governor Carrington and Governor Vindico were to his left. They were all men Rainer trusted and loved. They'd all had a hand in his raising. The knowledge that they were the men running the Realm made him feel secure and safe.

His father had been assassinated a few months later. A haunting chill replaced the warm memory. Rainer shook himself. He wasn't a kid anymore. It was his job now to protect all that his dad had given the Realm, and he wouldn't let him down.

CHAPTER 2

IN THE MIND'S VAULT

An hour later, Rainer pulled one of the Expeditions onto Venton Drive and let his eyes sweep over the vast campus. Venton was definitely most picturesque in the fall.

As he stared at the noble, brown brick buildings and the well-landscaped lawns, with stone benches where he'd stolen more than a few kisses, his heart ached. Being at Venton without Emily only further depressed him.

He could taste her lush, full lips as he stared at one of their favorite make-out locales. His tongue thirsted for the flavors of her. His heart thundered as he swallowed down the need and slid out of the Expedition.

"Well, well, well." Logan pointed to the administration building. At that moment, Clarence Pendergrath was looking around suspiciously as he slipped inside.

Rainer chuckled and threw himself into the job at hand. "Wanna have some fun?" He grinned at Logan.

"Finally, you're back." Logan opened the doors, and they slipped quickly into the admin building.

Rainer pointed to Clarence, who was very carefully attempting to pick the lock on one of the Venton Academy test vaults. It stood in the rear corner of the building.

Rainer and Logan eased along the wall. They watched Clarence attempt to summon to get the magnetic pulses of the vault in the correct order. He would glance around nervously, and then continue to try to unlock the keys to all of the mentors' exams.

With whispered chuckles, Rainer and Logan watched him work. Clearly, Clarence wasn't aware that the vaults only opened to certain energy sequences done in frequency and in order. Frustration set in as he continued his futile endeavor.

After several long minutes, Logan spun from his hiding spot adjacent to the vault hall. "Clarence!" he called loudly. "There you are! We've been looking for you everywhere, man. What are you doing?" He flipped his wrist and tapped his watch. "Pretty sure you're supposed to be in Durtrox's class now, aren't you?"

Rainer tsked as they stalked quickly toward a wide-eyed Clarence Pendergrath. "He probably just got lost on his way to class, Officer Haydenshire." He feigned pity.

They watched Clarence's mouth drop open and his eyes goggle. "Who are you?"

"We're your escorts, buddy. Don't worry, we're gonna take good care of you," Logan informed Clarence with a heavy smirk. "Why don't we escort you to class, and then maybe sit in there and make sure you don't suddenly decide to go wandering around campus again? We don't want our little buddy to get lonely."

"Hey, man, this is a great idea," Clarence changed his tactic. "I heard some other kids took some of the test copies, but they're not entrepreneurs. If you get me in these vaults, I'll copy the answer keys and sell them all over campus. I'll cut you in. Cops can't make that much. Just think of it as a little side money."

Logan stared at Clarence in rapt disbelief.

Rainer shook his head. "Wow! Daddy must be so proud. You're following right in his footsteps. Maybe we could get you a double cell in Diapoley." Rainer jerked Clarence forward by the collar of his shirt, spun him, and led him out of the building.

Clarence spluttered all the way into the history building.

"Aren't you Rainer Lawson?" He spun toward Logan. "Isn't your dad the new Crown? Why are you bugging me?"

"Don't think of it as us bugging you," Rainer mocked. "Think of us as saving you from yourself."

"What are you two doing here?" Mentor Durtrox looked none too enthused as Logan and Rainer entered her class.

"Aww, we missed you too," Logan sneered. Rainer ignored her obvious disappointment and gestured to Clarence.

"Found one of your students lost in the admin building. We just thought we'd help him find his way back to class," Rainer informed her kindly.

Clarence scowled as Rainer forced him into the room. Mentor Durtrox shooed Clarence toward an empty desk.

"We'll just stand here in the hall and make sure Clarence doesn't wander away again." Logan raised his eyebrow at Clarence in an obvious threat.

"Yes, fine." Mentor Durtrox shut the door in Logan's face before resuming her droning lecture.

"I kept telling myself last year that if I just got through here, graduated, and got hired on at Iodex, I'd never have to sit through one of her classes again," Logan whimpered.

Rainer gave him a wry grin. "Can you believe that kid? He's only a sub-freshman." He was still shocked that Clarence had thought quickly enough to offer to cut them in on his answer-key-selling plans.

"His dad is Wretchkinsides's money man. He killed his own wife. I'm not thinking the prospect for our boy Clarence there was ever very good."

Rainer wondered how long it would be before they would be arresting Clarence. He'd be an adult in the Realm in just a few years' time.

A few minutes later, Fergus marched by looking furious.

Logan rolled his eyes. "And there's the source of this disaster." He'd clearly come to the same conclusion Rainer had in Vindico's office. "Fergus!"

Fergus hadn't even noticed them standing in the corridor. He spun and gave Logan and Rainer a shocked smile as he furrowed his brow. The anger seemed to melt some of his awkwardness from his features.

"What are you doing here?"

"Clarence Pendergrath." Rainer watched Fergus closely to gauge his reaction.

"Is he being arrested?" Fergus asked hopefully.

"No, he's a minor. We're just here to keep an eye on him. We're trying to keep the academy from suspending him."

"Oh." Fergus's face fell as he nodded dejectedly.

"We heard Clarence has been giving some of the girls a hard time." Rainer shared a quick glance with Logan.

"Not some, just one."

"Why her?" Logan asked.

Fergus glanced up and down the hallway. "My office is right in there." He pointed to a closet-sized room farther down the corridor. "Wanna see it?"

"Why not." Rainer glanced at his watch. It was another half hour before lunch, so Clarence would be stuck in class a while longer. He was fairly certain he wouldn't venture an escape from Durtrox. They followed Fergus down the all-too-familiar hallway.

Rainer glanced out one of the windows and wondered if the biting pain would ever lessen its grip. The history building overlooked Ioses House, and there, on the lawn, stood the large statue of his father. He kept watch over the Academy. The eternal flame burned in the courtyard nearby. Ioses Predilects, like Rainer and his father, were supposed to keep the fire burning, work for what was right, and protect the innocent from being consumed. Rainer's name was inscribed on one of the many flat stones surrounding the base of the statue. Every head of Ioses Order's name was on the stones. It was a sacred tradition.

Rainer shook himself and followed Logan into Fergus's office. Fergus shut the door and spun back. He looked sick.

"What's going on?" Rainer sighed.

"I screwed up." He sank down into the seat behind his desk. The room was small with hardly enough room for Fergus's aged desk and chair. Logan and Rainer stood side by side in the cramped space and waited on him to continue.

"Screwed up, how?" Logan prompted.

"Clarence is a monster. He's in one of my entry-level science classes, and he's always cutting up in class or not turning in his assignments. Anyway, he's forever in detention with some mentor, and I accidentally double-booked him with one of my, uh...tutoring sessions."

Logan rubbed his temples. "I'm guessing this particular tutoring session was with Tilly?"

Fergus nodded. "Anyway, he was about fifteen minutes late to detention. Like I said, I'd forgotten I'd even given him detention, so he's pretty sure he saw something he shouldn't have."

"What exactly didn't he see?" Rainer tried to determine the level of damage control this was going to take.

Fergus grimaced as they awaited his answer. "Everyone was dressed. We haven't done *that* yet." Fergus appeared simultaneously embarrassed and terrified.

"Yeah, well, I wouldn't. Not here on campus, ever," Rainer ordered.

"I know. I wouldn't do that, and I know I shouldn't be seeing her, but I swear she's the one. I know I was a total screwup growing up and that you guys bailed me out more than I care to remember, but I would do anything for her. I'm really"—he drew a deep, steadying breath before concluding—"I'm really in love with her."

In that moment, it appeared that Fergus might've grown up as well. He wasn't the kid everyone had picked on. He seemed much more confident and sure of himself.

"So, Clarence saw you..." Logan drawled, "...kissing?"

Fergus nodded his agreement. "He thinks he did, so now he's trying to prove it." His pain over the situation was evident in his tone.

"Prove it how?" Rainer quizzed.

"By harassing her constantly. He's hoping I'll come to her defense and prove that we're seeing each other, thereby getting me fired." He shook his head in utter disbelief.

As all of the puzzle pieces clicked into place, it was just as Rainer had suspected. It was also a disaster. If Fergus defended Tilly, he would lose his job and be leaving Tilly alone at Venton unprotected from the likes of Clarence.

"Tilly's filed several complaints with my mom and the chancellor, but for some reason they won't expel him." Fergus was clearly hoping Logan and Rainer would fill him in on the reasoning behind the lack of discipline shown to Clarence. Normally, if someone was harassing another student, they were readily expelled. Venton didn't put up with shit like that.

Logan grimaced. "Yeah, we can't really go into all that."

"Yeah, I figured."

"But, we *are* here to keep Clarence from being such a prick," Rainer offered hopefully.

"I guess that's better than nothing."

"We'll do what we can," Logan vowed.

They spent the rest of the day making certain that Clarence went to all of his classes, and that he didn't make anyone's life miserable, until they deposited him in his dorm and headed back to the Senate.

They worked for several hours on all of the evidence Vindico had collected over the past ten years on Pendergrath. They were both disgusted as they read just some of the crimes he was suspected of committing.

At seven o'clock, they both stood in full uniform beside every other Iodex officer, the entire Senteon, the heads of every Predilect department, and the Senate bank employees to watch Governor Haydenshire vow to uphold the constitution, to do good even when it's not easy, and to protect those who struggled to protect themselves. Immense pride filled Rainer's shield. Logan stared up at his father in awe. Rainer was truly honored to serve the man who'd raised him.

Riddled with both deep respect and exhaustion, they headed home a little after nine.

Logan had ridden into the office with Rainer so Adeline could use the Accord. He was thrilled to see it parked in the garage when Rainer pulled in.

Rainer smiled as he watched Logan sprint into the house. He grabbed his phone as he heard the text chirp. After reading Emily's text, Rainer replied:

Fionna and I helped the girls with their schoolwork and then it was their night to use the one bath with running water here in the orphanage. We helped them with that and just got them to bed. This place is so awful. It just kills me that they have to live here. I want to bring them all home with me.

Rainer could almost hear the desperation in her typed response.

I read to Aida tonight, which she loved, so that was fun. She's just so sweet.

Aida was a little girl in Emily and Fionna's group that they'd both fallen head over heels for. The way Emily went on and on about how sweet she was made Rainer want to be there with her all the more.

He wanted to meet the kids she was helping.

CHAPTER 3

REPERCUSSIONS

Wednesday, Rainer and Logan headed back for another day with Clarence at the Academy. Rainer's nerves were frayed before he'd ever gotten up that morning.

Emily had called him in the middle of the night from the bathroom in the orphanage. She was in tears. She loved working with the kids, Aida especially, but being in a place so full of desperation was wearing her out.

Her ability to feel what each of the kids was feeling was so strong it broke her heart. She could feel the fear, sadness, and loneliness in all of the children she was working with.

On top of all of that, Garrett had arrived Monday morning, and he and Chloe had been driving the other Angels crazy. It had taken every ounce of Rainer's resolve not to get in his car, drive to the airport in the middle of the night, and purchase a ticket on the next Gifted flight to Rio.

Vindico wanted them to keep their presence unknown, as much as they were able, on this particular day. He wanted to see what Clarence might do if he thought his guards had taken the day off.

Logan studied Rainer. "Is Em okay? I heard your cell ring in the middle of the night."

"Not really." He hoped Emily wouldn't mind him talking to Logan.

With a concerned nod, Logan waited for him to continue. "It's just hard for her. She feels everything every one of those kids feels, and she's really taken with this one little girl. Emily's casted her a few times when she was upset, so now, if Aida is sad or hungry, Emily feels it even more strongly. Plus she's so worried about your mom and the baby."

"Yeah, I figured that would happen. Em's always been like that, you know? She's tough, but sometimes I can tell everything just gets to her."

Rainer momentarily wondered how Fionna Styler was coping. She was a vastly more powerful Receiver than Emily. She was supposed to be the most powerful Receiver of their generation.

He assumed that since Fionna was nine years older than Emily she had a little more control over her powers and a lot more perspective. Everything Emily had sobbed over the phone the night before tumbled through his mind again.

He pulled the binoculars from the center console and watched the students change classes. Clarence moved from the sciences building to the arts and literature building just as he was supposed to, though he scowled the entire way. Satisfied that he was at least in the correct building, Rainer lowered the binoculars.

"Apparently, Chloe and Garrett have been fighting ever since he arrived. I'm not so sure Chloe is as okay with not being exclusive as Garrett is."

"I have no idea how my brother can be with her one night, then call up Heather the next, then somebody else the next, and know that she's calling up some other guy. I just don't get it." Logan shook his head. "He's a Shield. That's not what we're supposed to do."

Rainer considered. "Yeah, but he's not *her* Shield. He doesn't have that attachment to Chloe or any of the other women he bangs."

"Are we gonna make our presence known at lunch?" Logan glanced at his watch. He was apparently already thinking of eating.

"Yeah, that's what Vindico wanted."

∼

A short while later, they wandered into the dining hall without any enthusiasm. They returned a wave to Jeff Strenton and Becca Sapman who were obviously still together. They'd paused from their kissing to wave, share pizza, and sip from a shared Dr Pepper.

Eating in the academy dining hall wasn't something either Logan or Rainer ever really planned on doing again. Mrs. Berbera, the woman who'd run the academy cafeteria since she'd graduated as head of Occamy Order in the eighties, was very kind and certainly could provide food to the masses, but it was still cafeteria food. The lack of choices served on the yellow melamine trays did nothing to pique either Logan or Rainer's interest.

They moved through the line just ahead of the students who poured into the building. They carried their trays of beef stroganoff to the far corner table where they'd always sat as students.

Had Emily, Connor, Adeline, and Fergus been with them, it would have been just like any normal school day. The pain of missing Emily seared through him once again.

Fergus waved to them but didn't join their table. He moved to sit with the other science mentors. From their vantage point, Logan and Rainer took in Tilly talking with her friends as they seated themselves at a table very close by.

Rainer was impressed. Fergus and Tilly never even exchanged a glance with one another.

"Where's Clarence?" Logan began shoveling the stroganoff into his mouth. After he studied the room, Rainer shrugged.

Several minutes later, Clarence entered the cafeteria. He looked mutinous.

"Here we go," Logan warned. They watched Clarence search the room until his eyes landed on Tilly. He began to laugh derisively as he took in Fergus's nearby proximity.

"Ah geez." Rainer spun to watch Clarence saunter toward Tilly like a hawk circling his prey. Tilly cringed and scooted nearer her friends at the table. Rainer's blood ran hot as he took in Clarence's vindictive scowl.

"If he touches her, I'm arresting him," Logan stated firmly.

"Agreed."

They kept a keen eye trained on Clarence as he made his approach. "So, Tilly…" he drawled her name pompously. "Where's Professor Boyfriend? Did he leave you all alone? Never know what might happen to girls who are left unprotected."

Logan's jaw clenched as he shook his head. "I wish she'd backhand him."

"She wouldn't need anyone to protect her if he wasn't such an asshole." Rainer narrowed his eyes and drew a sip of his Dr Pepper. They watched closely.

Her friends didn't seem as frightened of him as Tilly appeared to be, and they defended her.

"Why do you keep saying that to her? She's not dating anyone. Leave her alone. You're such a prick."

Clarence gave off another derisive laugh and grabbed the back of one of the girls' shirts. "Then why don't you tell me why she won't go to the Fall Ball with me?"

She jerked away from him, and Rainer saw Logan's eyes flash dangerously. He shook his head.

"Probably because you're an asshole." She pretended to wipe his fingerprints off her clothing.

Clarence laughed. He didn't seem to mind her assessment.

"Yeah, well, I don't think that's it. I'll bet Professor Boyfriend is in here,"—Clarence shot Fergus a goading smirk—"somewhere, keeping an eye on his favorite student. Now, what would make him come out and play?" His sarcastic drawl made Rainer want to wrap his hands around Clarence's throat, but he kept watch and didn't make a move. If he'd learned anything from his months of intense training with Vindico, it was that patience is key when you're waiting to strike.

"So, Tilly," Clarence sneered, "got a hot tutoring session coming up? You let Professor Boyfriend tap that, or you taking things slow? Does he even know how?"

Tears rimmed Tilly's eyes. "Leave me alone, Clarence," shook from her mouth, but she didn't have much volume.

With a quick move, he slid into the seat beside Tilly and placed his hand on her thigh.

"Wonder how high I'll have to reach before Professor Boyfriend comes to your rescue," he jeered as he slid his hand up Tilly's thigh until he pushed it under the hem of her skirt.

Logan and Rainer were out of their seats, and Logan had Clarence by the collar of his shirt and out of the booth in a second flat.

"I believe the lady asked you to leave her alone, you fucking asshole!" In one quick move, Logan spun Clarence, who was almost a foot shorter and had no muscle tone to speak of, up against a wall and had him cuffed.

The entire cafeteria applauded as Logan and Rainer led Clarence out of the building. They threw him in the back of the Expedition.

"You can't arrest me," Clarence taunted. "I'm a minor. I'll tell Uncle Nic. He'll tell my dad."

Rainer nodded. "Good, and when Daddy finally gets out of Diapoley, if he still has any freaking clue who you are, you let me know what he has to say about it."

"And you can tell Uncle Nic all of Iodex says fuck off." Logan jerked the Expedition into reverse and flew out of the parking lot.

Although Vindico wasn't happy about their arrest, he agreed with their reasoning as he sealed Clarence in one of the holding cells and told him to pipe down.

At five o'clock, he received a certified letter from the Russian government that had him mutinous. It seemed Wretchkinsides had managed to bribe enough people in the Russian Senate and prison board, and they'd agreed to hold another trial for Pendergrath.

Their prisons were overcrowded, and he'd only been arrested for white-collar crimes. Vindico was to appear at the trial in Moscow in just over two weeks' time. The long strings of curse words that flew from his mouth were volatile in their doggedness alone. Rainer was oddly impressed, but he had no idea what to say or do to make this easier on his boss.

"Can Dad do anything?" Logan suggested hopefully after Vindico's long rant.

"No," he spat, "and I have exactly two weeks to come up with something more substantial than tax evasion and fraud to nail Pendergrath with, so that's what we're going to do." He eyed Rainer speculatively. Rainer's brow furrowed but he had no idea why his boss was looking at him like that.

~

Ultimately, it was up to Governor Haydenshire, as the new Crown, to determine how long Clarence could be held as a minor. The charges weren't substantial enough to warrant a trial, and Tilly hadn't wanted to appear before the governing board for fear that they would ask her under oath if she was seeing a mentor at Venton.

The fact that Clarence had sexually harassed Tilly did not sit well with a man like Governor Haydenshire. He, just like all of his sons, was fiercely protective.

The governor ordered him to spend a week in the low security cells at Felsink. He'd told Vindico that he was sorry, but if anything like that happened again, Clarence would have to be suspended from the academy. Though he didn't want to agree, Dan really had no other choice.

While Clarence was locked up, Logan and Rainer threw themselves into finding evidence to link the crimes Pendergrath had committed back to him. The work was rather tedious.

At ten o'clock Friday morning, Rainer was poring over several confessions from murderers who had no recollection of actually committing the crimes they'd been convinced to confess to.

There was one man who'd killed his own wife and children under Wretchkinsides's mind-cast. He'd owed Pendergrath a great deal of money. Normally, a person couldn't be casted to do such a heinous thing, but the man had been using heroin, and his mind had been easy for Wretchkinsides to manipulate. Drugs were far worse for Gifted people than they were Non-Gifted.

Rainer wanted to vomit as he shook his head and moved onto the next document on his desk. His cell phone rang. He glanced at the screen, and his heart halted and then flew. It was Garrett, and a million horrifying thoughts raced through Rainer's mind as he answered the call.

CHAPTER 4
I'LL BE THERE

"What's wrong? Is Emily hurt?" he demanded.

"Damn," Garrett gasped. "Calm down. She's not hurt."

Rainer allowed himself to breathe as he waited to hear the reason for Garrett's call.

"Listen though, you may have been right. This may not have been a great year for Em to come down here. She's having a rough time."

Rainer's heart fractured as he tried to think of some way to help her. "I can come get her," fell from his mouth in a desperate plea.

"No, you can't. Not if she wants her contract renewed to challenge for the Angels next year," Garrett reminded. "Just listen for a minute."

Rainer tried to draw a steadying breath but found it difficult. His lungs seemed to seize and tighten of their own accord.

"I took Chloe out last night. We stayed in a hotel. Spent a little time reconnecting."

Rainer rolled his eyes. He couldn't care less what Garrett and Chloe had done the night before. He needed to know that Emily was all right.

"Dana and Carys and a couple of the other ladies were teasing Em about you. You know, shit like telling her that she should screw a few other guys before she decides that you're the one or whatever." Garrett chuckled, but Rainer ground his teeth.

"They're just jealous. They didn't mean to hurt her feelings. She's just been really sensitive lately, and I don't think she's sleeping all that well. She also isn't eating. She's lost weight. She keeps giving all of her food to the kids. I don't think she's had a full meal all week. Fi tried to talk to her, and she even casted her, but Emily wouldn't really let her in.

"I tried to get her to draw from me this morning, but she couldn't. She's really weak. I think it's gonna have to be you, man. I guess I didn't really think about how much shit she'd been through before she got out here. Being with the kids here and listening to their stories, it's rough. She's just not dealing."

"How is it going to be me? You just told me I couldn't come get her."

"All right, calm down. Geez, you two really can't make it without each other, can you? Just listen."

Rainer assumed that his fury must be evident even over the phone.

"You can't come get her, and you sure as hell can't show up here at the orphanage, but I can get her out of here for a night just like I did Chloe last night." He stated the first thing that made Rainer feel any hope at all.

"The catch is going to be getting you out of the country unnoticed. If any of the owners find out you came down here to see her, she could get fired, and you're Rainer Lawson. Do you think you can manage to get to Rio without a media circus?"

"If Emily needs me, I'll move hell and high water," Rainer vowed.

"Yeah, I had a feeling. All right, get a private flight to Rio. I'd try for late tonight. Seems like that might get you out with a little less notice. Book a suite at the Copacabana Palace. Obviously, don't use your name. It's downtown. Nice place.

"I'll get her to you tomorrow afternoon. It might be late, depending on what they're supposed to be doing with the orphans tomorrow. Just do whatever it is you do that makes my little sister's world right because she's coming unglued. I'm worried about her."

"I'll be there."

"Listen, you might need to pack her some clothes because she won't be able to bring anything from the orphanage. She also probably won't shower so..."

"I'll see you tomorrow."

Rainer's heart raced as his mind reeled. Everything about the next few days was going to be entirely different from what he'd thought it would be just moments before. He was going to get to see Emily. He let the realization flood through him in a mixture of elation and deep concern.

If Garrett was calling and arranging to get Emily out of the orphanage, then she was worse than Rainer had realized. He wondered what Emily had done that finally made Garrett call in reinforcements.

The fact that she hadn't even drawn from her brother's substantial shielding energy made Rainer's stomach churn uncomfortably.

Dana and Carys's teasing was certainly part of it. The ability to feel deeply, and the energy needed to have the level of empathy that Receivers were known for, generally meant that they didn't pick on people because they could feel what their words or actions did to the recipient of the chastising. They could feel their energy falter. However, it also often made Receivers the target of teasing and harassment.

There was a very basic and genetically encoded reason why marriages between Auxiliary Predilects and Ioses Predilects were so common and generally lasted.

Auxiliary Predilects were kind and caring. They made the world a better place, but their powers needed to be protected, and Ioses Predilects had a deep and permeating need to protect. They also often needed to be softened up a little. They needed to be forced to see the world through a kinder lens, one that an Auxiliary Predilect could provide. Inside of an Ioses Shield was the only place a Receiver could stop feeling the emotions of everyone around them. But Receivers were also the only Predilect capable of pulling emotional energy out of a Shield. They could take on every horrifying emotion and ease the strain.

"What was that all about?" Logan's voice brought Rainer back to the matter at hand. He motioned for Logan to move closer, and he rolled his chair around until he was right beside Rainer. They pretended to be going over a document on Pendergrath.

"Em's not handling all of this very well. I think everything that happened before with the press and my uncle and your mom and the baby and now the orphans, just being there, it's getting to her. Garrett wants me to come down there. See if I can't help a little. She's not eating. She's giving Aida and the kids all of her food. He wants me to give her a break, you know?"

Logan nodded. He looked extremely concerned.

"But I have to get to Rio without anyone knowing. If the Angels' owners find out, Em could get fired."

"Do you have a plan?" Logan whispered. He nonchalantly flipped the document to make it appear that he was showing Rainer something he'd missed.

"Yeah, sort of. I need to make a few phone calls." He contemplated the best way to make the arrangements without being overheard.

"Samantha's memorial service is Sunday afternoon. You have to be back for that. All of Iodex is attending, and your absence would definitely be noticed."

Rainer felt the familiar, sickening guilt that washed through him whenever he thought of Samantha Peterson settle on him once again. He also knew that her death had devastated Emily, not because they'd been particularly close, but because Emily blamed herself for not being more empathetic with Samantha before she'd been abducted.

"I'll be there." If he flew out of Rio Sunday morning, after Garrett got Emily back to the orphanage, he'd be back in plenty of time.

Logan checked his watch. "All right, why don't we take an early lunch? You could make all the arrangements then."

"Yeah, but we'll have to eat in my car. No one can overhear me." He wasn't certain Logan would want to eat in the Mustang while he was on the phone the entire time. But just as their friendship had always worked, Logan was perfectly willing to do whatever Rainer needed.

Rainer threw himself back into his work. He didn't want to shirk his responsibilities in any way. He tried to focus on Pendergrath and all of the crimes he was associated with, but his mind was much more interested in thinking about spending the night with Emily in Rio.

He could make her feel better. He could reassure her and soothe her. He could ease all of her pain. His heart sped, and his mouth went dry. Worry fought for dominance over the hunger that played in his rhythms.

He tried to decide that he wasn't going to make the night about sex. She needed much more than that. It was going to be about her. Whatever she needed from him, he was going to provide, but that didn't stop the dizzying fantasies.

Garrett's warning that the ladies weren't able to shower often had Rainer rolling his eyes at the time, but he knew Emily would definitely want a shower.

He didn't give a damn what she looked like or even smelled like. He just wanted to see her, feel her, and let her know that he'd be there whenever she needed him.

A little while later, he and Logan were sitting in the Mustang, inhaling burgers and fries, while Rainer began his phone calls. He scrolled down his contact list and prayed this wasn't going to be too much of a favor to ask as he touched Pete Namphis's name.

"Captain Namphis, it's Rainer Lawson." He was extremely thankful that Pete had answered. Rainer explained what he needed and apologized for the short notice. He offered to heavily compensate Pete for his services if he could get Rainer to Rio late Friday night and back home Sunday morning.

Pete assured Rainer he'd be only too happy to help out with the flight to Brazil, but he wouldn't be able to bring him home in his private plane on Sunday. He said he'd swap flights with another pilot and that Rainer could fly home on a Gifted, commercial flight if Pete could help Rainer blend in.

Rainer agreed as long as he was home with ample time to get to the service for Samantha. Pete assured him that he'd make the arrangements.

After turning the sleeve of French fries over his mouth in order to finish them off, Rainer Googled the number for the Copacabana Palace in Rio and booked a suite using an alias.

Logan phoned Adeline to tell her what Rainer was planning, and that he might need a little help packing.

Garrett planned on telling the nuns running the orphanage that he and Emily would be going to a nearby town for supplies. Garrett would make it appear Sunday that Emily had been there all night. Rainer shuddered slightly as he considered the fact that they would be lying to nuns who ran an orphanage.

Adeline immediately began making a list of things Rainer should take for Emily.

"I really appreciate all this."

Logan scoffed, "Hey, she's my baby sister, and you're my best friend. This is what we do."

As soon as they'd finished eating, they returned to their desks. They hadn't taken their full hour. They wanted to get as much work done as they could before they left for the weekend.

Rainer worked well past five, but he needed to get home to get his things packed before he headed to the airport to meet Pete. A volatile cocktail of excitement and nerves swirled in the pit of his stomach.

The flight to Rio with only Pete and one of his pilot friends, who had agreed to cool the engines of Pete's personal King Air plane, would be much longer than the Gifted flight home. Rainer hoped to be in Rio by lunch the next day. He wanted a chance to get in the suite and get it ready for Emily before Garrett dropped her off that evening.

Everyone knew how much Emily loved surprises, and Garrett had promised her a doozy the next night if she'd focus on the kids and let Dana and Carys's continued teasing roll off her back.

Emily and Fionna had spent the day with Aida and a few of her friends. She helped them with their schoolwork and then played with some of the toys the Angels had carried with them which seemed to soothe her.

Rainer thanked Adeline profusely for her help with packing Emily a few comforts from home. Emily had packed all of Rainer's loses shirts to take with her, so Adeline pointed out one of the navy blue T-shirts, with the Senate crest on the front pocket and Iodex scrawled across the back, for Rainer to pack for Emily to sleep in.

Iodex officers typically used them for working out. It wasn't something Rainer would've picked, but Adeline assured him that it was the way to go.

She packed a new toothbrush and a small bottle of Emily's favorite shampoo and conditioner. She added a hairbrush and hair dryer to Rainer's suitcase, along with deodorant and a few other things she thought Emily would like to have.

As he would only really be in Rio one evening, Rainer just threw in the clothing he planned to fly home in and a few extra T-shirts and pairs of boxers.

"Do you want to take the Accord?" Logan offered as Rainer grabbed a pair of dark sunglasses, a Virginia Tech baseball cap, and a black, hooded sweatshirt.

"Nah." Rainer shook his head, "I'm gonna park a good ways off. I don't think anyone will see the 'Stang."

"Tell Emily we miss her, and we're thinking of her," Adeline urged.

Rainer promised he would as he waved to Logan and Adeline, threw his bag in the back of the Mustang, and headed back to DC.

Adrenaline and speed pumped through his veins. He reveled in the sensations he always felt when he was driving his Mustang.

With a quick glance at his watch, he grimaced. He was running late, and he didn't want to be any more of a burden on Capt. Namphis. Adding pressure to the gas, he flew down the interstate.

He pulled the Mustang into one of the farthest lots from Reagan airport. Its distance meant that very few other cars were in the derelict lot, only those whose owners were vastly more conscious of their wallets than their comfort.

He paid the minimal fee to the attendant, who had barely noticed he even had a customer. Rainer grabbed the bag and began a calculated sprint toward the airport. It was almost a mile away. He left off the glasses after he decided that wearing sunglasses at eleven thirty at night might draw more attention than not.

He pulled the hood of the sweatshirt over the hat and kept his head down as he moved stealthily through the cold night air. His breath came in visible, steady huffs. He slipped carefully into the airport.

CHAPTER 5

RECOLLECTIONS

While keeping the fact that he'd be seeing Emily and holding her in his arms planted firmly in his mind, he eased along the darkened corridors of the airport. Only a few of the gates were even operational at the late hour.

He nodded to Captain Namphis as he rushed toward the last gate. Pete smiled but moved quickly. He gestured for Rainer to follow him out an exit door and onto the tarmac.

"We'll make introductions once we're airborne, but right now let's not draw the attention of ground control," Pete urged.

Soon they were in Pete's plane. Rainer cringed as he recalled the flight he and Emily had made in the same plane just a few weeks before. Pete had flown them back to reality from their beach house hideaway after Rainer had killed his uncle to save Emily's life.

Leaded fuel and oil fumes hung in the air. It mixed with the aroma of leather seats and cheap carpeting. Rainer sighed as he fell into his seat. Pete handed him a headset so they could chat while they flew.

"Is Miss Haydenshire okay?" Pete asked with sincere concern.

"I hope." Rainer was still worried about what state Emily might be in when he saw her. "It's been a rough few months with everything that happened during the election, and then an acquaintance of hers was killed the night before she left. I think the orphans and the living conditions have taken their toll." He owed Captain Namphis the entire reasoning behind the last-minute flight request.

Pete gave Rainer a kind smile and then spoke into the mic on the headset. He requested clearance to climb.

After he was granted permission, the plane tilted back slightly, and Rainer watched the lights of DC disappear beneath him. Pete studied the instrumentation as the plane leveled off.

"This is John Henderoy, Rainer. He's a good friend of mine. We've been flying together for years. He was a copilot for me most of the times I flew with your dad."

Rainer greeted John and thanked him for his time.

After Pete turned on the autopilot and summoned to boost the engine speed, John immediately followed suit to cool the engine. Pete turned back to Rainer.

"When you called this afternoon, you reminded me so much of your old man." He had a distant look in his eye. Intrigued, Rainer leaned forward. "You were just a baby," Pete began the story with a wry smile. "Your father had gone to Prague to work on helping their Realm with a Constitution similar to the one he'd written here.

"In the middle of the night, your mother phoned. It seemed you'd come down with croup and were running a high fever. I'm not sure who was crying harder, you or your mom. Lillian had gone over and determined that you needed to go to the emergency room to be healed up. She and your mom tried to heal you, but you were an Ioses from the beginning. You kept shutting them out. Lillian was worried about the fever," he explained.

"Your father hated to be away from Maggie so much, and when she called crying, it just about did him in. So, he had us up at two in the morning. We were flying home with a full staff. Your mother needed him, and he was going to be there if he had to swim the Atlantic to get home." Pete's kind smile eased the lines in his face.

John chuckled as he nodded his recollection of the same story.

Pete continued, "So, there we were, abuse of power charges could go straight to purgatory. Crown Governor Lawson was going home, and he was going to get there quickly."

"We'd never have pressed charges." John shook his head as if flying in the middle of the night after flying all day long wasn't something to be given much worry.

"Of course not. Joseph was a dear friend of all of ours. If you were sick and your mama needed him, then we'd move the Atlantic to get him home, and that's what we did. A few hours later, he raced into Georgetown Hospital. I went along. I was worried about you. You kept getting worse. While the medios worked on you, he wrapped Maggie up and held her right there in the hallway of the pediatric ward. He let her cry 'til she'd ruined his shirt." Pete gave Rainer a friendly wink.

"See, truly great men know that it's the women who stand beside them that make them so much more than they could ever be alone, and your father was a truly great man."

John nodded his adamant agreement. "Yeah, and the next day, after he'd gotten you home and Maggie settled, we all got a rather hefty bonus check and an extra week of vacation."

Pete seemed to remember the rest of the story as well. Then a broad grin spread across his face as he began laughing. "I hadn't thought about this in years. Like I said, not until you called me this afternoon, but when Lillian Haydenshire and your mama showed up at Georgetown, the medios rushed Lillian. She was about seven months pregnant with Emily, and they thought she'd gone into labor."

Rainer joined in the laughter. "I wish I'd known my mother better," poured from his mouth without him meaning to admit that out loud.

"Me too, son. Me too," Pete soothed.

"She was a knockout," John recalled. "Always had her head stuck in a book."

Pete nodded. Rainer watched the memories of his own mother form in the eyes of the men flying the plane.

"Yeah, she was a dreamer, and she wasn't going to let anybody or anything tell her what she could or couldn't do. She fought for women's rights and to stop the oppression of the Non-Gifted with all her might. Your daddy saw her at a protest at the academy, and he was sold lock, stock, and barrel. I was a junior when they started, but we were in Ioses Order together, your dad and me. She finally agreed to go to the Fall Ball with him. She'd turned him down several times before, but after that, the rest is history."

Rainer tried to envision his mother turning his dad down repeatedly, but his father was persistent to say the least.

He was only four when his mother had been murdered. A deep, aching pain seared through him every time he thought of her. He couldn't even recall her voice, though he'd tried repeatedly throughout his life. He fought the slipknot enclosure that always tightened in his throat when he allowed himself to miss his parents.

A peaceful silence loomed over the aircraft as they flew through the inky blackness.

"Get some sleep, son. It sounds like Miss Haydenshire needs you in top form," Pete urged Rainer.

He tried to doze, but his nerves wouldn't let him rest.

But Pete repeatedly encouraged him to sleep, so he feigned resting by keeping his eyes closed and leaning his head back. He wondered if Pete and John had any other stories they'd be willing to share about his mother. He wasn't certain he wanted to hear more, but some part of him craved the pain. It meant he hadn't forgotten her altogether.

Pete and John seemed to fall into an amicable silence, so Rainer decided to allow himself a few minutes to fantasize about Emily.

His heart sped. Her nipple pulsated against his lips. He sucked ravenously. She crawled over him, naked and greedy. Her lower lips separated around his cock, hungry, wet, and eager to be penetrated.

Rainer's body jerked slightly. He had to stop. He was going to moan out loud. He ordered himself from his rather lurid daydreams and listened as Pete and John began discussing him. They thought he was sound asleep.

"He looks so much like Joseph," John commented.

"Yeah, he's built like him, but he's got Maggie in there too. I know he feels bad about asking us to do this. I wish he wouldn't. He's paying us, and the kid's been through hell the past few weeks."

"Do you believe the press? You think he really killed his uncle?" John quizzed disbelievingly.

Rainer didn't dare open his eyes. Pete must have nodded.

"I think if Stan Lawson was in cahoots with that Interfeci gang, and he was after Emily Haydenshire, he didn't have much choice. That's a heck of a thing to have to do when you're twenty-one years old."

They were silent for a long minute.

"I also think he was with the team that went in to try to rescue Governor Peterson's daughter. I overheard Governor Willow and Governor Sapman talking about it when I captained their flight to LA last week. Apparently, it was pretty gruesome," Pete's voice shuddered slightly.

John sighed. "Poor kid. You know, I always thought Stan Lawson got somebody to fake those documents he came up with right after Joe was killed. I just never believed Joseph and Maggie would've named Stan his guardian. Not with the way Joseph used to talk about his brother, and he always left Rainer with the Haydenshires when he traveled. Rainer and Logan being such good buddies and all. Just never made any sense to me. Joe loved Rainer more than anything in the world. He adored his son. He would've wanted him somewhere he knew he'd be happy."

Rainer fought to keep his eyes closed. He clenched his jaw and waited to hear Pete's response.

"You and me both, and I told the governors that, but they couldn't prove it. God knows what he went through living with that sorry excuse for a human being."

Rainer's heart raced as he let that revelation wash over him. It hadn't made any sense to him either when Governor Haydenshire had blinked back tears and forced himself to tell Rainer that he was going to have to go live with his uncle.

"Yeah, but I thought I'd be gettin' money for him." His uncle's words from the trial pulsed through his mind as he began to consider who might've forged documents to state that Stan was to become Rainer's guardian.

Stan must've known that his dad had set up an allowance for Rainer, given his untimely demise, and that the majority of the trust couldn't be accessed until he turned twenty-one.

Stan wouldn't have thought far enough to have the forger add a child support payment for himself. He would've just assumed that he'd have access to the monthly allowance left to Rainer.

Revulsion washed through him as he began to consider that perhaps the meeting at The Tantra, where his uncle agreed to run Emily's car off the road, hadn't been Stan's first encounter with the Interfeci.

It would be just like Dominic Wretchkinsides to forge documents for his uncle years before, and then wait patiently until he had a job he needed his uncle to complete to pay him back for his handiwork.

He was cold, calculated, and never let debts go unpaid. He would leave a fly webbed for years before he ate him alive.

CHAPTER 6

THE MANY MOODS OF EMILY HAYDENSHIRE

The thirteen-hour flight was shortened to ten given the size of the plane and the fact that there were only two pilots to enhance the engines with their energy.

Rainer shook Pete and John's hands and thanked them profusely as he exited the plane. He pulled on his hat and sunglasses, took his bag, and then headed out into the teeming streets of Rio de Janeiro.

He phoned a cab from Galeão airport after finally finding a company that had a dispatcher who spoke English. He changed several hundred dollars into Brazilian reals and waited until the cab pulled up. He quickly got inside and informed the driver that he needed to head to the Copacabana Palace, *rapido*. He flashed the cash, and the driver took off.

The city was fascinating. It was bathed in brilliant colors, from the mountains to the beaches, and the men and women were all dressed in an array of bright hues.

The tourist area brimmed with advertisements for beaches, restaurants, and nighttime entertainment. It was hard to imagine that just a few hours away was a tiny town full of people and orphans lacking food and proper living conditions. Rainer wondered how the world managed to go on ignoring those that needed help so that those who already had everything could keep it.

After thanking the cab driver and paying for the rather harrowing ride, Rainer breathed a sigh of relief as he exited. He wished momentarily that he could take Emily to a few places in the city. He was certain that the food and nightlife in Rio must be amazing, but he reminded himself that what Emily needed was a quiet night to get some rest and to be restored. She needed time to process every emotion she'd taken on in the last few weeks.

He walked by a street vendor. Keeping his dark sunglasses on and his hat pulled low over his face, Rainer ordered several hot dogs and something called pão de queijo, that he thought looked interesting.

He assumed that getting food quickly and getting inside their suite would be the best way to keep any of the team owners from knowing he was in Rio, even though the crowded streets seemed like the perfect place to get lost in plain sight.

He gave the hotel attendant his alias and was given the key to the suite he'd picked for them.

He offered hesitant smiles to the patrons on the elevator with him, but he never removed his sunglasses. He issued quickly to the suite, unlocked the door, and quickly ducked inside.

Rainer pulled off his Virginia Tech hat and glasses, and took in the bright room lit by the sun's luminous rays that reflected off the sand and water just outside their suite.

The relatively small room contained a king-size bed, a small couch, and a couple of club chairs. There was a desk in the corner, along with a table for setting room service trays.

Rainer placed his lunch on the desk and threw his bag onto the bed. He moved to the sliding glass doors. With a delighted grin, he took in the panoramic views of one of the most stunning beaches he'd ever seen. It was soothing to be in the warm, salty air after leaving the icy chill of Virginia in November. Emily would be thrilled.

The food smelled delicious, and he was starving. He glanced at his watch and willed time to move faster. The orphans ate lunch at noon, and Garrett was going to try to get Emily out as soon as she'd helped serve their lunch and made certain her group of girls was fed and set up for their afternoon activities.

After sinking down into the chair at the desk, Rainer dug in. The pão de queijo turned out to be a kind of cheese pastry puff that was out of this world.

He licked his fingers after eating the last one in the sack and inhaled the hot dogs. They tasted decidedly different from American hot dogs but filled his stomach with something warm and satisfying.

The food consoled him from the revelations he'd learned on his flight. Only being a few hours away from Emily, and knowing she was on her way to him, soothed his soul as well.

Boredom crept in as the hours ticked by. He watched TV, but he didn't understand even one word in Portuguese, so he gave that up quickly. A deep yawn was the last thing Rainer recalled before his cell phone chirped two hours later.

He shook himself from his deep, exhausted sleep and pulled his cell from his pocket.

Be there in about a half hour. Em's in a mood.

Garrett's text made him chuckle out loud. He let the news that Emily would be in his arms in under an hour delight him. He crawled from the bed, straightened it from his nap, and tried to make the room look the way it had when he'd arrived.

He moved into the well-appointed bathroom, complete with a large steam shower, to clean up after his flight and his nap.

After he finished, he headed back into the suite and began going over all of his ideas of ways to get Emily to relax once she'd arrived.

"Garrett, what the hell are we doing? Why are we here?" he heard Emily demand as they made their way down the hallway.

Rainer smiled broadly. She was in a mood indeed.

"This is creepy. Why are we in a hotel? Where are you taking me?"

He leaned his head against the door and could hear her clearly.

"Geez, your surprise is here. Would you try not to be so fucking annoying?" Garrett ordered. "See if I ever try to do something nice for you again."

Rainer knew the precise glare Garrett would receive from Emily for his retort.

CHAPTER 7

TO RESTORE A RECEIVER

A knock thudded against Rainer's head. He jerked away from the door.

"Who is in there?" Emily demanded.

Rainer pulled the door open and grinned. He watched as Emily's eyes goggled, and her mouth fell open in astonishment.

"Hey there, baby." He gazed at her. He'd never seen anything so beautiful. She took his breath away as tears formed in her eyes. Her hands flew to her mouth in a stunned gasp, and she began to sob.

Rainer pulled her against his chest and wrapped her up in his arms. The feeling of her against him eased the pain in his heart as he held her. Tears streamed down Emily's face. They soaked Rainer's T-shirt, but he wouldn't let her go. She stepped back a full minute later and gazed at him like she was terrified he might disappear if she looked away.

"What… are you… doing here?" she finally managed.

"I missed you."

He didn't necessarily want to let on that Garrett and most of her friends had been worried about her.

"I missed you too." She nuzzled her head against his chest as he wrapped her back up in his arms.

Garrett chuckled and shook his head at both of them. He started to bid them farewell.

"Wait!" Emily spun away from Rainer and threw her arms around her big brother. "You're the best brother ever."

Garrett chuckled again and kissed the top of her head. He gave her a fierce hug. "You had me worried. It's not like you to go so many days without even a smile."

"Thanks, man. I owe you." Rainer offered Garrett his hand.

"Not a problem. What time's your flight tomorrow?"

"Ten," Rainer replied. "I have to be back early afternoon." He hoped that Garrett would remember where he had to be without him having to say it in front of Emily.

He shared an understanding nod with Rainer, while keeping Emily's head under his chin.

"You'll gain an hour going back," he reminded him. Rainer knew that. He'd calculated very carefully. He wanted to be able to spend as much time with Emily as possible.

"So, I get to stay here tonight, all night, with you?" Disbelief rang in her tone.

"Well, only if you want to."

"I can take you back to the orphanage if you'd prefer that," Garrett teased.

Emily shook her head into Rainer's chest which made both him and Garrett laugh.

"But I feel bad. No one else is getting a reprieve," she fussed.

Rainer's heart raced. He couldn't believe he was standing there, holding her to him and feeling her energy. He felt complete for the first time in a week. He longed to kiss her. He wanted Garrett to leave.

"They are, actually. Mom and Dad got permission from the Angels' owners, and they're paying for a couple of suites here. I'm bringing some of the Angels out here every few nights. Letting them shower and get a decent night's sleep whenever I can tell the whole thing is getting to them. I'm just their ride. It's unusual for their to be so many orphans all at the same time. That's why there aren't any extra beds and supplies are so low. I'm not actually staying with anyone but Chloe. I just thought maybe I'd give you a break. You've kind of had a hell of a few weeks, and I talked to Logan. He said Rainer was being a real pain in the ass."

Rainer and Emily both laughed. Neither was able to take their eyes off the other. Garrett laughed at them both outright as he shook his head.

"I'll let you two enjoy each other." He made a quick exit.

Rainer drew a deep breath. His chest and gut unknotted from just holding Emily in his arms.

"I missed you so much." He squeezed her tighter.

She clung to him and inhaled deeply of his shirt.

"Relax for me," he soothed. He casted and surrounded her in his fierce shield. "Come on, baby. Draw from me. I've got you."

She pulled from his back as she wound her arms under his T-shirt. His energy entered her readily. She gave a contented sigh as he restored her.

"Keep going. Take what you need," he coaxed and fought not to groan in ecstasy as she pulled more.

"I look terrible," Emily gasped suddenly as she jerked away from Rainer. He dropped his cast. "I haven't had a shower in days."

"Em." Rainer shook his head unable to believe her. "You are always beautiful to me but,"—he pulled her close once again and brushed a soothing kiss across her forehead—"I will be glad to give you a shower if you'd like to take one."

Emily bit her lip and nodded hesitantly. "Did Garrett call you because I was so upset?"

Rainer knew he couldn't lie to her, so he nodded. "He was worried about you. You want to talk about everything that's been going on, or do you want to shower first?"

He wasn't giving her an option on the talking portion of their evening. There were too many things she needed to get off her chest.

Emily shrugged as her gaze traveled to the floor. "I don't know. I want to shower. I want to talk, and I want to do other things. I want you to hold me. I don't know."

Rainer grinned at her. He fully understood that they had to try to squeeze three weeks of their rather event-filled lives into one short evening, and it was hard to prioritize all of the things they wanted to share.

He decided to take the reins. Maybe what she needed was to not have to make decisions for a while. He took her hands. Her rhythms were weak and exhausted despite the fact that she'd just drawn from him. Her normally vibrant energy was lackluster and frail.

She needed to be taken care of and tended to if she was going to continue to care for the orphans. Her emotional bands were depleted, and even the Lawson ring couldn't do much for exhaustion.

As Emily Haydenshire showered on a daily basis, often twice a day if she had practice or a challenge, Rainer assumed the lack of bathing options were probably getting to her.

"Come on. Let me give you a shower, then we can crawl in bed. I'll hold you, and we can talk. We can order food and spend the whole night catching up on everything."

Emily let Rainer lead her into the bathroom. He pulled the toiletry bag Adeline had packed with all of Emily's favorite products and placed it in her hands as he turned on the many jets of the large shower. It was plenty big enough for two.

"You are amazing." She took everything out of the bag.

"I had help." He wanted to give Logan and Adeline credit where credit was due.

As he began pulling off her T-shirt, he felt the distance between them. The time apart had indeed taken its toll. Fear and isolation swirled in his mind. He needed the reconnection as much as she did. He could also tell she wasn't eating.

As Rainer discarded his own clothes, tears returned to Emily's eyes. They fell rapidly from her long lashes. Her pain seized him. His heart began to ache once again, and Rainer wiped away her tears. His shield leapt to fix whatever the problem was.

"What, baby? What's wrong?" he soothed. "I kind of hoped my being here might make you smile."

Emily tried to draw a steadying breath. "It does. You have no idea what this means to me. I just can't believe you're here."

"Come here, sweetheart." He eased her into the pouring water and wrapped his arms around her again. He let the water soothe her as he reveled in having her naked in his arms.

"I don't like Carys and Dana anymore," Emily declared.

She kept her eyes closed as the water fell, and she buried her head in Rainer's chest.

With an understanding nod, Rainer began to lather his hands in Emily's favorite shampoo. As he tried to massage away the trauma of the past few weeks, he was taken back through their long relationship to a middle school dance.

Emily had stood there trying with all of her might not to let the girls who'd called her a spoiled little bitch see her cry.

Rainer had smarted off to them, but that had only made it worse. Connor and Logan came to her defense, and that sealed the deal.

In their eyes, she was a spoiled little rich girl with a thousand older brothers ready to fight her battles for her, but Emily could feel their jealousy and their hatred.

She could feel that the ringleader had a crush on Rainer. She'd felt the preteen lust and thirst for vengeance. Rainer had no interest in anyone but Emily, but the fear had taken her over. She'd dissolved on his shoulder in a puddle of tears. He'd called Mrs. Haydenshire to come pick them up early.

He shook his head. If only everyone could feel what their words did the way a Receiver felt them.

After he washed her hair, he moved down her luscious body. He bit his tongue and refused to comment on the fact that she'd lost a bit of weight.

Several of the Angels had been giving their food to the orphans, and Garrett was planning to bring back a great deal of local grub that evening from Rio to supply to the Angels.

After Rainer had made certain that Emily was thoroughly clean, he asked if she was ready to get out. She smiled and nodded. He turned off the water and quickly summoned heat into his hand. He ran it over a towel and wrapped it around her.

"I still feel bad," she fussed as Rainer pulled the T-shirt Adeline had instructed him to pack over Emily's head. He donned a pair of boxers.

"Why?"

"Because all of the other Angels don't get the person they miss most in the world on their nights off, and the orphans never get the night off."

"Did you want me to call Garrett and get him to take you back?" Rainer winked at her.

"No," she fussed.

He pulled back the bedspread and sheets. "Then how about we just sort of give ourselves the night off from worrying about everyone else? Let's just be here together. I know we can't go out, but I just want to hold you and hear about everything you've been doing."

"So, did you pack me anything to wear under your T-shirt?" she flirted mischievously.

Delighted that she was already feeling somewhat better, Rainer waggled his eyebrows. "I haven't seen you in days. It took all of my willpower to put the T-shirt on that gorgeous body. Now you want me to cover the bottom half too?"

Her sweet giggle righted his world. It always did. "Well, I guess this is okay."

"For now," Rainer's tone turned ravenous in a heartbeat. He shot her a look that told her he didn't plan on leaving the T-shirt on all night. She shivered deliciously as the fire he loved began to slowly return to her emerald eyes.

He strode to her and lifted her up into his arms. He tucked her into the bed and laid her back on several of the pillows he'd left propped against the headboard.

"Now, what would the lady like to eat?"

Excitement lit Emily's face. "I'm starving."

"I know you are." Rainer held her eyes with his own, telling her that he knew what she'd been doing with all of her meals. She also knew he didn't approve.

"They don't have enough to eat," she said. "They shouldn't have to share their food with us."

He felt guilty for disapproving, but she couldn't continue to work if she didn't eat. He handed her the room service menu and then moved around the bed to crawl in beside her.

"I know, baby. I also know that some quack television psychologist or somebody told you that I'm not supposed to try to swoop in and fix everything that makes my baby sad, but I'm going to see if we can't help with the lack of food as well." He pointed to the menu and urged her to pick anything she'd like.

She shook her head. "I think they were telling that to guys in general."

"Yeah, well, they'll get over it."

He ordered a vast array of food for them and watched to make certain Emily ate enough to make up for just a few of the meals she'd gone without.

In between bites of some kind of delicious chicken and rice mixture, she turned to him. "What do you mean? How are we going to fix that too? How are we going to get them more food?" Rainer grinned at her. He leaned to brush a kiss in her hair. It was still damp from their shower and held the scent of her shampoo.

"We have quite a bit of money, sweetheart, and I'd really like to use it to help people. So, if you'd like to make a yearly donation, or a monthly one to fund the orphanage to help take care of Aida and the other kids, then I would really like to do that. I have a rather substantial check in my wallet to give to Garrett tomorrow."

Tears pricked Emily's eyes again. "Really?" she gasped.

Rainer gave her an adoring smile. "Really."

She picked up the empty plates from their multi-course dinner and stacked them back on the tray before she crawled back in the bed.

She got up on her knees and threw her arms around him. Rainer hugged her to him. She was effectively drowning his face in her ample cleavage. It was a heavenly sensation.

"You are the most amazing man ever, and I just can't believe I'm lucky enough to get to be your wife."

Rainer cradled her to him and reveled in her energy. It already felt stronger.

He eased her back beside him in the bed and inhaled deeply. He wanted to immerse himself in Emily for the few short hours he could have her before he'd have to go back to life without her.

"You wanna tell me about Carys and Dana, or do you want to tell me about Aida first?" He was perfectly willing to start wherever Emily wanted, but he was determined to hear everything she'd been going through.

Emily sighed. "I don't know. I don't think they meant to hurt my feelings, but I'm just tired of hearing about it, you know? The ring makes me feel everything even stronger than I normally would. All of it is just hard."

"Hearing about what, baby?" Rainer began slowly pulling the story out of her. He knew the Lawson ring amplified her abilities beyond all belief. He hated that it did this to her, but it also made her able to throw a shield cast even stronger than his if she were ever in danger.

She stared into his eyes and held onto his hands. Rainer felt his energy give way slightly. She was drawing from him again.

It was exquisite, and he had to fight with every fiber of his being not to lay her down and pull his T-shirt off her. He longed to fill her with all of him.

His energy soothed her, and she smiled as she began her story. "All of the Angels were up talking one night, because those beds are really way too small for all of us, and we're having trouble sleeping with so many of us in one room. Anyway,"—she shook her head and forced herself to focus—"Chloe kept going on and on about how amazing my brother is in bed." Emily pretended to gag.

Rainer laughed. She was completely adorable. He reclined and guided her onto his chest. He wanted her to be able to draw from more than just his hands. "It must run in the family," he teased her.

"Anyway..." She rolled her eyes. "A couple of the girls started comparing all of the different guys they'd been with, and Dana asked me if I'd ever been with anyone but you."

Rainer bristled at the thought. His jaw clenched.

"I said I hadn't, and then they started telling me that it was stupid to tie myself to you and never try anyone else out." Emily sounded as horrified by the idea as Rainer was. "I just want them to shut up about it. I don't want to be with anyone else. I've only ever wanted you. Why can't they just get over it?"

He squeezed her tighter and tried to soothe her again, but his own anger made it difficult.

"Baby, I really think they're just jealous, or they don't get it. We *are* kind of different from most couples."

"I know, but that's just a big deal to me. I know it's not to everybody, but it is to me. I can't really imagine letting anyone in like that. Not anyone but you. You're my Shield."

"Seeing as how we're due to get married here in a few months, I'm really glad you feel that way," he teased her. Her body jostled against his as she giggled.

"Do you want me to talk to them when you get back?"

"No, Garrett pretty much got them to shut up, but they're still calling me Mary. They're grown women. Why are they acting like that?"

Dana was a powerful Enforcer, a Vis Virres Predilect. This would make her more determined than any other Predilect. She was excellent at her job, but occasionally she was a pain to deal with in social settings.

"Why don't you ask them?" Rainer studied Emily's reaction.

"I did this morning, and Fionna told them off. She told them that they had no idea what it was like for a Receiver. She also threatened to tell the coaches and the owners. They're big on us being one big, happy family. They apologized, but I really think we just need a little space. There are twelve exhausted women who aren't getting enough to eat, and who are hot, and miserable, and feel terrible for the sweet kids who have to live that way all the time," Emily lamented. "I think we're all just cranky."

Rainer was certain that was true, but he was still furious that grown women were behaving like bratty teenagers. He brushed a tender kiss onto Emily's cheek.

"Okay, well, then the kids should have enough to eat after Garrett gets that check, so I want you to promise me that you will eat your food every meal. You can't help those kids if you're starving."

Emily's head lowered, and Rainer cupped her jaw and lifted her eyes back to his. "Promise me, sweetheart. Promise me that you will eat. I know it's uncomfortable but try to get some sleep while you're there. Just tell me to stop texting you. I'll understand. If all of the Angels eat more and sleep a little more, maybe everyone will be a little nicer and have a little more patience." He felt guilty as he thought of the late nights they'd spent on the phone.

"But I *want* to talk to you. I miss you so much. I need you."

Rainer cradled her closer. *This just doesn't work.* The thought ricocheted through his mind. The world didn't work without him and Emily together. It just didn't make any sense. There were entire legends about how Shields and Receivers had to be together.

Tell her you want her to come home. Tell her you want to make love to her all night long, and then beg her to come home with you. Tell her you need to keep her safe and warm, to hold her and watch her sleep. Tell her that you need to soothe her and let her soothe you. Her father's the Crown Governor. He could square everything with the team owners. Just beg her to come home. She won't tell you no. She's not happy. Ask her. Beg her not to go back with Garrett. You can't deal with all of the shit going on by yourself.

His own selfish desires waged a brutal war in his head, and he fought valiantly to silence them. Unable to quiet them fully, Rainer focused on the few he could have as he slid his hand under the T-shirt she was wearing and caressed her thigh and backside. The friction of his hand stoked the fire in her eyes.

"Tell me about Aida." He hoped that hearing about the amazing work she was doing might help quiet the restless murmurs of his selfish side.

Emily sighed and tucked herself farther into Rainer's chest. The movement made his desire increase tenfold in a matter of moments.

"She's so sweet. It just kills me that she has to live there," Emily mourned. "It kills me that all of them have to live there."

"What happened to her folks?" He forced the memories of living with his uncle when he'd become an orphan himself out of his mind.

He didn't want to think about all of that now. He didn't want to think about what Pete and John had discussed during his flight. He wanted to focus on Emily.

"She had three older brothers." Rainer smiled as he understood Emily's immediate connection with Aida. "She told me that her entire family was killed when a mine collapsed near their home." Rainer grimaced over the harrowing story. "But the nuns said that wasn't true."

"That's not how they died?"

"Well," Emily hemmed, "that is what Aida was told. She wasn't lying or anything, but they were murdered."

"What?!" Rainer gasped in shock.

Emily grew pale. Aida's disturbing tale had her rhythms reeling. "I wish you could meet her. She's the sweetest thing ever. I wish I could bring her home with me. She's been through enough."

"How old is she?"

"She's six, and she's just endlessly fascinated with everything. Fionna let her play in her makeup, and I've never seen anyone so thrilled." Emily chuckled. "We're going to throw her and the other girls in her room a slumber party. They've never even had a birthday party, much less a slumber party." Rainer's heart broke over just hearing Emily talk about Aida, and he'd never even met her. "I wish she could come stay with us for the summer or something. Just give her some stability even for a little while."

"If that's allowed, then it's fine with me. I don't think I'm quite old enough or ready to become a dad to a six-year-old just yet, but she's welcome to come visit whenever you'd like."

"You're the best." Emily hugged Rainer tightly. "I've told her all about the wedding and all about you." Her energy leapt when she thought about the wedding. His heart picked up pace. "I wish I could get her up there to be the flower girl. She'd be so thrilled."

Rainer reveled in just hearing Emily's voice right beside him instead of over a phone thousands of miles away.

"Was Aida okay with you leaving tonight?" He didn't want to cause any more strife in the little girl's life.

Emily grimaced. "She was a little upset, but I promised that I'd be back tomorrow because that's what Garrett told me to tell her. Fionna told her that she could sleep in our bunk, since I wouldn't be there, so she was pretty excited about getting to stay in the room with all of the Angels. She adores Fionna. They seem completely connected. Way more than even I connected with her."

Rainer's worry ebbed some as he let his mind work through everything Emily shared.

"Do they know who killed her parents?" he asked softly.

"No, and they don't want Aida to know what really happened. They don't want her to be frightened."

It was one thing to tell a fourteen-year-old with an excellent education that his father had been assassinated. It was another thing entirely to try to explain to a little girl that her entire family had been murdered.

"She's so smart. She speaks fluent Portuguese and English, and she loves to read."

"How long has she been in the orphanage?"

"Since she was four." The sadness in her voice shattered Rainer's heart. "She absolutely adores Garrett. She was so excited when he got there Monday. He comes and sees her more than I ever realized. He comes down here more than he's ever told Mom and Dad just to check on her. I guess he's a pretty good guy."

CHAPTER 8
CONTENTED

A peaceful silence washed over the room as the moonlight danced across the lapping ocean.

"I wish you'd gotten here before dark," Rainer lamented. "The view is amazing."

Emily gazed up at him. There was a tender tranquility about her now—a need to be cared for and adored. A timid hunger swam in her eyes.

"Nothing is as amazing as looking up at you and being here in your arms. I've been a mess all week. I just needed you so badly. I feel so weak." She sounded disgusted with herself.

Rainer scooted farther down in the bed and pulled her onto his chest. "I'm right here, baby, and I've got you. Even if I'm not with you, I'm always thinking about you, and missing you, and wishing more than anything else that you were with me." He listened to her contented sigh. "You're not weak. You're human, and the past few months have been more than any of us could deal with."

"This one night, just getting to see you, makes the next two weeks seem bearable though, you know?" Her cheeks colored rapidly as heat rose from her body. The effect transformed the slow fire that had been burning low in Rainer's groin into an all-consuming blaze.

Her energy was soothed now that she'd showered, eaten, and had spent the last hour in his arms.

He'd tried to fight the lust that permeated every single cell of his body, but he longed to feel more of her. He wanted to be a part of her again. He was desperate to join her energy with his. He yearned for her, but he forced himself to wait. He had to make certain that was what she wanted as well. He needed to take care of her first.

"I've been kind of a mess too, you know," Rainer informed her as Emily smiled and ran her hands up and down his chest. She pulled at his pecs with hunger. It drove him wild. "Just ask Logan." He let his eyes close as his body burned with her touch.

Emily giggled before a soft sigh egressed her lips. "I'm sorry, but that does kind of make me feel better."

Rainer chuckled and shook his head. He began running his hands down her sides. He brushed them lightly down her rib cage and followed the delicious curve of her waist. He carefully kept his hands from her breasts. He wanted her starving for his touch. He felt the longing as he cuddled her. The need emanated from the energy between them.

He reminded himself that if he spilled his release inside of her, she could draw more energy from that for the next several hours. His heart raced. His body thrummed in desire.

"Rainer," she whispered in a heated plea.

"What, baby?" He brushed his thumb over her cheek and swept her hair behind her shoulder as he began to lightly massage her neck.

"Can we stop talking for a little while and maybe talk again later?"

A low guttural groan escaped him. "What do you want to do while we're not talking?" He let his fingertips glide from her earlobe down to her neck. He followed her delicate chin. He needed to hear her beg, needed to feel her energy spike rapidly. Her words always drove him wild.

Her breaths shortened, and she trembled under his touch.

"I want you so much. I want to feel it again. I feel like it's been forever. I just want to forget everything else. I just want to be with you."

His body vibrated with need. In one quick move, he pulled the electricity from the lamps in the suite but left one glowing. He wanted to see her body as he took her. He wanted to watch her back arch, her luscious curves tremble, and her breasts sway all for him.

The noisy streets of Rio were brimming with tourists and locals, eager to capture the night in lush drinks, thrumming music, and carnal dancing. They faded away as the air around Rainer and Emily filled with arousal and sensual desire.

The moment existed for them alone. The rest of the world would have to wait. It had already taken its toll, worn the two of them thoroughly, and they were taking this night to shut everything else out. They would exist in this time, in this space, alone together.

While keeping the promise he'd made to himself to take care of her every need, Rainer casted her in his shield. It spun from his pores and blocked out everything else. Her mind quieted. Her rhythms eased, and elation filled her as she let his energy permeate the very air she breathed.

Rainer began running his hands all over her soft, sweet skin.

"I'm going to make everything better, baby. I promise." His voice was rough and reverent from his desire.

He forced himself to move slowly, to take his time, and to relish being with her as he satiated their need.

"I'm gonna take this off, baby. I want to see you. Then I'm gonna set the cast, okay?" he explained his plans and listened to her pant and moan as she gave a heavy nod.

He lifted the T-shirt up over her luscious curves. He gazed at her with desperate hunger. A slight moan of appreciation echoed from his soul as her breasts swayed when he removed the shirt.

He wanted to touch and taste every part of her beautiful body. He wanted to soothe every ache and allay every fear she held in the recesses of her mind.

He began tracing his fingers from her neck lightly over her collarbone. Unable to keep his hands from her breasts, he groped them in heady need. A shuddered groan of adamant approval rose from him as he felt her nipples pebble in his hands. A moment later her breasts swelled ripe and full. Her body flushed under his urgent caress.

It had been far too long since he'd fondled her, and all of the lurid fantasies he'd allowed himself over the past week were nothing compared to feeling the heavy weight and the warmth of her in his hands.

"Touch me, Rainer, please," she begged, and with that she'd united their long, unending past with their time apart. The phrase she'd whispered in his ear at the pier on the beach so many years before sealed them together again with no space between.

Unable to deny her anything, Rainer brushed his fingers down her abdomen and sealed her womb as he let his hands travel to her slit. He felt her tense in delicious anticipation as he moved over her.

"Spread your legs for me, baby. Show me where you want me to touch you. Show me where it hurts. I'm gonna make everything feel better," he vowed in a heated pant, and she flew. Her energy soared as a loud moan echoed from her lips and seared through him. It took up residence in his groin.

She did as she was told. She bucked under him and lifted what he'd asked to see up to his face. The heat of her arousal filled his lungs. She was soaking wet, so hungry for him.

He traced two fingers along her slit. Her rhythms pulsed in need. It nearly sent him over the edge as the thought of her tightening around him overtook his mind. He let the tip of one finger separate her and listened to her beg fervently.

"Please," spilled from her mouth in a desperate whimper, and he couldn't make her wait any longer. He slipped two fingers deep inside of the liquid heat between her legs. She cried out his name. Her body bucked and rolled all for him.

"God, baby, you're so damn tight." Rainer gasped out his appreciation. The feeling was exquisite as her energy began to engulf him, but she was pulled taut and bound. The stress of the past week held her captive.

He forced himself to breathe. He slowed his fervent strokes and let her body open at its own pace. He had all night, and if that's how long it took to set her free, to hear her scream out his name, to feel her come undone, so be it.

He curved his fingers and stroked the spot that usually drove her wild. He smiled as her breaths began to stutter. His thumb gave gentle caresses to her still hidden clit.

Frustrated impatience set in her eyes. She wanted the release that seemed slow to come.

"Shh, baby," he let his voice take on a commanding thrum. "I know what you need. Relax for me so I can give it to you. Let it go for me," he urged, and she shattered. It flooded through her. She quaked and convulsed as her energy unfurled for him.

"That's it," he continued to command her as she went wild. Her lips swelled from the powerful orgasm. Her body was unable to remain still.

She was still tight from the stress she'd carried the past week, and he debated moving on. He didn't want her to hurt the next day. He continued to remind himself that they had all night, but with a wild look in her dark, ravenous eyes, Emily grasped his biceps and pulled him on top of her.

"Take me, please. Please, I need you," she begged, and his steady control was gone in an instant. He grasped her hips, opened her thighs, and gazed at the very heart of her, swollen, ripe, and wet. She was throbbing for him.

"I'm gonna take it slow, baby. You're still really tight, okay?" he warned more for himself than her, but his promise brought on another round of desperate moans and pleas. He entered her slightly, separating her with his head, but she held his eyes with her own.

"More," she whimpered. It was just too difficult to remember why he needed to move slowly. He wanted to fill her with all of him. He wanted to make her feel all of his straining length. He needed to feel the heavenly pulse of her release. The need consumed him. It overtook every rational thought as he gave in to the wanton desire.

He thrust hard and poured himself into the warm, liquid perfection of her. She cried out for him as he gave her what she wanted. She met his thrusts. Her muscles clenched so tightly around him he could barely move.

She held him as her captive. It was a role he was only too eager to fill.

"That's incredible, baby," he gasped as he pounded into the very heart of her and opened her until he was buried to his hilt.

He ground his hips into hers and gave her the force and friction she demanded. She met his exultation with a loud moan. Her body spasmed tightly around him.

He moved his hands back to her breasts and kneaded and grasped them. He released her right breast as he lowered his mouth to it. He pulled her nipple in and sucked her fervently.

She went wild. She swelled around his penetrating thrusts. He let his tongue and his teeth bring her the sensations he wanted her to have as her body nursed his cock.

She trembled. Her back arched deeply. Her body flushed the shade of a delicate pink rose.

"I'm gonna..." she panted as her body writhed under his, but she couldn't continue her warning. The release began to steal her breath.

His vision split and his breath tore from his lungs. "I know, baby. I feel it coming. Just give it to me, and then I'm gonna fill you full."

With that, her energy spiked. The arcs reached their highest tilt. Her temperature climbed, and then she peaked and fell. Her body flooded her rhythms all around him. Just as he'd promised, he filled her with all of him. He spilled himself inside of her with an elated groan of gratitude. He felt their releases mix in the ecstasy of being together.

When he was able to breathe normally again, he eased away gently. He was certain she was tender.

"Are you okay?" He held her close and tried not to let guilt mar any part of the incredible evening.

She beamed. "I'm much better than okay. That was amazing."

Rainer smiled as he wrapped her up in his protective embrace. They lay in the serenity for several minutes, just reveling in being in each other's arms again.

"You know what I think?" Emily drew the light from the lamp Rainer had left on.

"What, baby?"

"I think that if Dana, or Carys—or any of the Angels really—ever met someone who made them feel the way I feel when we're together like that, they'd never want anything else. Then they would understand."

He nodded and then kissed her. Her rhythms soothed as they rolled in his own. They were tangled together, unable to be separated. "That's always what I think when I hear Garrett, or Tuttle, or even Vindico talk. I think they've just never been with someone as incredible as you because there is nothing more amazing than that."

"I want to stay up and talk to you all night," she fussed. "I have to make this night last for weeks, but I'm so exhausted. I haven't slept at all. I worry all night about you and Mom and all of the kids there."

A deep yawn overtook her. His heart, that was still swollen full of the penetrating love he felt for her, fractured slightly. He could feel her exhaustion in her waning energy.

"Go to sleep, baby. I'm going to hold you all night. We can talk in the morning, have breakfast, and just be together. When Garrett picks you up, I'll be counting the minutes until I have you back in my arms."

Sadness flooded through her, and he grimaced. He shouldn't have brought up Garrett picking her up. She tightened her grasp around his chest, and he moved so that she was completely enveloped by him.

He began running his hands through her hair as he flooded her body with calming energies. After a little while, he kissed her forehead and watched her sleep, his precious baby content in his arms.

CHAPTER 9
IN THE MOURNING LIGHT

Emily awoke early and looked much more like herself. The color was back in her cheeks, and her energy was strong and able.

They made use of the shower again. This time, she showed him how much better she was feeling by lowering her mouth to him and working her heady magic.

Unable to withstand that kind of tempting pleasure, he showed off some of his newly acquired muscles he'd gotten from being abused by Vindico in the gym. He reached down, lifted her up into his arms, and then lowered her onto his straining length. He took her up against the tiled shower wall.

Rainer ordered another huge breakfast and plied Emily with as much protein as he could coax her into eating. She was arguing about his insistence that she finish up the bacon when his cell rang.

He didn't want to answer. He was certain it was Garrett saying that he was almost there. He'd willed away the sunlight, just like he willed away Garrett's call. To his surprise, when he picked up the phone, he saw Vindico's name.

His brow furrowed. He didn't like the fact that his heart was racing and the hair on the back of his neck was standing.

He forced himself to answer. It was nine in Rio, eight in DC.

"Lawson," Rainer gave the expected greeting. He tried to sound much calmer than he felt.

"Have a nice night?" Vindico quipped.

"Uh, I guess," Rainer answered carefully. He didn't want to give anything away.

"Good." Vindico had his number. Rainer could tell. "Tell Emily good morning for me." Rainer grimaced. This was going nowhere good. "Rio's nice this time of year. I've been a few times."

"I suppose."

"You know, if you'd just told me, I would've helped you."

"You would've?" He saw no point in trying to hide where he was. Clearly, his boss already knew.

"I'm not completely heartless. I remember having a fiancée. I know how much you miss her. I could've helped you out and possibly avoided the reason for this call."

"Okay, sorry." That seemed the appropriate thing to say. He was still shocked by Vindico's insistence that he would've helped Rainer break the Angels' owners' rules.

"Yeah well, I guess I should be the one apologizing," Vindico stated cryptically. "But first, tell Miss Haydenshire congratulations. You two became an aunt and future uncle last night."

"What?" Rainer gasped. In all of his methodical planning, he'd never considered the fact that Brooke was due to go into labor at any moment.

"Yeah, and your absence was noted by the press as the Crown Governor's first grandbaby was born." He was almost laughing by this point. "It took me about half a second to figure out where you must've gone. So, I informed the press that you were on special assignment out of the country."

"Thank you." His heart steadied as he willed his breakfast to remain in his stomach.

"No problem, and tell Emily that Will is the proud father of a bouncing baby girl. She's good. Brooke's good. They named her Lily Ana."

"Uh, Will and Brooke had the baby last night," he informed Emily.

"Oh," she closed her eyes, "I missed it." Deep regret tensed in her rhythms.

"I couldn't get Garrett on his cell, so I figured you could tell him when he picks Emily up. I assume she has to be back at the orphanage before her presence is missed."

"How do you do that?" Rainer asked in awe.

Vindico laughed heartily. "Even without all of the special ops training, detective training, and endless work I've done in the past ten years, this wasn't terribly difficult to figure out."

Rainer nodded his acceptance of that.

"Are we planning a trip to South America next weekend as well?"

"I wish, but I don't think we'd better chance this again."

"If you change your mind, let me know. Like I said, I would've helped you."

"I don't think Garrett can get Emily out again, but thanks," Rainer stammered. He was still not certain what he should say.

"Understood, but listen, I'm going to pick you up at the airport, which will lend to the story that you were on special assignment. We need to talk."

Rainer tried to recognize the emotion that Vindico's voice had taken on. It sounded like regret and sorrow.

"Why? What's wrong? My car's there. I could just meet you at the office if you want."

"Uh-huh," Vindico replied hesitantly. "I'll meet you at the gate. Try to enjoy the rest of your morning."

With that, the line went dead, and Rainer had an uneasy feeling as he lay back on the bed and casted Emily. He held her in his shield until Garrett knocked on the door.

Vindico's cryptic statement that if Rainer had asked for his help, he could've avoided the reason for the call had his mind reeling.

When Emily began to cry in earnest from hearing the knock on the suite door, Rainer shut down his ponderings and tried to soothe her.

"He was supposed to make you smile," Garrett teased when Rainer had awkwardly walked to the door to open it with Emily clinging to him.

Emily spun with vengeance burning furiously in her eyes. "This is all your fault." Her temper finally worked its way through her sadness. "And now I can't see him for two more weeks, and we have a brand-new niece, and I'm not there to see her either," she continued her rant. "I hate you!"

Rainer grimaced. He'd been expecting this.

It appeared Garrett had as well. "Yep, been waiting to hear that all week," he concluded and then furrowed his brow. "Wait, what do you mean we have a niece?"

"Brooke had the baby last night," she spat.

"Wow." Garrett moved into the room and closed the door. "I bet Will's already completely wrapped around her tiny finger."

"Em, baby, come on, shh…" Rainer began whispering in her ear as he held her against his chest. His heart broke over having to leave her again.

"I don't want to go back." Emily knotted Rainer's T-shirt in her fists. "It's awful. I want to go home."

Rainer clenched his jaw. He tried to recall why he couldn't demand that Garrett leave her alone, and why he couldn't take her to the airport to bring her home with him.

"Yeah, it's awful," Garrett agreed, "but the kids who live there don't get to leave. They don't even get a night off, and Aida's there in tears because you hadn't come back this morning. You promised her you'd come back. Are you gonna break that?"

This only served to bring on gut-wrenching sobs, and Rainer shook his head at Garrett. Guilt was not the way to get Emily to calm down. It never had been. Why did no one understand that but him? It was incredibly obvious.

"Garrett, we'll meet you in the lobby in a few minutes, okay?"

"Uh sorry, man, but you can't be seen leaving with her. So, how about I take a slow walk down to the soda machine at the end of the hall and then come back?"

"Whatever." He was growing more and more agitated with Garrett the longer he stayed in the suite.

Garrett left, and Rainer let Emily cry. He held her close, rubbed her back, and told her how much he loved her. He wiped away the tears when she'd let him. When she calmed, he cradled her face in his hands.

"Listen to me. It's just two more weeks. Just take it one day at a time, and before you know it, I'll be standing at the airport, probably jumping the guardrails as soon as you land, okay? I'll talk to you every day, and I'll dream of you every night. Then when you get back, I'll show you everything I've been dreaming about." A slight smile spread across her beautiful face.

"And when I decide to let you put clothes on again, you know, a week or two later, then I'll take you to Will and Brooke's. They'll probably be so sleep-deprived by then, they'll let you hold the new baby and play with her as long as you want." Her energy began to calm.

"Promise?" Emily laid her head tenderly back on Rainer's chest.

"I promise."

Emily seemed to draw on deep resolve as Rainer brushed kisses over her cheeks and forehead.

"You don't have to jump the guardrails." She beamed at him.

"We'll see how hard up I am by then. I may not be able to," he teased as she giggled sweetly.

Garrett returned a few minutes later, and Rainer had Emily calmed and even apologizing for shouting at him.

"How do you do that?" Garrett shook his head in disbelief.

"She's my baby."

Garrett nodded his acceptance of that fact. "No joke. I won't tell Dad, but you definitely have her all figured out."

"You keep her safe," Rainer demanded.

"You know I will."

"Oh and here." Rainer pulled his wallet from his back pocket and handed Garrett the check. Garrett stared from the check to Rainer and back again in stunned disbelief.

"You make certain she eats," Rainer continued his orders.

"Man, you have no idea how far this will go here. Seriously, this is amazing."

After a deep, fervent kiss, meant to last for the next two weeks,

Rainer released Emily to Garrett with a harrowing sense of loss washing over him yet again.

The emptiness returned to his chest while he watched from the window. She climbed into the ATV that Garrett used to get around Brazil.

CHAPTER 10

WAR CRY

Misery was Rainer's constant companion as he thanked Pete for ushering him quickly into the jump seat of the jet. He joined the other pilots and coolant officers and tried to stay out of the way.

He wanted to be alone with his dejection. He'd almost forgotten Vindico's warning that he was meeting him at the airport. Just over four hours later, Rainer was shocked that not only was Vindico standing there, but Logan, Adeline, and the Haydenshires were there as well.

They all looked devastated, and Rainer's stomach clenched as he took in their expressions. "What's wrong?" he demanded as soon as he was close enough for them to hear him.

"How's my baby girl?" Governor Haydenshire dodged. He was very obviously putting off whatever they'd all come to tell him.

"She's a little better than she was," Rainer supplied impatiently. He couldn't help but wonder why the governor wasn't upset that he'd snuck out of the country to go spend the night with Emily.

"I'm so glad you got to see her, sweetheart," Mrs. Haydenshire vowed. "I know how much you've missed her. You've looked so sad all week. And I knew this was going to be hard on her. Everyone forgets what it's like for Receivers."

Rainer studied her. He sincerely wished someone would tell him what the hell was going on.

"So, you heard about my new grandbaby?" the governor continued to try to distract Rainer.

His patience was running thin. He finally turned to Vindico. "Will you please tell me why you're all here?"

Vindico nodded. He gave Rainer a sorrowful look. "Yeah, I'm not big on being forcefully distracted either." He threw the governor a wry glance as Governor Haydenshire nodded his admittance that he had been evasive.

Rainer hadn't checked any luggage, so they exited and headed toward the rear parking lot.

"Will you please tell me what's going on?" Rainer demanded of Logan.

Pain was Logan's predominant expression. He nodded.

"The papers finally broke the story of Samantha Peterson's kidnapping and murder. The mug shots of the two men who were standing guard that night were in the news a day or two ago," Logan explained.

"Wretchkinsides figured out I'd taken out his prizefighter," Vindico interrupted. He clenched his jaw for a moment before continuing. "So, I assume *that* coupled with you and Garrett taking out the three drivers he'd trained and was so sure would be able to force Emily's car off the road brought this on." Vindico drew a steadying breath. "We received his answering war cry." He shuddered slightly.

"Okay, what was it?"

Vindico stopped walking and looked him in the eye. He offered him a steadying gaze. "I cannot tell you how sorry I am, but late last night he blew up the Mustang." Vindico tried to force his gruff voice to sound soothing but didn't quite hit the mark.

"What?" Rainer gasped. He couldn't breathe. He turned to Logan and willed him to confess that this was some sort of horrible joke.

"I'm so sorry, man." Logan reached and steadied Rainer. "It's a mess. You don't want to see it. I called Sam. He said he can build you another just like it if you want."

Stunned, furious terror coursed like shards of ice through Rainer's veins. His mind was unable to believe what he was being told. It couldn't be. He wouldn't allow it.

At that moment, the press located him outside the airport and began to swarm.

"Rainer, can you tell us who did this?"

"Rainer, where were you on special assignment?"

"Does Emily know about the car?"

The questions came fast and furiously. Rainer felt like he was being pelted with some sort of rapid-fire weaponry.

The pain was physical and moved throughout his entire body.

"Rainer, where was the Iodex assignment you were sent to?" called another reporter, repeating the same question.

"Just get them the hell away from me. I want to see my car," Rainer demanded.

Vindico pulled his badge, and Logan followed suit.

"If Mr. Lawson answers that question, he'll no longer be employed by Iodex. He's had a rough day, so I really don't want to fire him after all of this. Could you please move away and let him through?" Vindico demanded.

His threat gave more credence to the story that Rainer had been on special assignment. Somewhere in the recesses of Rainer's mind, he appreciated that, but at that moment he couldn't access any information except that Wretchkinsides's thugs had destroyed his car.

Vindico and Logan formed a kind of barrier around him as he forced his way to the parking lot where he'd left the Mustang.

"Crown Governor, as the man who raised Rainer, could you tell us if you feel he's visibly distressed?" a reporter buzzed beside Governor Haydenshire.

Rainer didn't wait to hear the governor's retort to the inane question. He began moving faster. Seeing his car was the only thing that made sense to him in that endless moment.

"Where do they find these idiots?" Vindico quipped. Rainer saw Logan nod his agreement, but he kept his eyes locked forward as he continued his determined march.

"Rainer, are you sure you want to see this? Maybe it would be best to remember it the way it was," Mrs. Haydenshire pled as she tried to keep up with him.

"Mom," Logan huffed, "he's not three. Leave him alone."

By keeping up his rhythmic advance, Rainer made it to the parking lot farthest from the airport in record time. Relentless reporters all hoping to capture his anguish on film were still following him.

Vindico shook his head and spun back. "That's it! Right here. This is as far as you're going," he challenged. He grabbed Logan and positioned him in the very spot where he'd drawn the invisible line in the sand. "If you move past Officer Haydenshire, he will arrest you."

Governor Haydenshire nodded. He turned to stand beside Logan. It was a defiant dare to anyone willing to move past an arresting officer and the judge.

"Come on, Lawson." Vindico cuffed Rainer's shoulder and ushered him into the blocked parking lot. He eased him behind the trees and shrubs so that the reporters could no longer snap photos.

There it stood—the smoldering, burned-out cage of what was once his most prized possession. Bile burned his throat. He clenched his jaw against the hot tears that threatened to overtake him. He willed himself to understand the horrific display, but his mind rejected the image.

"This is entirely my fault. I just never thought…" Vindico began. He was shaking his head as he stared at what was left of the car.

Finally able to formulate words, Rainer turned his eyes from the remains of the car. "How is it your fault? You didn't do this. I'm the one who didn't cast it." Rainer shuddered as the deep regret threatened to consume him.

"When you didn't show at the hospital last night, I figured out where you were and what you'd done. I also knew that if you got caught, they'd end Emily's career in short order. I immediately told the press I'd sent you on location out of the country," Vindico elaborated. "I know the press is Wretchkinsides's best ally right now. This wasn't even done well."

Vindico leaned over and picked up what appeared to be the wired end of a blasting cap. He shook his head and then threw down the wiring.

68

"He's getting desperate, and men like Wretchkinsides are most volatile and the most dangerous when they're desperate. He was hoping you'd left your car unprotected at the airport. He had his explosives guys rig up some C4. They even left the taggant. Normally, he has his guys make their own C4 with no tracer, but this wasn't planned. He ordered them to get it destroyed quickly, and that's what they did.

"They could have blown it up with their own energy, but they wanted it destroyed, not just burned out. They put enough C4 in the car to make certain nothing was left, moved away, threw an electric cast mixed with a heightened sound wave, and they were done." Vindico shook his head in disgust. "I really am sorry. He's punishing you for helping me, and for being damn good at what you do."

"Stephen finally had enough. He paid the attendant a hundred dollars to hang up a few no trespassing signs," Mrs. Haydenshire explained as she came to stand near Rainer. Logan and Adeline followed.

Unable to stop them, the memories of everything the Mustang had been to him flooded through his mind. It was his father's last gift. He needed the freedom it afforded him.

The recollections overwhelmed him. Emily, with her hair whipping out behind her as Rainer drove with the top down, revving the engine to make her smile. The things they'd done in that car. The way the gearshift felt in his hand as he put the engine through its paces. The feel of the soft leather seats, the steering wheel sliding through his hands. The intoxicating fragrance of her perfume entangled in the wind as it mixed with the smell of the leather seats and the fumes. They all made a heady cocktail in Rainer's mind.

He recalled Logan asking him to put the top up so they could talk their way through being teenagers. They were so often stupid and reckless and sensitive and caring all at the same moment.

The dirty jokes, the goading laughter, so many things tied up inside of that piece of their adolescence. The sheer number of times he'd copped a feel in the front seat or slipped his hand up Emily's skirt. The first time she'd grabbed him through his jeans, and he'd almost lost control, at barely sixteen years old. He could feel her hand on him, groping him, telling him how hard he was, though he certainly knew.

Something brushed against his bicep. He jerked away furiously. He spun toward the motion and glared at Adeline.

"I'm so sorry." Her voice shook. "I thought I could help." She dropped her gaze to the ground. She'd been trying to cast him. She'd thought maybe she could slip her healing, soothing energy into him.

Logan shot him a warning glance, and Rainer let his eyes close for the length of one heartbeat. He clenched his jaw together and refused to yell at Adeline. She'd only been trying to help. He repeated the mantra in his head.

"Just please don't," Rainer forced out of his mouth.

Adeline nodded her understanding, but heartbreak marred her features.

"I don't think any of us are going to be getting in for a while, sweetheart," Mrs. Haydenshire soothed. She put her arm around Adeline to bolster her.

She was right, Rainer knew. His shield formed an internal steel cage around him. It was impenetrable to anyone. He felt the impregnable wall between him and the world. There was only one person who could ever have broken through it, and she was thousands of miles away. Rainer's heart ached as the horror of reality settled on him.

"Son, do you want me to have Emily flown home? I don't know what else to do. You've been through enough." Governor Haydenshire joined them. The look on his face was extremely concerned.

Not certain why, Rainer shook his head though that was precisely what he wanted.

"Does she know?" Rainer choked.

Vindico nodded. "I finally got through to Garrett a few minutes before you landed. He told her. She's waiting on your call."

Everyone stood reticent beside him and waited for him to instruct them as to how to make him feel better, but all Rainer knew at that moment was that he wanted to be alone.

His cell phone chirped, and he fumbled momentarily. He tried to remember where his phone was and what the sound meant. He pulled it from his pocket and opened the text.

Rainer blinked back tears. He was astonished that she knew what he was feeling from another country, from another continent. He shook his head, simply unable to look at the heap of charred metal any longer.

He turned his back on the remains of his car. Logan held up the keys to the Hummer, and Rainer extended his hand. He caught them as Logan let them go. Rainer knitted his brow. He didn't fully understand how Logan had known to bring the Hummer to the airport.

"Hey, Em may be better at it than all of us, but she's not the only one who knows what you do when shit happens." Logan smiled as Rainer nodded his understanding.

"Thanks," he managed.

"You know, I think we still have those old Diamondbacks we got you and Logan on your tenth birthdays, the ones that went through our trampoline." Governor Haydenshire smiled at the memory as he shook his head. "I could dig them out of the barn if you think you might need to use them for a while," the governor continued to tease as he saw that Rainer was responding.

Vindico chuckled. "That sounds like a good story."

Logan was laughing at the memory, and Rainer felt his face pull into a smile. He was shocked that in light of everything that had happened, he was able to laugh at his and Logan's antics when they were young.

Emily was right. He didn't necessarily have to have the item he'd always associated with the memories. The memories themselves were much more valuable. She was also correct about him not really wanting to be alone. Rainer met Logan's wry smile.

"You know," Logan offered, "if you want, we could head home, throw on our suits, take the Hummer for a spin for a few hours. Maybe go see Sam, and then head to the memorial."

"Hey, Lawson, like the governor said, you've had a rough go. If you don't feel up to the service, you don't have to come, but I actually think it might help," Vindico offered.

Rainer shook his head. "No, I want to go," he stated without giving it much thought. He was working on instinct alone.

He turned back to Logan and nodded. "Let's go." He tried not to sound pleading.

Logan looked genuinely thrilled to be going along. Still holding his cell in his hands, Rainer texted Emily back.

> I'm all right. Just need to think for a little while. Gonna go for a drive with Logan. I miss you so much. I wish you could come home, but you should stay. Aida needs you.

He typed what was in his heart. He wasn't entirely certain that the last sentiment was the truth. He doubted that Aida needed her as much as he did at that moment, but he turned off the screen and stowed the phone in his pocket.

"Are you sure you're okay?" Vindico asked as they headed back to the parking lot that held his Agusta and the Haydenshires' cars.

"I don't really have much choice, do I?" He hadn't meant to be disrespectful, but the loss was hitting him hard.

Dan slapped him on the back. He didn't seem to mind Rainer's tone. "Been there, said that more times than I care to remember. Maybe we can go out and grab a beer after the service. Unless you want to go back to an empty bed?" He knew perfectly well that Rainer didn't want to feel the cold emptiness of a mattress that didn't contain Emily's heat or her curves, but he lowered his voice so that Governor and Mrs. Haydenshire didn't hear the sentiment.

"Yeah, that'd be good." He wondered if that was really how he would feel in a few hours, but he decided to go with it anyway. Drowning the pain in a few drinks sounded rather appealing.

CHAPTER 11
LET IT GO

Rainer pulled the Hummer into the garage. The pain set in with a harsh, blunt cruelty. Although he was always the first to admit that he was keenly devoted to his Mustang, he wasn't certain even he'd understood the depth of his respect and love for the car that had raised him.

Rainer threw the bag he'd used in Rio in his and Emily's room. He dressed in his suit slacks and dress shirt quickly. He wanted to leave. He wanted to drive away from the pain. After grabbing a tie and his sport coat, he waited on Logan in the Hummer.

"Let's go." Logan hoisted himself up into the passenger seat. Rainer drove out of the gravel driveway in silence and headed to the highway.

"Wanna go see Sam?" Logan quizzed, but Rainer just shrugged. He didn't want to think. He didn't want to make any decisions. He just wanted to drive.

After a solid hour of staring at the asphalt as it slid beneath them and then disappeared in the rearview mirror, he turned to Logan. "I'm kinda hungry."

Logan laughed and gave Rainer his version of the Haydenshire smirk. "That's probably a good sign. I'm pretty sure burgers, shakes, and onion rings are one of the stages of grief."

Rainer laughed. He was struck by how good it felt to laugh with Logan. After nimbly maneuvering through the drive-thru line, he ordered a variety of cheeseburgers, hot dogs, and onion rings. He placed the food between him and Logan, and just as they'd done since their sixteenth birthdays, they proceeded to devour food out of the bags with no concern as to who ordered what.

They downed the large chocolate shakes, and Rainer felt a pang of sorrow when he started to order Emily's small vanilla shake with extra cherries out of habit, but then remembered she wasn't with them.

Although the Hummer was certainly a fine piece of machinery, it didn't respond to Rainer the way the Mustang always had.

"Hey, man, I know you probably had way more fun with Em in the 'Stang, but we had some good times too. I really am sorry," Logan offered sincerely.

Rainer smiled. "Yeah, we did." He let the memories of him and Logan in the Mustang reel through his mind as he followed the curving roads toward Alexandria.

"How was Rio?" Logan tried for a new topic. Rainer sighed, but Logan had agreed to go along on his ride to nowhere so the least he could do was talk.

"I really only saw the inside of the hotel room, but seeing Em was great." He tried to let the evening before soothe his grief.

"Is she okay?" Logan seemed uncertain if Emily was a topic he should bring up after everything that had happened.

"She was better when she left this morning than when she first got there last night."

"Don't brag, man," Logan chastised.

Rainer shook his head at Logan's insinuation and joined in his laughter.

"She hadn't been eating or sleeping. Some of the Angels were giving her a hard time. It's kind of a mess." He gripped the steering wheel tighter to keep his hands from using his phone to call Governor Haydenshire to have Emily sent home.

They talked a little more about Emily and the Angels, and then

Rainer turned in to the gravel lot. His muscles eased as he turned off the Hummer.

He and Logan slid out of the SUV, and Rainer drew a deep breath. He inhaled the gasoline, car fumes, and a hint of Old Spice aftershave. A smile automatically spread across his face.

While sharing his signature smile, Sam walked toward Rainer and Logan. He was shaking his head and wiping his hands on an old rag.

"Trouble just won't leave you be, will it, Rain Man?" Sam slapped him on the shoulder. He looked truly sorrowful for Rainer's plight.

"You're not joking," Rainer lamented as Sam turned to Logan.

"I am joking, boy." He grinned at Rainer while extending his hand to Logan. "You keep your sense of humor in that Mustang or something?"

With a goading grin and the afternoon sunlight glinting in his eyes, Sam chuckled. "Now, the last time I saw Miss Emily, she was a darn sight prettier. What have you gone and done to her?" He gestured to Logan, and all three of them cracked up.

"Logan, I haven't seen you in a while. You keeping him straight?" He pointed to Rainer.

"Nah." Logan shook his head and smiled. "I leave that to Em. I was never any good at it anyway. I usually just got him in more trouble."

Sam chuckled and nodded his agreement.

A few minutes later, they were seated on the tailgate of an old pickup in the lot, drinking ice-cold Coke out of glass bottles.

"I tell you what, any man who'd destroy another man's car,"—Sam clasped his chest, feigning heartache—"that's low down. That's what that is."

Rainer raised his bottle in a toast to that, and Logan and Sam joined in.

"So, what are we gonna drive next?" Sam studied Rainer thoughtfully.

Rainer drew a long sip of his Coke. He futilely hoped the fizzy beverage might wash away the inflicting wound.

"I don't know," he sighed. "I want my Mustang." He knew he sounded like a spoiled child.

Sam smiled wistfully as he shared a glance with Logan that Rainer pretended not to notice.

"You don't want that 'Stang," Sam soothed. "I told you it was a sissy, white-boy car," he teased, but Rainer didn't laugh.

He chose to succumb to the pain instead, so Sam went on. "Nope, you don't want that Mustang. You want what was inside that car."

Rainer furrowed his brow and lifted his weary eyes to the man who always seemed to have the answers he needed whenever he needed them.

"There was a piece of your soul in that car. It fit you because it was you," he vowed. "A classic, American automobile built when America told itself we were innocent and protected, even though we never really were." Rainer and Logan listened intently. "That car was everything you said you wanted when his daddy brought you out here when you were sixteen years old with your daddy's money burning a hole in your pocket." Sam chuckled at the recollection.

"A Mustang, first off the line, not red, no, no, had to be crimson, reminded him of Miss Emily's hair. Wanted a classic that would fly just like you, boy. It was a fine car. A virgin car, that made a gesture to the world that had robbed you of a little too much. Wasn't always a nice gesture, but it made you happy," Sam stated with a wry grin.

"Wanted to show off a little, wanted an engine that'd make some noise for you when you couldn't seem to find the words to tell the world what you really thought. And it did everything you wanted and more. You want what was inside that car." Sam paused and seemed to consider.

"You want to hold it in your hands, and you just can't. All those things making your heart hurt and your head ache, you gotta let 'em go. They'll eat you alive. So, you take all those memories, all those times Miss Emily let you get past second base in that car," he drawled knowingly as Rainer and Logan laughed. "All the drives with the top down, all the dates, all of the laughs over burgers and fries..." He gestured to Logan. "All of your childhood, you hold those tight and don't let anybody take those away, but you aren't that kid anymore.

"Not quite so innocent. Been through a whole lotta stuff nobody oughta have to go through. Got a ring on Miss Emily's finger, got a house, and a job, and if I'm not mistaken, I believe you just mighta cashed in Miss Emily's innocence as well." Sam chuckled as Rainer blushed.

Logan laughed and punched Rainer in the shoulder.

"You're a man now, Rainer, and that car isn't here anymore. So, you take your soul with you when you let it go, son, but you gotta let it go. It's time to grow up." Sam gave Rainer a gaze that said he, at least, thought Rainer had turned out all right. That gaze soothed Rainer's soul.

"You can't live your life looking in the rearview mirror of a '65 Mustang. That's why the windshield's so much bigger than the mirror," Sam concluded.

Rainer drew a deep steadying breath. "But I don't know what I want. When I was sixteen, that Mustang was perfect. It was exactly what I wanted."

Sam smiled kindly. "Well, Miss Emily's already called me up twice worried sick about you. And you got your partner in crime over here watching you like a hawk." Sam nodded his head to Logan. "Our new Crown Governor called me before the sun got up this mornin'. You got a lotta people who care about you, myself included.

"Why not give it a little time for the wound to heal itself up, and then this time why don't you listen to all those people who love you, boy? When you were sixteen, you couldn't hear any voice but your own." A broad grin spread across Sam's face as he allowed, "Well, maybe Miss Emily's, if she was telling you to slide that hand a little higher, but that was it."

Rainer and Logan laughed again.

"We're gonna find you just what you want, but you're gonna have to slow down, take your time. Let your soul heal before you try and make it a part of another car," Sam warned. "And whatever we decide on, Rain Man, there are gonna be good memories in it as well."

Then, with a faraway look in his eye, he shared his story. "Drove a hot-off-the-line, '69 Cadillac Eldorado on my first date to pick up my sweet Dolores. Near 'bout stripped the clutch trying to get away from her daddy about a year later when I brought her home, and her beehive wasn't buzzin' no more."

Sam raised his right eyebrow with a smirk. Rainer and Logan guffawed.

"Few years later, I drove her away from the church house in a Mercury Monterey. Drove all the way to the Poconos Honeymoon Cabins," Sam announced proudly before continuing.

"Spent almost three months' salary from the gas station, and she still wouldn't let me leave the lights on." Sam shook his head and feigned bitter disappointment as Rainer and Logan continued to laugh.

"Bout nine months later, I traded in my Monterey, got an Oldsmobile Deluxe. Gonna bring my baby girl home from the hospital in style. I was glad that Olds had a radio 'cause let me tell you, I couldn't tell you who cried more, my sweet Dolores or Deidre. They both hollered to raise the rafters on that drive home. I thought I'd lose my mind." He smiled at the memory.

"See, Rain Man, it's not the car. It's the people inside the car, and you have all of them right here with you, and that, boy, that's where the soul comes from."

"So, you'll help me find something?" With sudden desperation, Rainer needed to know that Sam would always be there and would always help guide him. This time, he intended to listen.

"You know it." Sam slowly walked Logan and Rainer back to the Hummer.

CHAPTER 12

REMEMBER

An hour later, Logan and Rainer walked solemnly into the cathedral where Samantha Peterson was being remembered. Rainer had mourned Samantha the night he'd watched her be murdered. He mourned the loss of life, but as he considered everything, he knew that he'd never really even known Samantha, and that she had never really known herself.

So, it was out of sorrow for her parents and sorrow over the loss of someone who had so much further to go, who should have been given time to figure all of that out, that Rainer sank into the pew between Logan and Vindico to pay his respects.

The senseless loss and the horrendous things that had been done to Samantha haunted every Iodex officer seated in the pew.

From the loss, vengeance grew. It had to stop. Wretchkinsides had to be ended. This could not be allowed to continue.

As Rainer glanced discreetly at all of the officers seated beside him, he knew the people who were going to have to put an end to the violence and the terror were right there beside him.

It had to end. The words echoed in the tears her mother shed and her father fought. They resonated from the priest who gave the eulogy. Each bitter dirge rang with the directive. The air seemed to resonate with determination and purpose as everyone stood and followed the Petersons out of the church.

It had to end.

CHAPTER 13

DR PEPPER

The following Friday, Rainer and Logan finally arrived home from another extremely boring day of following Clarence Pendergrath around the academy and then returning to Iodex to work on his father's case.

Adeline had left the mail on the table and was getting ready to have dinner at the farmhouse with the Haydenshires. She and Logan were to discuss her mother and the case against her with Jack Stariff.

Rainer tried to feel hopeful as he pulled a few hot dogs out of the refrigerator. *Emily will be home in one week,* he told himself repeatedly.

As the doldrums of sitting through sub-freshman classes—that he himself had taken and passed five years before—had been mind-numbing, he'd spent most of the day thinking about all of the things he wanted to do with Emily when she returned.

"Hey, Logan," he called. Logan raised his eyebrows and handed Rainer one of the envelopes on the table as he inhaled a canister of chips. "Are you and Adeline still planning on going to that bed and breakfast thing next weekend?"

Logan rolled his eyes. "Yes, but you owe me so big."

"Hey, I believe you were the guy who said, and I quote, 'Hey baby, why don't we give Em and Rainer a weekend when she comes home.

I'll take you somewhere fun. I know the trial is getting to you, so you pick anywhere you want.'" Rainer cracked up.

A smirk Logan couldn't quite hide spread across his face. "Yeah, well, I was trying to show off my romantic side. I didn't know she was gonna pick somewhere so girly."

Rainer gave him a mocking grin. "Is that what you're calling it now, your romantic side? Did Adeline not like Dr Pepper?" He reminded Logan of the name he'd given his member when they were preteens. They both doubled over laughing hysterically.

"Hey," Logan managed between guffaws. "Trust me, she likes Dr Pepper." He waggled his eyebrows.

"Yeah, well, that thing between her legs that Dr Pepper can't get enough of, it's going with you to the bed and breakfast so at least there's that. But for future reference, if you say 'anywhere you want,' you end up staying places called The Betsy Carriage House that looks like everything that was ever pink or lacy crawled there to die."

"That's better than the dick inn, which is where she picked first." Logan shook his head.

When Logan had made his romantic gesture, Adeline had pulled up a list of bed and breakfasts near Arlington on the computer. The first listing that had interested her was named the Richard Johnson Inn.

When Logan and Rainer had managed to collect enough maturity between them to stop howling with laughter, Logan had declared that he could not stay there and begged Adeline to pick somewhere else.

A few minutes later, Adeline emerged from their bedroom. She was no longer wearing scrubs, and she was giving Logan and Rainer incredulous, albeit adoring looks.

"Are you ready, baby?" Logan beamed at her.

"Yeah, I'm just gonna grab a Dr Pepper." This had Rainer and Logan guffawing again as Adeline shook her head.

"I really, really miss Emily," she sighed as she removed a Dr Pepper from the refrigerator and headed to the garage.

Rainer opened the envelope Logan had handed him a few minutes earlier. He added it to a stack of car brochures that Emily's brothers had compiled for Rainer in an effort to help.

Anger and dejected sadness coursed through his veins. He fought not to pout. He reconsidered and removed the rather substantial check for the total worth of the Mustang from the envelope and put it in his wallet.

With a defeated sigh, he picked up his cell. Emily still hadn't texted. Fionna, Emily, and Chloe were throwing a slumber party for Aida and all of her friends. Rainer knew Emily wouldn't be able to text much that evening, but he desperately wanted to hear from her.

She'd phoned her mother, and Mrs. Haydenshire had flown several large boxes containing popcorn, candy, movies, new pajamas, board games, and silly string to Rio, via Captain Namphis. Garrett had picked it up for them. When the supplies had arrived, the girls were ready to party.

Loneliness swirled around Rainer. It threatened to drown him. He needed to get out of the house. He crawled into the Hummer and debated. He was certainly always welcome at the farmhouse. It would always be the home that had raised him, but he didn't want to interrupt Logan and Adeline's meeting with Jack.

The charges against Adeline were mounting due to her mother's venomous lies about why drugs were found in the apartment when she'd been arrested. She was blaming Adeline for everything. Thus far, Adeline had been given eight random urine tests in an effort to prove she'd never used. She'd popped one right after having surgery and being given painkillers. Her mother's lawyers ate it up.

Rainer cranked the Hummer. There was always work to do. Maybe he could come up with something more damning in the evidence against Pendergrath.

Before he'd left work that evening, he'd come across some information on a man who'd signed over his life savings to Pendergrath just before he'd committed suicide. As the man had shown no signs of depression or erratic behavior, Rainer had spoken to the man's ex-wife. Though she was not Gifted, she identified Pendergrath in a picture.

Vindico was set to interview her Monday, and Rainer decided he could sort through some more of the information on her case beforehand.

After he flashed his badge, he moved into the Iodex offices. The lights were still on. He was certain Vindico was still working. He worked all weekend, every weekend. He was relentless.

As Rainer considered the loneliness that had driven him from his own home, he understood Dan's obsession so much more.

He sank down at his desk and pulled up the files on his computer he'd been working on earlier in the day.

His head shot up as he heard something crash in Vindico's office. His heart thundered in his chest. Rainer pulled his pistol, chambered a round, and edged toward the closed office door. Then he heard laughter.

He leaned in and listened. A low moan and a voice that was distinctly Bridgette's calling out Dan's name had Rainer holstering his weapon and bolting from the door. He cringed as Vindico began informing her that she liked it like that.

He broke out into a frantic sprint, fled through the Iodex doors, and bound back into the Hummer. While willing his brain to forget everything he'd just heard, Rainer cranked the car and popped his phone into the speaker dock. He cranked up Radiohead as loud as the enhanced speakers would play.

CHAPTER 14

GIFTED SEX ED. - 101

By Monday, Rainer was trying his best not to be irritated with everyone around him. He and Logan reported for the morning meeting and then headed to Venton.

Clarence had spent the majority of his weekend in detention and was being quite belligerent about the experience. They escorted him to his first class and stood outside the door while Clarence began studying different ways to use the magnetrons that Gifted people had in their bodies.

"Have you ever done anything with the magnetron thing besides make popcorn?" Logan quizzed.

Rainer considered and then shook his head. "I don't think so."

"Magnetrons are what make Gifted people able to pick up on all of the different energies in an area. They are essentially our radar," Logan and Rainer listened to Mentor Sullivan explain.

"Oh." Logan looked impressed. Rainer chuckled at the fact that he had a rather strong radar as an Ioses Predilect, but that he hadn't really known how it worked.

Just then, Mentor Bryant approached Logan and Rainer. She smiled and appeared to have just come from the Admin building. She'd been Emily's creative writing mentor, but Rainer hadn't had her.

"Chancellor Wilshire asked me to give you this. We're a little worried Clarence might cause trouble today with everything going on. He wanted to make sure that you both attended his health and wellness class with him. He has to be in these classes. They're required by the Senate." She blushed slightly as Rainer furrowed his brow. Logan took the note from Mentor Bryant.

"Okay, sure, no problem." Rainer wondered why they needed to be inside the classroom with Clarence.

"Tell Emily I said hello." Mentor Bryant made a quick retreat.

Logan unfolded the note. "Ah geez, really?" He rolled his eyes and handed off the note to Rainer.

"Great," he sighed. "It's amative and erogenous energies week. That's perfect." Rainer had been through a health and wellness class every year of his six years at the Academy. One week of each semester was dedicated to the energies related to having intercourse. He recalled those weeks of his adolescence as being rather uncomfortable and embarrassing.

The students were divided into groups and instructed on the energy created during lovemaking, ejaculation, and the energy in the release itself. They were schooled on how overwhelming it was to join your energy with someone else's.

The ejaculate that would ultimately create a Gifted child was extremely potent in terms of the sheer amount of energy it held.

All bodily fluids held the owner's energy, but Rainer recalled that ejaculate held more than any other. It was seconded by vaginal lubricant. Tears held a great deal of energy as well.

By Friday, every female on campus would have to have performed the cast to seal her womb for the school nurse in order to pass the class. The first days of the week, the women would be casted by the female mentors or campus nurses so that they could experience what it should feel like to be sealed off, and therefore be able to know if they'd performed the cast correctly on themselves.

This tended to make the majority of the heterosexual males on campus extremely lascivious in their knowledge that the girls on campus, for the next few days anyway, couldn't be impregnated.

Anyone with any dating prospects at all was keenly aware of their partner's sexual energies as it was forced to the forefront of their mind.

Many Gifted couples held off on having intercourse until amative energies week because of their lack of knowledge of how to perform the cast and the fear of what might happen if it should be done incorrectly.

The air on campus would be thick with erotic energy and tension. Rainer recalled the temptation to try to talk Emily into taking a drive with him many times during these particular weeks of the school year. His fear that she might not be ready and that it would change things between them had kept him from ever making the request.

When Emily had started asking, it became almost unbearable to even be at school during amative and erogenous energy week. His mind would be full to bursting with erotic thoughts of her. He'd spend the week trying to hide the effects of thinking about her during class.

"When is his health class?" Rainer quizzed dejectedly.

"Next." Logan showed Rainer the copy of Clarence's schedule.

"Great."

"At least my brothers aren't here this year."

Since most of the Haydenshires were only a year apart in school, Connor, Cal, and Patrick had been in different years at the academy when Rainer and Logan had begun. They'd had a great deal of fun harassing Logan and Rainer their first couple of years during amative energies week.

It was a source of contention among Gifted families that the boys' sexual energies classes provided them knowledge of other forms of birth control but did not teach the boys the process of closing a woman's womb. The reasoning had always been that it should be the woman's choice if she was closed off. While Rainer heartily agreed with that, he also thought the responsibility of birth control shouldn't only fall to the woman.

However, a fair number of Gifted families felt strongly that the male participant should be able to seal her if he so chose, which always led to nasty letters and phone calls to the academy during the week.

Once, a few parents had even picketed. The knowledge of how to close the female womb was widespread around the academy. Rainer had been instructed in the proper way to do it by Garrett with the vehement addendum that he was only ever to do it if that's what she wanted.

There was a very small group of students on campus, led by Mentor Hannon, who would protest the class altogether. They believed that not educating the students on healthy sexual relationships, or on how to bring pleasure to your partner, or even how to seal the womb, would mean that students wouldn't participate in the act.

That always seemed stupid and ridiculous to Rainer. It was difficult to fight what you were genetically encoded to do.

The Haydenshires had long been of the belief that sex was a natural part of life, and that all of their children should be aware of the ways to have a healthy relationship. Communication was encouraged and often thrust upon them randomly. That hadn't seemed to make it any easier on the governor when Rainer had started sleeping with Emily, however. Rainer smirked as he recalled those trying few weeks.

As all academy classes ran for two and a half hours, Rainer glanced at his watch and tried not to think about Clarence in a sex ed Class. He shuddered.

"What are we going to do when he starts acting like the prick he is?" Logan gestured toward Mentor Sullivan's classroom.

"I don't know, but it didn't sound like we can take him out of the class."

"As if that class isn't awkward enough without a kid like him in there."

"Who's teaching his health class?" Rainer hoped it was one of the rather mundane mentors. Logan flipped the schedule back open and shuddered. He closed his eyes in his horror.

"No," Rainer pled, "please, no."

Logan nodded his defeat. Rainer grabbed the schedule to read the name himself. Mentor Soleus was the physical education mentor, and the health and wellness teacher for Clarence's group of academy males. Soleus had some very weird takes on sex in general and took to his role as mentor during amative energies week with just a little too much gusto.

Rainer recalled one class during his pre-freshman year when Mentor Soleus had spent all two hours going over different masturbation techniques and insisting that it was a normal healthy part of life. Although no one would dispute that, it was a particularly horrifying few hours of Rainer and Logan's adolescence when he continually insisted that solo sex was the best sex. Every question that was asked was somehow always guided back to jacking off.

"Logan, man," Rainer started, but then halted abruptly from his whining. He wasn't certain how Logan would feel about hearing what he had to say. He paused and studied Logan for a moment.

Logan gave him his signature smirk. "Need me to do that thing where I pretend you're banging someone who's not my little sister for a while?"

Rainer nodded.

"Done," Logan vowed.

"Thank you," Rainer continued his lamenting. "I've spent the past several weeks trying desperately not to think about sex. It just makes it so much worse. This is not cool." He held up the note from the chancellor.

Logan gave him a truly sorrowful look. "I know. Believe me, I've been there," he hesitantly reminded Rainer of his and Adeline's hiatus while she'd been suffering and then recovering from a ruptured ovarian cyst. "Hey, I'm sure Soleus would be happy to discuss ways you could take care of the problem." Logan laughed.

"Thanks for that." Rainer rolled his eyes.

"I'm sorry. She'll be home Friday is the only thing I can think to tell you."

The bell rang, and Mentor Sullivan opened the door to the rather rowdy group of sub-freshmen. He dismissed the class with a sigh and turned to Logan and Rainer. Sullivan had always been their favorite mentor, and Rainer got the impression the feeling was mutual.

"I despise amative energies week," he offered with a slightly dejected chuckle. They understood why his class was so talkative.

"Yeah well, we're about to go sit through sub-freshman amative energies with Soleus...again," Rainer lamented.

Mentor Sullivan laughed heartily. "Hey, you never know, you might learn something new."

They guided Clarence to the Health and Wellness building.

The upper grades' amative energies classes were combined among Predilects. Ioses, Vis Virres, and Valeduto Predilects typically took the class together in one of the large lecture halls in the afternoons. The sub-freshman and pre-freshman classes were not combined and were taught during their regular health period. The school felt they needed more direct instruction and more time to ask questions.

Without really thinking about it, Rainer and Logan sank into the seats in the very back of class where they'd sat when they were students.

Logan shoved Clarence into the seat directly in front of him. "You just keep your mouth shut, and don't cause any problems."

Clarence gave him a dramatic eye roll and then promptly flipped Logan off.

Mentor Soleus floated into the room and gave everyone a broad grin. He noted Logan and Rainer's presence. They were decidedly older than all of the other people seated at desks in his classroom.

"It's always nice to have visitors to our amative and erogenous energies class, and Crown Governors' sons to boot. What an honor." Mentor Soleus made a dramatic bow to Rainer and Logan who both sank farther down in their seats.

"We're just here to make sure our boy Clarence keeps his mouth shut and acts like a human being," Logan spat.

Mentor Soleus didn't seem to care for Logan's declaration and shook his head. "No, no, now, if Mr. Pendergrath has any questions, we want him to ask, but perhaps you two could help me with our class today."

Rainer's eyes goggled as Logan's mouth fell open. Soleus leaned on an empty desktop near Rainer.

"Now, I do recall reading that you are both engaged, correct?"

Not at all liking where this was going, Rainer and Logan nodded hesitantly. The group of fifteen-year-old boys studied Rainer and Logan with a mix of curious intrigue and nervousness.

"And would you both consider yourselves to be in sexually satisfying relationships?" Soleus quizzed flippantly.

Stunned mortification etched Logan's face as Rainer huffed, "Officer Haydenshire and I will not be answering that or any other questions. Just pretend we're not here…please."

"I really wish you would reconsider. You're among friends." Soleus stood and gestured grandly around the room. "I'm sure the young men would enjoy hearing about some of your experiences. Perhaps how old you were the first time you engaged in intercourse. You could tell us about the energy exchange. You're such an excellent resource for our class."

"No," Logan and Rainer stated in unison.

With a shrug, Soleus went to stand at the front of the classroom, after announcing that perhaps Officer Haydenshire and Officer Lawson would feel more comfortable sharing the next day.

He began discussing the energy flow passed from kissing and then how the energy was heightened from what he called engaging the oral erogenous zone with a kiss using the tongue. He explained how one Gifted person could draw from the energy held in saliva and breath with a slight suck of the mouth during the kiss.

Rainer was considering beating his head against the desk he was currently seated in when Clarence smirked. "I really like it when girls engage other zones with their tongues."

"I told you to keep it shut," Logan threatened furiously.

"Now, now, it's perfectly normal to have questions about other erogenous zones, and, Clarence, we will get to oral sex, but not just yet," Soleus assured. "Today, I want us to focus on masturbation."

He went on for another hour of Rainer's life that he could never get back. As several rounds of, "That's what she said," echoed around the room, Rainer let his head drop in defeat.

Eventually Soleus summoned and projected two diagrams of Gifted male and female bodies from his laptop. He pointed out erogenous zones, which were highlighted in red. Then he explained which areas contained the most erotic energy in Gifted individuals.

He then stupidly asked a group of fifteen-year-old boys different ways to activate the sexual energy in a male body.

"Oh geez. Seriously?" Logan whimpered as Clarence's hand shot up.

"Yes, Mr. Pendergrath?" Soleus smiled.

Clarence shot Rainer a goading glare. "I've seen pictures of his girl." He jerked his thumb toward Rainer. "She's all over the Angels programs. She's got a huge rack. I bet he likes to activate those with his tongue." Clarence laughed as Rainer glared at him furiously.

He clenched his fists but reminded himself that shattering Clarence Pendergrath's jaw would be like signing his own death warrant.

Logan popped Clarence on the back of the head. "That's my little sister, and I told you to keep your mouth shut," he growled.

"Well, now, that's very good, Clarence. The tongue and the mouth are excellent ways to activate all of the erogenous zones, but we're focusing on male bodies right now."

They moved on to the energy required to achieve an erection and then to achieve orgasm. Mentor Soleus began handing out condoms and instructing the boys to open them and become familiar with them.

"This is so much worse than I remembered," Logan whined. Rainer nodded his defeated agreement. Soleus offered Rainer a condom.

"I'm good, thanks," Rainer assured him.

To his horror, with an excited nod, Soleus turned back to the class. "Now, can anyone tell me why Officer Lawson might not ever need a condom?"

Several hands rose, and blood pooled violently in Rainer's face.

Clarence's hand shot up first, and Soleus called on him again. "'Cause you can't get your hand pregnant."

Rainer rolled his eyes. He wasn't fifteen. He felt no need to make a comeback quip.

Logan caught a handful of Clarence's hair. He jerked his head backward. "How many times do I have to tell you to shut it?"

"That is true and an excellent point for masturbation," Mentor Soleus agreed. "It is a perfectly natural and normal part of life. It's certainly not something we would poke fun at." Soleus turned and called on another student.

"Officer Lawson is going to marry Emily Haydenshire. She's Gifted, so he can seal her off. He doesn't need a condom to keep from getting her pregnant," the student replied dutifully.

"That is only partially true, David," Soleus corrected. Toeing the party line, he continued, "You are correct that Miss Haydenshire is Gifted. Her womb can be casted and sealed, but that decision should be up to her, not up to Officer Lawson."

Rainer clenched his jaw to keep from throttling Soleus and demanding that he stop discussing Emily and her womb. He drew a steadying breath and exchanged a furious look with Logan.

Soleus began explaining the proper way to put on a condom, and Rainer willed the clock to move faster.

The family-planning portion of the class was more tolerable, but then Soleus cupped his hand and pulled up another set of charts. There was one of the female reproductive organs and one of the male.

He added two clear overlays that showed thermographic scans of the storehouses of erotic energy in the organs.

Rainer shook his head as most of the class began attempting to copy the female print. They made precise notes on the places where the thermoscans glowed bright red.

As the students worked furiously, Soleus went on to discuss the sperm and egg portion of the class.

"Oh good, another diagram," Logan quipped indignantly as Soleus projected another chart of an egg inside a uterus, and then proceeded to pretend to be a sperm as he swam toward the egg through the classroom.

Rainer and Logan choked back laughter as did the rest of the class.

Soleus gave the class the last thirty minutes to ask questions. Clarence tried to raise his hand, but Logan jerked it back down. "No," he reprimanded.

It reminded Rainer of the way Mrs. Haydenshire would jerk Keaton's hand back when he reached for the stove.

A rather pompous student in the back of the class raised his hand. Soleus called on him immediately. He seemed delighted.

"Yeah, so are you going to teach us how to get a girl to let us do all of this stuff?"

Rainer rolled his eyes. Logan spat under his breath, "Why don't you try being old enough to shave first?"

"Ah, Joshua, are we having a little trouble in the department of amoré?" Soleus drawled. "I'm going to go back to masturbation."

After that it appeared every other student in the class was afraid to ask questions. Rainer breathed a sigh of relief when the bell rang.

Soleus dismissed the class with, "Now, tomorrow we will be discussing the art of pleasuring yourself and your partner."

With shuddering remorse, Logan and Rainer led Clarence to the dining hall.

"You stay the hell away from Tilly McIntyre," was Logan's warning as Clarence slunk off to sit with the few students who could tolerate him for longer than five minutes.

CHAPTER 15

THE SUBCONSCIOUS MIND

Fergus approached them as they went through the cafeteria serving line. He looked frantic.

"Hey Ferg, what's up?" Logan quizzed after asking for two helpings of spaghetti.

"Can I talk to you?"

"I was under the impression we were talking now." Logan was clearly still agitated from Soleus's class.

"I know,"—Fergus glanced around—"but could maybe just the three of us talk over lunch privately?"

Rainer furrowed his brow. "We have to keep an eye on Clarence. We can't leave him alone in the cafeteria."

Fergus, of all people, should understand that.

"Oh yeah, I know and thank you. I was just wondering if we could sit together, alone?"

Logan sighed. "Whatever. Let's just go. I'm hungry."

Fergus directed them to a quiet table in a back corner of the vast dining hall. Rainer made certain Clarence was still seated and eating before he sat down and dug into his food.

There was a hushed buzz all around the room. Students who'd already been to their health and wellness classes and those who were eager to attend were discussing what they'd learned or what they hoped to learn.

Rainer tried not to think about everything he'd heard over the last two hours, but his brain seemed unwilling to cooperate.

It was so much more than charts and graphs and lewd comments from fifteen-year-old idiots. He knew what it meant, how amazing it felt, and he was desperate for Emily to come home and be with him.

He was weak as he gave in momentarily and allowed the feeling of pushing into her to flood through his body. It was exquisite, the tight heat and the silky folds as she took him in. He almost whimpered audibly, but then shut those thoughts down.

Logan and Rainer were quietly eating. Neither of them had given Fergus's request too much thought until he cleared his throat. They raised their heads to study him. He looked green and seemed unable to eat.

With a quizzical glance at Logan, Rainer furrowed his brow. "Is everything okay?"

"I don't know, maybe," Fergus answered cryptically.

"You don't know?" Logan quizzed.

"I guess…I just wondered…if maybe…I could ask you something?" he stumbled over his words.

"Sure." Logan shrugged. He was still devouring his lunch. Fergus seemed to draw on deep resolve.

An ominous feeling settled in the pit of Rainer's stomach.

"Since I'm a mentor's aide this year, I have to help one of the health and wellness mentors with their class next period, and you know what they're teaching this week." He choked, and his face colored rapidly.

Logan and Rainer shared a concerned expression as they nodded.

"Yeah, and I, uh, I've never…you know…" Fergus' face was puce in his embarrassment. "And I wanted to ask you about this anyway because, you know, Tilly kind of wants to." He grimaced and drew a deep breath. "I don't know how exactly, and I don't know what to tell the class," fell from his mouth in one quick blurt without breath. "And it's the Ioses, Valeduto, Vis Virres preds."

"Why is the whole world determined to drive me insane this week?" Rainer huffed.

Logan offered him a sorrowful expression and then drew a deep breath. "Here, it's my turn for this anyway."

They shared a knowing chuckle, the one you shared with your best friend since birth, the guy who talked you through your first time.

"Thank you," Rainer breathed.

"All right, listen up, Ferg, 'cause I'm not saying all this twice," Logan commanded. "First of all, you're a mentor's aide, so just teach whatever the mentor gives you that's in the curriculum. It's not all as insane as Soleus's class." He shuddered slightly. "Second, you and Tilly need to wait until she graduates. Doing that here is stupid and dangerous." He gestured toward Clarence discreetly.

"What if I don't want to wait 'til she graduates?" Fergus argued.

"I dated Adeline for almost five years—five long, long years—before we did that, and unless you're sure she's the one you want to be with then you shouldn't do it at all," Logan vowed.

Rainer gave him an impressed smile. "Rainer and Emily have been together since she was born, so he waited like twenty years. I think you can make it a few more months."

"Whatever," Fergus dismissed. "So, if we decide not to wait, what should I do first?"

Rainer let his eyes close as images of him tearing off Emily's clothes and running his hands all over her body while he devoured her mouth and then sucked her nipples cemented firmly in his mind.

The things they did first. Rainer's mind reeled as he stifled a groan. He envisioned Emily's head falling back as she hoisted her cleavage in his face. His ravenous hands groping her and feeling her ripen and swell for him. He longed to grasp her hand and make her feel how hard she made him.

Rainer swallowed down the lust quickly and tried not to make it obvious that he was panting.

"Fergus," Logan drawled dejectedly.

"Come on, please. I have no one else to talk to about this."

Logan rolled his eyes. "I'd suggest taking your clothes off."

"Right." Fergus nodded as if Logan had just given him the answer to a deep, philosophical question.

"So, do I take her clothes off first, or does she do that, and I take mine off, or does she take mine off?"

Logan cringed. "It doesn't matter. Whatever works for you is fine."

Rainer stepped in with a sigh. "Has Tilly ever been with anyone?" He didn't really want to know the answer to the question he'd asked.

"No." Fergus shook his head.

Rainer hoped answering Fergus's questions might make them able to change the subject faster. "Then you need to be careful. I still don't think you've been together long enough to be talking about this, but the first time is a little rough." Rainer was growing more frustrated the longer he talked.

"Rough, how? Why?" Fergus urged.

Logan stepped up to bat. "It's gonna," he hemmed and clenched his jaw momentarily before he forced, "it's gonna hurt her a little."

Rainer and Logan both flinched from the memory.

"Why?" Fergus demanded.

"Geez, you took the class you're teaching in a few minutes for the past six years," Logan spat.

"No, I didn't. That's why I need you. My mom would never let me."

As Rainer thought back, he did remember that Fergus was one of the two or three students whose parents refused to let them take the amative energies portion of the health and wellness classes. They would sit in the library and work on a term paper on energies of the Gifted body instead.

Logan and Rainer spent the rest of lunch giving Fergus a brief overview of sex, much to their chagrin.

By the end of their very long day, Rainer grabbed a beer from the fridge and loaded cold pizza onto a plate. He retired to his room to text with Emily.

Rainer stood in the hallway of the farmhouse just outside Emily's bedroom. His heart raced. He could hear her. She was giving hungry, fleeting moans.

Intrigued, Rainer pushed open the door. She was laid out on her bed in a low-cut, white gown. It hung off her and obscured nothing at all. Her legs were spread wide. Her hair was splayed across her pillows, offering him a delicious view.

It was stifling in the house. Her windows were flung open wide. The hot, humid air hung thickly with the sweet, musky scent of her and of sex. With every haggard breath, he inhaled her arousal and her need.

A light breeze moved her curtains, and Rainer watched her nipples tighten and pucker. He stared intently. His breath was ragged as she lightly dragged her fingertips over herself. She traced and opened her lips. She was swollen and wet, throbbing and moaning. She teased at her clit and then dipped her fingers deep before she drew them back out. Her body writhed as she caressed herself.

A low guttural growl escaped Rainer, and she turned her head. Her eyes flashed wildly as she saw him.

"Come watch," she cooed seductively. She beckoned him with her hand, and he moved to her.

"Need some help, baby?" He panted and ached for her to do more. She gave him a heavy, sultry nod. She spread her hand, separating herself, and showed him exactly how she wanted to be touched. Another loud moan echoed from her. Rainer stared, unable to take his eyes off the erotic display.

"You have to be quiet, baby. Your parents will hear you." His voice was low and thrumming from his ardent desire.

"I don't care," she urged in a heated pant. "I need you." She kept her body moving in sensuous, writhing arcs. "I want you to take me hard, now. I want everyone to hear how you make me scream."

She moved her hand from her lips and grasped him. He realized suddenly that he wasn't wearing anything at all.

"Mmmm, you're so big," she gasped out her adulation and contorted her body. She lifted her breasts upward. As the nightie fell away, she spun her other hand around her nipples. "You feel amazing inside of me." She kept her body writhing in need.

"Fuck me, Rainer. Make me take it. Right now." She flipped on all fours and shook her luscious ass in his face.

A loud quaking groan echoed from his chest as he reached and pulled her over him. He forced himself in with deep, unrelenting thrusts.

. . .

Rainer awoke with a gasp. He was clinging to the bed and panting for breath. He shook his head several times and tried to pull himself from the lurid dream.

It had been a very long time since he'd had a dream like that, and he wasn't certain what he should do next.

After rubbing his eyes and trying to steady his racing heartbeat, he turned over. He was extremely embarrassed, though he was entirely alone. His phone chirped. Still trying to regulate his breathing and heartbeat, he picked his cell up off the nightstand.

Are you awake?

was the text from Emily.

Yeah, baby. What's wrong? Why aren't you sleeping?

he texted back. He was still gasping for breath.

I just miss you. I woke up thinking about you.

Well, that makes two of us, he thought wryly.

Yeah, me too. Dreaming about you actually.

Aww, feeling fourteen again? ;)

He could almost see the smirk he knew she was wearing.

Certain she knew entirely too much about male anatomy, thanks to living with seven older brothers. Rainer shook his head.

Yeah, actually, thanks for pointing that out.

Don't worry, baby. I'll be home in three days to take care of you.

Rainer fought not to text for her to come home now and take care of him. He ordered himself not to tell her how badly he wanted her and needed to be with her. He longed to demand that he be able to feel her all around him.

With a determined clench of his jaw, he typed,

I can't wait

before getting up and heading to the bathroom.

CHAPTER 16

BECAUSE OF WHO YOU ARE

The next morning, Rainer fell into his seat at the table. He yawned and noted that Logan quickly got off the phone after commenting, "Yeah, he deposited it. I gotta go." Logan joined him at the table. "Rough night?" He looked concerned.

"I didn't sleep all that well," Rainer admitted.

Logan gave a slight chuckle. "We still counting days, or have we switched the countdown to hours?"

"Three days, eight hours." Rainer joined in Logan's laughter.

"Is that a countdown 'til she lands or 'til you land her?"

After thinking that Logan had really been an outstanding friend through Emily's trip, Rainer grinned. "Three days, eight hours, plus however long it takes me to fly home from the airport, and then an additional two maybe two and half minutes," he allowed as Logan cracked up.

"Better make it two and a half. You know girls like foreplay."

A few minutes later, Adeline joined them at the table, and Logan seemed to remember something. "Have you checked your phone this morning?"

Rainer took another bite of his cereal and pulled his phone from his pocket. "Not since I took a shower." He turned on the screen. He had a text from Mrs. Haydenshire.

Logan backed away from the table and pretended to shield Adeline. "Careful, baby, he's about to blow."

Adeline gave Logan a scolding glance. "Be nice," she urged.

Rainer read through the text and tried not to whimper.

Rainer glared furiously at the screen like the phone had mortally wounded him.

"So, maybe three days, eight hours, plus the time it takes you to get home from the airport, plus five or six hours and two and half minutes." Logan offered Rainer a sorrowful gaze.

While he bit back the long string of volatile curse words that threatened to spew forth from his mouth, Rainer shot Logan a desperate glare. Adeline seemed to understand why Rainer was quite literally choking on his words.

"Uh, I'm just going to head on to the hospital. I'm working a double shift, so I won't be home until late," she explained to Logan, while still staring at Rainer concernedly.

Logan nodded and kissed her goodbye before he turned back to Rainer. "Get Em to tell her no."

Rainer tried to think clearly.

He turned the phone back on and forwarded the text to Emily. He explained that he'd just received it from her mother. Logan pulled out his own phone and texted Emily as well. He recited his text out loud.

106

Rainer finally relocated the ability to chuckle.

was Emily's immediate response to Rainer's forward. He turned his phone so that Logan could read her reply.

Unbeknownst to Rainer, Emily added another text.

Logan gagged reflexively and groaned as he held up his hands and pushed the phone away.

"What?" Rainer glanced back at the screen and saw the second text. His eyes goggled.

"Sorry," he choked. He debated just returning to bed and being done with the day at seven thirty in the morning.

"'S'ok." Logan was still shuddering. "Just a little more information than I ever, ever needed." An uncomfortable moment later, Logan seemed to decide to give Rainer a break. "Hey, maybe you and Em could demonstrate that stallion thing for Soleus's class. He keeps wanting you to participate."

They cracked up. Certain he was still the color of an overripe tomato, Rainer sighed. "She's, uh…just a little…" He tried to think of a word to describe Emily at that moment. The past few days, her texts had become increasingly more sexually charged as the frustration had set in.

"If it's all the same to you, I'm not gonna call my sister that."

"I was going to say tired," Rainer assured him.

Logan look relieved. "Tired's good."

"Aside from anything else that might happen, she is tired, and she can only shower once a week, and she's sick of Garrett and Chloe messing around or fighting all the time. I think she really just wants to come home and relax. It's hard on Receivers not to have space to process everything they feel from everyone all of the time. It's wearing her out. She's with the Angels and the orphans twenty-four seven." He prayed that Logan would understand there was more to his desire to take care of Emily than the physical side.

"And you're concerned it might piss Dad off if you give her a bath there?" Logan mocked.

Rainer rolled his eyes but eventually chuckled.

With a quick glance at his watch, Logan stood. "Come on, we need to get to the academy to escort pipsqueak to class. I'll think of something."

~

Wednesday proved to be the most trying yet. The angry phone calls and emails had been flying around the academy about teaching the boys the cast to close off their sexual partners. Chancellor Wilshire looked haggard as he brushed by Rainer and Logan, who were standing guard outside Mentor Sullivan's class. Murmurs of the debate were all over campus.

"I know you're trying not to think about it, but seeing as we're about to go sit through two hours of the sex talk, can I ask you something?" Logan quizzed hesitantly, after making certain no one else was in the corridor. Rainer nodded.

"Did Garrett or Levi teach us to set the cast?"

"I was thinking about that the other day," Rainer recalled.

Garrett had overheard Emily and Rainer discussing the possibility of taking things further when they'd been up in her loft one afternoon. Rainer was a sophomore, and she was a freshman. Garrett had pulled Logan and Rainer to the side later that night and shot straight with them.

"If you're gonna take my sister to bed, then I'm going to teach you to do this the right way."

Logan and Adeline had been dating a few years by then as well, so Logan hadn't fussed too much over the reasoning for the lesson.

"The way they teach the girls to do it at school has no finesse, no skill, just wham, bam, and it's done. To me, if you're gonna close a girl off so she can be with you, then you should make her glad she chose you to share that with."

Already keenly aware of Garrett's many escapades, Logan and Rainer had paid close attention. Levi and Will had joined in the conversation a few minutes later and had agreed with Garrett's reasoning.

"Yeah, the way they do it at school is really clinical," Will had lamented. "And if you're gonna work it into the sex, then it should be sexy."

"Okay, so how do you do it?" Logan had demanded after growing tired of his brothers' overt bragging. Garrett then proceeded to explain that if they waited until after they'd been making out for a while, it would be easier to close them off because they would already have the essence of their energy.

"If you've gotten to feel her up or play down south, then you've pretty much got it in your hand." Garrett had chuckled at his own innuendo. He also offered them several tips on how to get a girl turned on so she would sleep with you even if she was nervous about it.

Will had jumped all over Garrett at this point. "If she's nervous about it, then you need to forget it for a while."

Garrett had continued with nothing more than an eye roll as his response to Will.

"In school, they just capture their energy and close off their womb. It makes them uncomfortable, but you can add in some of your own energy to what you gather from her. You know, just kind of calm them down and soothe them, so they don't feel it at all," Garrett had instructed. He then went into great detail, using extremely crude terminology for female body parts, as to how to get in and seal them off.

"Levi was there, but Garrett actually taught us," Rainer reminded Logan. He nodded and appeared to be recalling the same evening.

"Dad's been fielding calls from parents as well. They all want to know if he'll change the ruling on the curriculum."

Rainer wasn't surprised to hear that. "Seems to me, if you're gonna be with a woman, then it shouldn't matter who sets the cast. It should be a mutual decision, you know? If you can't even agree on that, then maybe you shouldn't be hopping into bed together." Rainer glanced into Sullivan's classroom to make certain Clarence wasn't causing any trouble.

Logan nodded. "Yeah, that's what I thought too. Dad's kind of with the 'it's the girl's choice' crowd, but Mom thinks boys should know how. She thinks if both people know how there might be fewer unplanned pregnancies, but obviously only if the woman is good with being closed."

When the bell rang, they led Clarence to another round of sex education.

They slunk down in the same seats they'd been using and shoved Clarence into the seat in front of Logan.

Rainer tried to think of anything but Emily. He missed being with her, but he also missed talking to her and actually hearing her voice.

He longed to see her beautiful face, hear her sweet laugh, and feel her energy around him. He wanted to feel her body move languidly beside his before the sunrise each morning. He wanted her warmth and her scent to linger on his skin. He missed her more with each passing moment.

Logan missed her cooking. He'd pointed this out repeatedly over the past few weeks. With a slight chuckle at that, Rainer began making a mental list of all of the things he needed to get done before he picked her up at the airport.

Emily had informed her mother that under no circumstances were she and Rainer coming to the farmhouse Friday evening. She'd explained that she was exhausted and wouldn't be able to shower before she arrived home. She requested that they have their normal Sunday family dinner with everyone, and that then she would feel up to meeting Lily Ana and being an aunt for the first time.

Rainer had repeatedly assured the Haydenshires that he was leaving work at noon Friday and had the entire next week off due to the sheer amount of overtime he and Logan had been working.

He'd vowed that he, and only he, would pick Emily up from the airport, but he'd been shot down. Governor Haydenshire insisted that he and Mrs. Haydenshire and the twins be there as well.

Rainer forced his mind back to his ongoing list. He needed to wash his clothes, something he hadn't done while Emily had been gone. He was down to his last shirts and trousers.

Emily and Mrs. Haydenshire had usually done his laundry for him growing up, though he'd never expected them to do that. They just always had, and he'd never really gotten the knack of it.

He had managed to rather discreetly get the sheets washed after his wet dream, but he added changing them to his list before Emily arrived home.

He also began making a grocery list. He didn't plan on either of them leaving the house before they had to be at the farmhouse Sunday evening. He wanted to have all of Emily's favorite foods on hand.

Their room was littered with brochures for new cars and consumer magazines discussing the pros and cons of the newest makes and models. It needed to be straightened up.

He and Logan were going out to Sam's that night to drive a few, but Rainer wasn't really looking forward to it. He still hadn't gotten over losing the Mustang. He still shuddered when he thought about the tattered remains of his much-beloved first car.

In that moment, when Rainer was parched for distraction, he decided that he'd just let Emily pick something for him. She knew him better than anyone.

Soleus moved into the classroom and closed the door.

Rainer wanted to pick up flowers to have when Emily arrived, but then wondered if that was too clichéd. Lost in thought, he didn't realize he'd been asked a question.

"Rainer." Logan coughed and discreetly gestured his head to Soleus.

Quickly shaken from his reverie, his head jerked upward. He felt guilty that Mentor Soleus was standing in front of him awaiting an answer.

After reminding himself that he was no longer a student and that he certainly didn't require this class for anything, he sighed. "I'm sorry, did you need something…sir?" he added at the end to be polite.

"Yes, Officer Lawson, I was wondering if you'd enlighten our class on your stance on the debate on whether or not our amative energies curriculums should include teaching the cast for closing a womb to all sexes."

"I'm not really certain. Like I told you, I'm just here to keep Pendergrath in line." He sincerely wished that Soleus would leave him alone, but something about Soleus's demeanor told Rainer he wasn't going to drop this.

"Now, come on, Officer Lawson. You are an example for these young men." He gestured to the class and then began walking around the room. "Since none of you were in attendance last year, you may not be aware that Officer Lawson graduated as head of Ioses Order, with an outstanding grade point average. He was immediately recruited to Elite Iodex. His father wrote and ratified our constitution. You are looking at our future, Officer Lawson." Soleus gestured to the students in the class and then returned his gaze to Rainer. "Why do you refuse to enlighten them on something as simple as your opinion? Have you ever casted Miss Haydenshire, and if so, where did you learn to do this as it isn't currently in our curriculum?"

Rainer bristled and drew a deep breath. He narrowed his eyes. Thoughts of all that his father had stood for and had died for filled his mind, though he fought to keep them at bay.

"First of all," he commanded, "my relationship with my fiancée is no one's business but ours. I would never share any of that with anyone else. If you really want my opinion, then here it is..." He glanced around the room at the boys staring up at him, thoroughly rapt. "Your physical relationship with whomever you're with isn't something that you share details of with people you hardly know or even with your friends. As for casting someone, that should be discussed long before you go hopping into bed. And if you can't agree on that, then I would give a lot of thought to the fact that perhaps you shouldn't be sleeping with that person at all. So, my opinion is two-fold. It shouldn't all fall to the person with a womb in the relationship, but it also should always be their choice that you discuss before you sleep together," he restated the opinion he'd shared with Logan earlier. He crossed his arms and glared at Soleus. He dared him to continue his inquisition.

"Well said, Mr. Lawson. You see, sometimes we're an example

because of who we are whether we want to be or not. I believe it was your father who used to say that everyone is an example, and you, and only you, get to choose whether you're a good one or a bad one, did he not?" Soleus quizzed Rainer, who nodded his agreement.

The uncomfortable understanding that his opinion mattered to people because of his father, because of his career, because of who he was, settled harshly in his gut.

"Officer Haydenshire, would you say you agree with Officer Lawson's opinion?"

"Absolutely." Logan nodded to Rainer. "I agree with every word."

With that, Soleus led the boys in another discussion about the energy related to sex, while Logan and Rainer discreetly texted one another throughout class.

Logan did an outstanding job of distracting Rainer throughout the lecture.

CHAPTER 17

PUNISHMENT AND REWARD

Friday morning, Rainer's entire body was hot-wired as he began his countdown to three o'clock. Portwood and Ericcson were taking his and Logan's place at the academy to keep up with Clarence. Garrett had flown in the night before to help Dan polish up his case against Pendergrath.

Rainer drove the Hummer onto the parking deck of the Senate and tried to focus on the Pendergrath case. He found it impossible to think about anything but taking Emily home and then taking excellent care of her.

The weather in late November was terrible. Storms were on the radar all day. It was pouring as Rainer exited the Hummer. He grimaced.

Emily hated storms. They terrified her, and Rainer didn't want her to have to fly through one. He resolutely decided that once he got her home, he'd make certain she forgot all about the storm. They could lie in bed all afternoon and all night. The storm and everything else in the world could just wait outside.

He flashed his badge at the security entrance and then sank down at his desk.

"Why does it have to rain today?" Logan sounded thoroughly put out. Rainer's brow furrowed. He wondered why Logan cared so much. He usually made fun of Emily's terror over storms.

All Receivers hated storms. There was too much volatile, violent energy in them, and Receivers had to feel it all. Emily associated Cal's death, her wreck, and Rainer leaving her with storms. Terror overtook her with every bolted rap of thunder and every shock of lightning that sliced through the sky. To Emily, if something horrible were going to happen, it would be during a storm.

Suddenly, Vindico snarled their names from his office, and Rainer and Logan shared an ominous glance. "In here, now!" Vindico demanded.

With a harsh swallow of his own fear, Rainer followed Logan into the office. Vindico was pacing and scowling furiously.

"I was in here last night and I finally asked myself—why is Clarence Pendergrath sexually harassing this one girl? What is it about her? He doesn't seem to be interested in anyone else."

Rainer's heart sank rapidly to his feet.

"He's a prick, just like his old man, no doubt, but then I began going over all of the complaints from the staff about his behavior. Now, most of his mentors have commented that he's rude and obnoxious in class, but all of the complaints about his behavior toward Tilly McIntyre have come from one mentor's assistant." His voice rose to a shout, but he reined it in slightly.

He leaned ominously across his desk and narrowed his eyes.

"I'm going to let you two tell me what you sure as hell should've told me weeks ago, and then I'm going to tell you how you're going to make that up to me. I believe it was Mentor Sherman," he spat, "who you got Garrett to get out of jail this summer and was a friend of yours growing up."

Logan and Rainer nodded their defeat.

"They're involved with each other," Logan immediately confessed.

"We didn't want him to get fired," Rainer added.

"But he should be fired, Lawson. That goes against numerous academy rules. You know that."

"She's only a year younger than he is. It just didn't seem like a big deal," Logan came to Rainer's defense.

Vindico resumed his pacing. "Until Clarence Pendergrath found out and is now going to blackmail Sherman."

"He's not certain what he saw. He's trying to get proof. That's why he keeps bothering her," Rainer admitted.

With an infuriated huff, Vindico spat, "So, now I have to keep two of my Iodex officers playing babysitter because your friend makes incredibly poor decisions."

Unable to refute that, Rainer and Logan simply nodded. Vindico shook his head and ran his hands through his hair. "You have *got* to tell me stuff like this. I've never done anything to make either of you believe that I am incapable of understanding that shit like this happens, but I need to know."

Rainer and Logan agreed, and Vindico seemed to calm down slightly.

"All right, here's what I need." He jerked the chair out from his desk and reseated himself. "I'm extremely concerned at this point about anyone involved with any of my officers. I'm urging both of you to watch Miss Haydenshire and Miss Parker like hawks when they aren't at work. Bridgette says more and more members of the Interfeci are in the club every day. She's picked up on quite a bit as she's been waitressing, and none of it is good. I'm due to fly to Moscow Thanksgiving night for Pendergrath's new trial." He rolled his eyes. "So, I'm going to make my customary appearance at my mother's dining room table, endure her relentless meddling into my life about why I'm not married or dating anyone, and listen to her incessant reminders that I'm not getting any younger. While my sisters argue with their half-wit husbands and my niece and nephew drive me insane. We'll all wait to see who Lindley shows up with. It will be whatever hookup she thinks will infuriate my father the most."

Rainer furrowed his brow and wondered momentarily why Vindico's mother would be under the impression he wasn't dating anyone. With sudden realization, Rainer knew that Bridgette was nothing more than a pawn in Dan's stupidly dangerous gamble. She didn't mean anything to him at all.

"But since I'll be out of the country until Saturday morning to attempt to keep a murderer in prison, I'm going to need someone to keep an eye on Bridgette. I'm certain you know the work she's doing for us is rather dangerous. I need the information she's providing us. So, the Crown Governor's wife"—he narrowed his eyes—"has offered to let her stay at the farm until I return.

"As annoying as she is, I would prefer she be taken to work and picked up from work by an officer, and that she be guarded while I'm gone. Obviously, be discreet. I can't take another innocent life being lost on my account. So, you two will be spending Thursday and Friday night at the farmhouse as well," he dared them to argue.

Horrifying images of Bridgette staying at the farmhouse with Emily swirled through Rainer's mind. He knew they couldn't argue. They were being punished for not spilling the goods on Fergus, so they nodded their defeat.

"You can go," Vindico commanded. They traipsed dejectedly out of the office. "Lawson," he called, and Rainer turned back. "I do hope you and Miss Haydenshire have a nice homecoming," he stated sincerely.

"Thanks." Rainer sighed before making his exit.

"Well, that should be fun to try to explain to Adeline," Logan whimpered.

"Would it be bad to tell Emily that…tomorrow?"

Logan chuckled. "I say it's okay, but I gave up trying to reason with my sister ages ago."

Quickly deciding that he wanted to have just one night with her before the world intruded yet again, Rainer determined that he wouldn't bring up their new Thanksgiving arrangements until the next day.

He tried to focus on Pendergrath's trial, but it proved tedious, and Logan seemed equally distracted. "So, Adeline wants to keep the Accord and for me to get a new car."

Rainer wasn't surprised. That sounded just like something Adeline would offer.

"She's really insistent," Logan added, "so I was thinking maybe I'd get a truck."

Rainer glanced at his watch for the fifth time in a ten-minute period.

"I'll call Sam for you if you want."

"Nah, I've been talking to him," Logan informed Rainer but then grimaced like he shouldn't have admitted that.

"Oh, okay." Rainer studied his best friend. Something was up.

"We can leave in a little while. You wanna grab some lunch on the way home?" Logan changed the subject abruptly.

"Yeah, sure." He studied Logan and wondered what he was trying to cover up, but thoughts of Emily held his attention with much more ease.

His cell rang on his desk, and he answered it quickly. "Hey, baby. Are you okay?" He checked his watch again and prayed that she was calling from the Angels jet and that they hadn't been delayed for some reason.

"Yeah, I'm okay. I can't wait to get there." Delight rang in Emily's voice. "We're on our way."

His heart found a regulated beat. "I can't wait either."

"They said the weather there is really bad." Fear replaced the delight in her voice. "Anyway, they redirected us to Ronald Reagan instead of the arena. We'll be landing there at three."

By two, Rainer was restless. He stalked around the house, arguing with himself as he tried to determine if it was too early to leave for the airport.

Logan and Adeline had packed for their weekend at the bed and breakfast and asked Rainer to tell Emily they missed her before they'd left.

While pacing in the living room, Rainer came up with an excuse to leave. If he continued to stay in the house, he was going to drive himself insane. He decided that since it was still storming, traffic would be bad. He grabbed an umbrella and raced to the Hummer.

On the way, he allowed the dozens of dizzying fantasies he'd been fighting back through the barriers erected in his mind. They began to play out in his head.

By the time he pulled into the parking lot, every nerve ending in his body was on high alert. This time, Rainer parked as close as he possibly could to the airport itself. He shut down all thoughts of what had happened the last time he'd been there.

His shield gave constant craving pulses. He focused on the fact that in a matter of minutes he would have the very reason for his existence back in his arms.

He pulled his jacket tighter around him and opened the umbrella. He casted the Hummer and fought the driving rain as he raced into the sprawling building.

People were everywhere. Non-Gifted flights had been delayed because of the weather, and utter chaos had ensued.

With a careful study of the screens displaying flight times, he noted that the Angels jet was due in on time but was being landed without a jetway.

Rainer grimaced and headed toward the Gifted gates. He hated that she was going to have to run through the rain to get into the airport. The gates were backed up with the Non-Gifted flights that were arriving late.

He was too nervous to sit as flights arrived and taxied away. Rainer checked his watch constantly. The Haydenshires arrived a few minutes later. They'd left the twins at home with Nana and Pops due to the weather.

Governor Haydenshire insisted that Mrs. Haydenshire sit, though she kept up steady reassurances that she and the baby were fine.

Another moment later, Rainer saw the Angels plane with the pin-up style artwork of Angels painted on the sides touch down on the rear runway that had no connector to the airport. "The Alluring Angels of Summation" was scrawled on the belly of the plane.

Rainer smiled. His heart leapt as he moved toward the door the Angels would be escorted through.

"You seem a little eager," Governor Haydenshire teased.

"I really missed her." He didn't point out the details of what exactly he'd missed most to his future father-in-law.

"I know, son." Governor Haydenshire slapped him on the back and eased Rainer away from Mrs. Haydenshire. "And I know Lillian was insistent about that welcome home party. I'm glad Emily turned her down. She tends to get a little…forgetful, let's say, during this stage of her pregnancies." He clearly didn't want to say anything negative about Mrs. Haydenshire.

Rainer grinned and nodded his understanding. He was extremely appreciative that the governor wasn't upset they wouldn't be coming over that evening.

"I can't believe they're making them run through the rain." Rainer watched the pilots and coolant officers descend down an airstair off the plane and into the deluge.

"For all of the hell we've put the Non-Gifted people through, our flights being moved off the usual runways doesn't seem like too much to ask," Governor Haydenshire reminded Rainer.

While supposing that he agreed, Rainer continued to watch, and then, there she was. She took his breath away. She was wearing a plain dirty T-shirt and a pair of jeans. She held her hands over her face to shield her eyes from the pouring water. She shivered. Her clothes clung to her curves, soaked with freezing water. Rainer's heart ached as she began to sprint toward the airport.

A moment later, she'd followed the rest of the Angels up a set of concrete steps. They raced into the airport. Everything and everyone else faded away as she flew into Rainer's arms. He wrapped her up and devoured her mouth with his own.

Suddenly, he was whole again, like a part of him had been missing, like he'd been in a pain so constant he wasn't fully aware of it until it was gone.

He'd never tasted anything sweeter as he continued to lave her mouth. He lifted her up in the exuberance of his embrace. She was his lifeline. Nothing else even mattered without her there. The very air he breathed seemed unnecessary unless she was beside him.

She was soaked thoroughly, and as she finally pulled away from him, he realized that the water had caused her shirt to become quite see-through.

Though he longed to see her in nothing at all, everything he considered to be his and his alone was on display. He pulled his coat off and zipped it around her. Governor Haydenshire seemed pleased with the gesture as he hugged Emily.

She hugged her mother, but she kept her gaze firmly locked on

Rainer. He studied her as she embraced her family and bid her teammates goodbye. She looked exhausted. Her hair clung to her face and back. It was drenched with water, but he was certain he'd never seen anything more beautiful.

Rainer wanted desperately to take her home. He wanted her so badly a fierce pain only she could tend consumed him. He wanted to undress her, to bathe her, and to wrap her up in the heat they created when they were together.

She moved back to him and laid her head on his shoulder. She buried her face in his neck as he wrapped his arms around her protectively. He kissed the top of her wet head as he cradled her.

"Let's go home, baby."

Relief smoothed over her tense features.

"Now, are you sure you don't want us to bring some dinner over?" Mrs. Haydenshire offered again. She looked concerned. Governor Haydenshire shook his head and offered Rainer an apologetic glance. "I'm certain Rainer will take care of Emily," he stated firmly.

"Wow, Daddy," Emily teased, just as shocked by her father's declaration as Rainer was. Governor Haydenshire chuckled as he reached back to take Emily's hand. He effectively pulled her away from Rainer.

"I'm trying," he stated wryly as Rainer listened to Emily laugh. The sound soothed his soul. As she released his hand and returned to Rainer, her father glanced back at her wistfully.

Rainer knew, in that moment, her father didn't see his twenty-year-old daughter pulled snugly under her adoring fiancé's embrace. He saw his baby girl letting go of his hand and walking away from him.

"He better, anyway," Governor Haydenshire threatened.

"Always," Rainer vowed. He squeezed Emily's hand. He was worried about the fact that she was still shivering from being so drenched, despite being in his coat.

As he considered that he was about to take her back out into the freezing wind and rain, he halted.

"Stay with your parents. I'll pull the car around."

"No," she fussed insistently. Rainer wished she wouldn't show her stubborn side right at that moment, but he knew better than to argue. "I got to see you for only one night over the past three weeks. I'm not letting go of you until Christmas."

Rainer popped open the umbrella and pointed out the Hummer in the nearest lot so Emily would know which direction to run. He carried her large suitcase and held the umbrella over her as he rushed her to the car. He pulled his cast from the car and threw her luggage in the back. Then he ran through the now standing water to get in the driver's seat.

While cranking the car and turning on the heat as high as it would blow, he summoned and raised the temperature. Her teeth chattered, and his heart ached.

Rainer tried to add to the ambient temperature of the Hummer as he backed out, but driving through the pouring rain required most of his attention.

"I'm so glad to be home. I missed my Hummer," Emily gushed as her teeth finally quieted enough for her to speak.

Rainer laughed and squeezed her thigh. "It missed you too, baby."

She was quiet for a few minutes as Rainer made his way back to the interstate. He was barely able to see in front of him. Thunder clapped, and Emily shuddered.

"I'm getting you home as quick as I can."

She nodded and gave him his grin.

"I know." She pulled his coat tighter around her, still unable to get warm. Her clothes were too wet, and she was too tired. Her Gifted energies appeared to be completely depleted.

Rainer leaned toward the back seat and produced the flannel blanket he kept in the Hummer.

"I don't mean this as dirty as it's going to sound, and I will really try to keep my eyes on the road, though I make no promises, but why don't you take that shirt off and cover up, sweetheart? I'm worried you're going to turn blue in a minute."

Emily giggled and shook her head.

"I can't get naked for you yet," she sassed. The ache in his groin throbbed in disapproval. He let images of her naked body writhing under him swirl rapidly in his mind as he tried to soothe the hunger.

He drew a steadying breath. "It's either now or about two seconds after I get you in the house," he teased just to hear her delighted laughter again.

With another convulsive shiver, Emily added the blanket to the jacket. She swathed it around her as Rainer attempted to seal heat in its fibers while flying down the interstate.

Thankful when he spotted the exit for McLean as the wipers threw water off the windshield forcefully, he exited. A few minutes later, he turned down the two-lane road that led to the farm.

Emily sighed contentedly even though she continued to shiver.

"I just want you to take me to bed and not get out for about a month."

Rainer chuckled. That sounded perfect to him. "Hmm, what should I do with you in bed for a month?"

"Actually, you're not going to want to stay in bed with me for a month," she teased with a great deal of her redheaded sass.

Rainer gave her an incredulous glance. "Wanna bet?" She shot him a knowing grin that had him curious. "Why wouldn't I want to stay in bed with you for a month or, hell, a lifetime?"

"You'll see."

He turned down the gravel lane to their house. His heart picked up rhythm. His longing began to consume him. He glanced in his rearview mirror and saw something as the rear windshield wiper flashed past.

"Why are your parents behind us?" He sounded more irritated than he'd intended.

"They're not staying long, but it has to do with the reason you won't want to stay in bed with me." She seemed to be enjoying frustrating him.

"What's going on?" This wasn't at all what he wanted.

"You're not the only one who can pull off a good surprise. I hate that it's pouring, and believe me, I want to go in the house and for you to take these soaking wet clothes off me and to do all of the things I've been asking for, but I have something I want you to see first."

"What?"

At that moment, Rainer noted Logan's Accord back in the driveway along with Garrett's Highlander.

"Why are they here?" He was well aware of the fact that he sounded like a spoiled child, but he didn't care at the moment.

Emily giggled. "Logan was right. You *are* cranky."

With that, she summoned and opened the garage door. "This is why they're here."

Logan, Garrett, and Adeline were standing in the garage beside a car that Rainer could barely make out in the windshield wipers' dance. It couldn't be what he thought he saw.

"What is that?" he asked as he remembered how to turn off the Hummer.

The car was angled sideways in the garage. He couldn't park the Hummer beside it.

"It's your new car if you want it. I haven't signed the check yet, but that's all Sam's waiting on." She beamed at him.

"But how did you...?" He was still sitting in the Hummer not certain what to do next.

"Let's go see it, and then I'll tell you how I did it."

Rainer tried to remember that he needed to get her safely into the house before he went to drool over what he was fairly certain was sitting in his garage. He grabbed the umbrella and ran to her door. He helped her out and kept the blanket over her as they raced into the garage.

Rainer's mouth fell open as he stared at the car in shock.

"Is that? Are you serious?" he gasped as Emily nodded. "You bought me a...." Everyone joined in her laughter.

"Only if you like it. We can take it back to Sam's tomorrow if you want something different, but I kind of thought it was perfect for you." She bit her lip nervously.

"If he doesn't like it, he's insane," Logan vowed. "Seriously, I just drove it here from Sam's. Sweet, sweet ride."

Rainer moved to the brand-new, not even released to the public, jet-black, Porsche 718 Boxster GTS Cabriolet convertible with custom Carrera sport wheels. He was speechless.

Logan slapped him on the back as Rainer stared at the car in utter disbelief.

"Yeah, I'd say it's good he's spent the majority of the last week in the shower."

Garrett and Emily cracked up.

The Haydenshires had moved into the garage and were staring at Rainer with pride-filled smiles.

He turned to gaze at Emily. "You're incredible."

Emily was beaming. Logan stepped in. "It topped out around one seventy before she had Sam enhance the engines," he stated with lust filling his tone as Rainer gave an audible groan. "Now it does zero to sixty in under two seconds."

Rainer shook his head in awe of the automobile before him.

"It's built like the Porsches from the sixties," Emily explained. "The Spyders like they used to race. So, I thought this was sort of a little something like what you had but a whole new ride for the next part of our lives."

Rainer pulled her to him and wrapped his arms around her.

"It's incredible," he assured her. Rainer moved away from Emily to walk around the new car. Logan had lowered the top to show off the top-of-the-line, beige leather interior.

"I, uh, I wasn't planning on spending quite so much." Rainer began calculating what it must've cost Emily to get this.

Garrett shook his head. "Hey, you do a lot of great things for a lot of people, and she makes a fortune doing what she does. She wanted you to have this."

Rainer turned his gaze back to Emily, still unable to believe what she'd done.

"Plus," she sassed as she adjusted the blanket back around her shoulders, "I think you'll be really sexy driving it."

Rainer raised his eyebrow and gave her a naughty smirk as he tried to quell his rapidly heightening libido.

"And with that, we'll just go." Governor Haydenshire shuddered slightly, and everyone laughed.

"Very nice car, Rainer. She picked well. It suits you," he

complimented as he kissed Emily's cheek, then held an umbrella over Mrs. Haydenshire as they returned to the Suburban.

"Okay now, you all leave so he can thank me for his new car." Emily's demands brought on another round of laughter. Garrett and Logan edged out toward the rain, with Adeline and Emily hugging awkwardly since Emily was still bundled in Rainer's coat and the blanket.

"Too bad you're screwing around with my little sister. I'd enjoy hearing a story about you taking somebody on the hood of that car, but if you tell me that, then I'll just want to hit you." Garrett seemed truly confused by the conundrum.

Rainer shook his head and rolled his eyes. "Why don't you go ponder your confusion in your Toyota."

Everyone waved goodbye and raced through the rain to their own cars. Rainer turned back to Emily.

"So, you like it?" she quizzed hesitantly.

"Em, baby, it's more than I could ever have even imagined." He was still stunned.

"Do you want to drive it?"

"I would love to," Rainer assured her, "but not out in that. A little part of me died inside when Logan said he'd driven it here from Sam's in this weather." He allowed himself to revel in the fact that he could always make her laugh.

"Plus, there are several things I want to take care of first." He pulled her to his chest. "And they all happen to involve you, but trust me, tomorrow we're going on a long, long drive."

CHAPTER 18
PLEASURES

Emily was overjoyed as Rainer lowered the garage door. With one last, longing gaze at the Porsche, he pulled her into the house.

"I can't believe you did that." Rainer continued to let the shock work through him as he guided her toward their bedroom.

"So, you really like it?"

"It's amazing. I don't deserve that."

With a sassy grin, Emily bit her lip. It slid seductively between her teeth. Rainer stared at her. Every nerve ending pulsed with an all-too-familiar ache, and the pain took up residence in his groin.

"I might even let you take me on the hood," she teased.

With a shuddering growl, Rainer eased the blanket off her. "I'm about to lose it already. If you want to be taken on the hood of the Porsche that the most incredible woman in the world bought for me, then I'll make certain that happens. But right now, I plan on showing you what I've been wanting to do since I put you on that plane weeks ago." His voice was low and thrumming from his desire.

She panted deliciously as he unzipped his jacket. Her chest rose and fell with her rapid breaths. The storm that swirled in her eyes was more intense than the one raging outside.

"Gotta get you out of these wet clothes, baby," he soothed as her body tensed and pitched in her need. "Come here. Let me give you a shower, get you nice and warm, then we're gonna eat, and then, baby, I'm gonna make you wet all over again," he vowed in a heated growl.

"Yes," Emily gasped as Rainer led her to the bathroom.

He turned on the water in the shower and heated it with his hands. He was thoroughly drenched as well, so he took off his shirt before moving back to her.

He pulled the T-shirt away from her waist and watched as it clung to her heaving breasts before he removed it altogether.

He dispensed with her bra. Her nipples were drawn tight. They were strained and puckered into deep cherry-red beads from being so cold. Rainer shuddered.

"That hurts, doesn't it, baby?" he soothed.

She gave a heavy nod. A shiver shook through her. Her beautiful emerald eyes were dark and hungry. Rainer lowered his mouth to her right breast as a needy moan of expectation quaked from her.

"Let me make it feel better." He huffed hot breath over the tight aching mounds. She let her head fall back and brought them closer to his mouth as a low guttural groan echoed from him.

He laved her nipple with his tongue as she shook in his arms. He sucked and bathed them. He drowned them in his mouth as she writhed in his hands.

Quickly unsnapping her jeans, he peeled them off her. She was wearing white cotton panties that were soaked through. He could see her lips swollen and red from the cold and from her need. The tender skin was raw from the bitter cold.

He pushed aside everything he longed to do to her. He wanted her to be warm. The cold had to hurt. He couldn't stand to think that she was in pain. His shield sizzled in desperation to soothe her. He pulled the panties down her legs and led her to the shower.

He helped her in, and she moved to stand in the falling water. Her body eased from the warmth.

"Get in with me," she begged.

"I will, baby. I promise. I'm gonna go make you some tea first, okay?" He closed the clear glass door and watched her in desperate need for a moment as she began to wash her hair.

With a slight shudder, he vowed to himself to take care of her first, to make her warm and comfortable, to make certain she was fed before he allowed her to satisfy the physical needs he'd been fighting for weeks.

He hoisted off his jeans and moved to the kitchen. After heating two mugs of water with his hands, he added the tea bags. Lightning flashed ominously outside, and the windows shook as thunder shattered the night sky.

Suddenly, the house went absolutely quiet as darkness fell. The electricity faded from all of the appliances.

"Rainer!" Emily screeched. She sounded terrified. He quickly left the tea on the counter and sprinted back into the bathroom. He opened the shower door and pulled electricity into his hands. It was floating in erratic waves throughout the house.

"It's okay, baby. I'm right here."

"I want to get out." Shame worked through her rhythms. She was embarrassed at her own reaction. It broke Rainer's heart.

"Come here." He threw the electricity from his hands to the lights above the sinks and turned off the water. He grabbed a towel and sealed heat in its fibers before pulling her to him and wrapping it around her.

As he dried her off, he considered. He could certainly run enough electricity through his body to run the heater or make the oven work. He could keep the lights in their home lit, but it would leave him depleted, and there were so many things he wanted to do with her.

When he was certain her body was dry, he grabbed another towel, heated it quickly, and ran it through his own hair and over his body. He pulled off his boxers and replaced them with a dry pair.

While guiding her into their bedroom, he cupped his hand and lit all of the candles scattered on surfaces around the room, the ones Emily usually lit when she wanted a slow, romantic session.

When the room glowed enough for him to see, Rainer grabbed one of his warmest Venton sweatshirts and pulled it over her head.

She wriggled into it with a contented sigh as it warmed her. She brought the loose sleeve to her face and inhaled deeply of his scent. He grinned as he watched her.

"This isn't what I planned on wearing for you the night I got back," she lamented.

Rainer winked at her as he grabbed another sweatshirt for himself. "Don't worry, baby. I can take that off you just as easily as French lingerie. I want you to be warm." His assurance elicited a broad grin.

She pulled on a pair of lacy white panties that had Rainer's mind racing. She bent over and offered him a delicious view. He couldn't quell the hungry groan that escaped his throat. She held up a pair of flannel pajama pants.

"Are you sure this is okay?"

Rainer tugged on a dry pair of jeans and moved to her. "If you don't put them on, I can't take them back off."

She shivered deliciously, but this time it wasn't because she was cold. Rainer forced himself to do all the things that needed to be done to keep her warm and safe if the storm kept the power out for much longer.

He decided to allow himself just one kiss before he set to work.

He pulled Emily close and held her eyes with his own. He cradled her head at the nape of her neck, angled it back softly, and leaned in.

"I missed you." He brushed tender kisses over her lips.

She responded heatedly. She reached and pulled him closer as he began to lave her mouth with his lips. He needed to feel her. He needed her energy inside of him. With desperate, craving propensity, he dipped his tongue between her lips and let it dance in slow rhythmic laps as he melded their souls. Ravenous with desire, he pulled her bottom lip into his mouth and sucked.

She panted and moaned. Her body swayed in need against his. Her hand caressed his ardent strain, and he pulled away. If she grasped him, he would be capable of nothing more than ravaging her body with eager force, and that wasn't what needed to happen…yet.

The storm was relentless. He had to keep her warm. He took her hands and led her to the couch in the living room.

After settling her, he grabbed two of the quilts thrown on furniture in the room and covered her in them. He headed to the fireplace, cupped his hand, and when he held enough heat in his cast, he set the wood that was already in the box on fire. He added another log from the pile on the tiled kitchen floor, and moved his hand over it to draw the fire to a higher pitch.

Quickly moving to the pantry, he pulled several cans of soup off the shelf and grabbed bowls from the cabinets.

"I can do that." Emily looked uncomfortable being waited on.

Rainer shook his head. "Em, baby, you've been taking care of kids for almost a month. I can tell you're exhausted. Let me take care of you."

While summoning enough electricity to run the can opener, Rainer heated the soup cans in his hands and poured the contents into the bowls. He grabbed crackers from the pantry and handed Emily her dinner.

"Thank you," she gushed as if he'd just handed her a gourmet meal. Rainer planted a kiss on the top of her head.

"It's not much, but it's better than nothing, I guess."

"It's perfect."

Rainer returned to the kitchen for his own bowl and joined Emily under the quilts. He decided that it wasn't a bad way to spend the evening at all.

When she finished, he removed the bowl from her lap, set it beside his on the coffee table, and cradled her to him.

"I missed you so much," he couldn't help but tell her repeatedly.

"I'm so glad to be home, and I know it's probably not how you pictured it,"—she gestured to the fire and the quilts—"but I think it's perfect."

"Me too."

With a sweet grin, she giggled.

"What are you laughing at, Miss Haydenshire?"

"I was just thinking that I'm really glad I get to sleep on top of you tonight instead of on top of Fionna."

It took Rainer a split second to realize she was referring to the bunk beds. He quickly shut down the lurid picture his mind had conjured. He shook his head at her.

As he watched her laugh and felt her warmth beside him, Rainer was overcome with need once again. Just as he was about to jump in with both feet, their cell phones chirped simultaneously.

Rainer edged his way out of the quilts. He left Emily covered as he located their phones. After handing Emily hers, he turned on his screen to read the text. Rainer laughed, but Emily shuddered and groaned.

The text was to the Haydenshire group chat from Mrs. Haydenshire.

> To all of our grown children, we love you all dearly and just wanted to take a moment to remind everyone that many of you were conceived during blackouts. So, if that is not your desire for the evening, please exercise caution.

"Do they have to do that?" Emily was thoroughly annoyed.

As he extended his hand to her, Rainer gave her an adoring smile. "Come here to me."

She smiled and threw back the quilts. He brushed a hesitant kiss across her lips and let his arms wrap around her loosely. He refused her another, though she leaned in for more.

While watching and studying her, he reveled in her energy as it began to crave and pulse for him.

"I want to take you to bed, baby. I promise I'll keep you warm," his voice was low and husky as he whispered in her ear. She shivered and clung to him. "Did you set the cast, sweetheart?" He decided to take care of the exercising caution portion of their evening now so he could spend the rest of the night worshipping her delicious body.

She shook her head against his shoulder. "It feels better when you do it," she admitted hesitantly. Rainer decided that he should thank Garrett for his lesson so many years before. He smiled at her.

"Come here. I'll take care of everything." He scooped her up and into his arms. He left their bedroom door open so the heat from the fire would keep their room warm as he stood her by the bed.

Desperate for her taste on his parched lips, he guided her mouth back to his. He sucked and explored her with his tongue until a heady moan spilled into his mouth from hers.

She slid her hands down his chest, reached, and then pulled his shirt over his head until she was caressing his flesh and dragging her hands over his pecs. Everywhere her hands caressed felt like he'd been set on fire.

"I wanted you so much," her words fell heavily from her kiss-swollen lips.

He needed to feel her. His heart raced. His shield tensed in need. He longed to touch her skin. His hands glided down her sides. He lifted the sweatshirt off her and groaned as he took her in. Her nipples throbbed cherry-red and begged for his care.

He grasped her breasts, pulled one into his mouth, and drowned the tip of her with his tongue. He laved one as he spun his thumb over the other until a stuttered cry escaped her.

He watched them swell and vie for his attention. They grew even more plump and ripe under his touch.

"I wanted you so bad it hurt," she confessed as he eased the pajamas and panties off. He forced them down in a puddle of flannel and lace at her feet.

"I would lie in my bed and ache for you. I hurt and was wet for you," she murmured.

He shuddered and moaned his approval. Her confession had him reeling. "I'm gonna make everything feel better, baby. I promise." She trembled, naked and desperate for his touch. "I won't let you hurt anymore."

A needy moan spilled from her lips. He traced his hands down her body and slipped them low. He caressed her tenderly. Then he dragged his hands to her backside and began kneading it with ardent hunger.

Her energy was spiraled in tight, jagged waves that needed to be soothed and released.

"Lie down for me, baby. Let me make it better."

She panted as he pulled back the sheets and blankets on their bed. He ran his heated hands over them and watched as she crawled in. He nestled her in the warmth as he removed everything he was wearing in a second flat.

While easing beside her, he studied her, lit by the glow of the candles. Her eyes were pleading and needy, darkened with her desire.

A kindled fire glowed there in their emerald depths. His eyes traveled from her kiss-swollen lips, to her breasts, to the dip and indentation of her waist, to the luscious curves of her hips, and the soft red curls between her legs that covered her lips swollen and wet for him. A low groan echoed from his chest.

"You are the most beautiful thing I've ever seen," he vowed as she writhed beside him. Her energy was spun too tightly for her to lie still.

"Touch me, please. I need you," she pled in a fervent moan.

"Baby, I'm gonna touch you, and taste you, and then I'm gonna lay you down and give you everything you need." His promises made her soar.

He slipped his hand to her lower lips. He traced her and felt the energy rise under her skin and liquid heat spill onto her swollen, fevered folds. The course red curls were soaked with need. He dragged one finger over her slit and gathered the nectar as she began to beg. He teased her clit gently and watched her body tremble from the sensations.

"Please," she whimpered in need.

Unable to draw it out any longer, he slipped two fingers deep inside of her. He nearly lost control. "God, baby, you're so fucking tight," he gasped. In fact, she was so tight he nearly withdrew. He could recall only one other time when he'd felt her drawn so intensely, and as the night he'd taken her for the first time—the night he'd made her his own—replayed itself in his mind, white-hot fire burned low in his groin. He began to melt down in the ecstasy of her.

He worked with delicate precision. He curved his fingers and slowly opened her. Emily was frantic. She couldn't remain still. He needed to take the edge off and let her relax before he moved on.

"Give it to me, baby. Let me make it better. I know you're so needy. Just let it go for me," he commanded. With another shallow stroke, he had her. The pent-up energy unfurled, and she convulsed. He knew she needed so much more.

It washed through her quickly, and he continued dipping his fingers inside her, reaching deeper with each pass, building her slowly this time. She bucked under his pliant touch, and her muscles spasmed around his hand. She pulled him deeper with each stroke.

"Does that feel good, baby?"

Her eyes flashed as another desperate moan quaked from her body. She gasped for breath. She rode his hand in earnest as he pounded his fingers in faster and deeper. Her body flushed as her temperature rose.

"That's it," he soothed. "Give me another one. I want to drink you." He had her. She called out his name. It drove him wild as the very essence of her spilled into his hand.

He pulled his fingers away and dipped his head between her legs. He positioned her calves over his shoulders and kissed the most sensitive parts of her inner thighs. She bucked and showed him exactly what he wanted to see. The liquid heat was visible to his eyes and his thirsty tongue.

Unable to help himself, far too hungry, he spun his tongue between her swollen lips. He let the tip of it dance just inside her before delving deep and drinking everything she gave up for him.

"I want it. Take me," she demanded in heated need.

Rainer fought with himself and with her desperation.

"Baby, I'm trying to be gentle," he panted as he gave her the friction she begged for with his tongue. "You're so tight. I don't want to hurt you."

"I don't want you to be gentle. I need you. I want to feel it tomorrow every time I move," she begged. He almost lost it all on the mattress then and there. He'd never be able to turn down such an incredible offer.

"I'm gonna set the cast." He summoned. He was already a part of her energy. He added in his own calming rhythms and sealed her womb.

With every nerve ending in his body hot-wired and thrumming in greedy arcs, he moved over her and settled his hips between her legs.

With precise gentleness, he spread her swollen lips with his hand. He listened to her gasp and moan as he entered her slowly, an inch at a time.

Her body trembled as she clenched around him. The liquid heat pulled him deeper. The intensity of them together nearly made him lose control.

He gave a gentle thrust and opened her as delicately as he could. She felt like hot, liquid silk. He groaned in the ecstasy of her pulling him deeper.

Feeling her open for him, listening to her call out for him as he plunged her searing depths and formed her around his length was blissful perfection.

"You feel so damn good," he moaned as she began to buck under him. She drew him deeper still.

"Harder," she panted. He pounded into her with ragged thrusts. He watched her eyes flash unrestrainedly and heard her breath hitch in her outcries.

He opened her to his hilt as he groaned. He relished the heavenly way she moved with him.

She swelled, and his eyes rolled back in his head. Nothing would ever feel as good as that. It was like being drowned in warm honey that could only come from heaven.

He throbbed inside of her as she clenched around him.

He pounded harder and pushed her further. He lost it all as her body tensed beneath his and the climax consumed her.

It seared through her, shaking her and making her convulse under him. She panted and cried out all for him. He felt her release mix with his as he rode the waves around her, and he got lost in the frenzy of being with her again.

A moment later, she stilled and tried to catch her breath.

"Are you okay, baby?" As the erotic haze cleared from his mind, he was terrified she'd asked for more than she could really take, and he'd certainly supplied it in heavy doses.

With a contented smile, she nodded. He eased out of her and tucked her on his chest as he folded the sheets and quilts around them.

"I love you," he whispered. He held her tight and kissed her forehead.

"I love you too," she vowed.

"I've been waiting too damn long to hear you say that out loud."

"I'm so glad I'm home. I missed you so much."

He cradled her closer. His release, her scent, the feeling of her curves lying in his embrace, all brought clarity to his mind.

"Did you really buy me a Porsche, or did I dream that?"

With a delicious giggle, she leaned up on her elbow. "Technically, *we* bought you a Porsche, and it's in our garage."

"Can I sleep in it?"

"No," she feigned offense as he laughed.

The storm had calmed slightly, but rain continued to hit the roof in a soothing, rhythmic dance.

"Let me go put another log on the fire, and then we can go to sleep."

"I don't want you to leave," she fussed.

Rainer kissed her forehead.

"Stay right here. I'll be right back. I'm not leaving. I'm keeping you warm."

After pulling on his boxers, he scooted from the room and threw several large logs onto the fire. He casted a low-grade shield over it to make certain the flames stayed in the box but the heat escaped it, before he returned to her.

He settled back beside her, and she curled up on his chest. He kissed the top of her head.

"Okay, so now that I can think straight," he confessed and listened to her infectious giggle, "tell me how you got a Porsche that they don't even have on the lots yet?"

Emily hugged him. "Sam helped me a lot. After the thing with the Mustang..." she hesitated, almost afraid to say the word. "Garrett was talking about how the new Boxsters are like race cars from the sixties. So, I started researching them and talking to Sam. He said he could get you one." She beamed at Rainer who was listening intently. "I know we were too wet from the rain to get in, but the key is even on the left, and I got you the one with sports mode," she informed him.

After giving her a deep, reverent groan, Rainer fought not to fly from the bed and into his new car. "It has the enhanced top, so it should be really quiet, and of course, it has the seven speed PDK transmission."

"Oh baby, trust me," Rainer teased, "if it were possible, I'd have another hard-on." He made her laugh hysterically.

Thunder clapped in the distance as the storm moved away, and she tensed. He kept her cradled in the safety of his embrace.

"I've got you. Go to sleep. I'm right here."

With a contented sigh, she kissed his chest again, and he felt her breathing steady. Her energy began to roll in soft, placid waves, and he drifted off to sleep wrapped up in her.

CHAPTER 19

MY EVERY FANTASY

The next morning, sunlight warmed Rainer in the scattered sheets of their bed. He thought he heard a door close, and he heard the refrigerator running. The power must have come back on in the night.

With a contented sigh, he reached for Emily, but the bed was empty. While trying not to pout, he let one eye open hesitantly. He'd wanted to spend the morning cuddling her in their bed and then maybe doing a little more than cuddling.

"Em?" he called, but she didn't answer. Panic began to set in as he sat up and scanned the house. Then he saw a note on her pillow.

His brow furrowed. He rubbed his hands over his face, snatched up the note, and opened it quickly.

Meet me in the garage. Love, the future Mrs. Lawson.

With a deep yawn, Rainer wondered what she was up to. He crawled from the bed. His body contorted as he stretched out the slight kinks in his neck. He hadn't slept well the entire time Emily had been gone.

After pulling on a pair of jeans, he glanced around the kitchen. It didn't appear that she'd eaten or made coffee. Maybe she wanted to go out for breakfast? He pulled open the door to the garage.

All thoughts of eating evaporated from his mind as soon as his eyes landed on the Porsche. All rational thought of any kind disappeared entirely.

With his eyes goggling, his heart racing, his breath ragged and stunned, his mouth fell open as he took in Emily lying on the hood of his new Porsche in a black silk and lace nightie that covered nothing at all.

The tiny straps hung off her shoulders. She was positioned on her back, propped up on her elbows, with one leg folded over the other. There was nothing under the nightie.

Please don't let me be dreaming. Please don't let me be dreaming, his mind begged the ether.

"Damn…" gasped from his lungs in a heated pant as he moved into the garage. She gave him a delicious grin that said, "come get me and take whatever you want." He tried not to lose control just looking at her sprawled out on display all for him.

"Please tell me I'm not dreaming." He was unable to even blink.

With a sexy laugh, Emily shook her head. "I was thinking," she drawled seductively, "the 'not in my car' rule was really only for the Mustang."

A deep, fervent growl echoed from his chest. "Are you sure, baby? You sure you want it rough and dirty on the hood of my car?"

He prayed she'd say yes. Fire flashed in her eyes as she moaned. Her head fell back in what appeared to be desperate desire. He watched her breasts heave as the slight lace slid farther down her ample cleavage. Her nipples flushed and throbbed as the rough lace made them raw.

"I want it right now. I want you to lose control. Take me hard," she purred. "We have a lot of time to make up for."

He flew to her instantly and positioned himself between her legs. He grabbed her hands and jerked her upward. He kissed her heatedly.

"Then come here to me." Quickly losing all sense of self-control or gentlemanly behavior, he jerked the already loosened straps down until he could see her breasts spilling over black lace.

He took her hand again, popped the snap of his jeans, and shoved the zipper down.

"Grab me. Feel what you do to me." His rather forceful demands seemed to drive her wild as she groped him and moaned at his ferocity.

He moved his mouth to her breasts. He sucked and devoured them. He slid his teeth along the swell and nipped as she moaned loudly.

She threw her head back and shook them in his face.

"Tell me what you want," she commanded. Her voice was raspy and erotic in her desire.

"Suck me," he ordered, and she went wild. She pushed him back and spun so she was lying on her stomach. She leaned over to shove his jeans off as she lowered her head to his straining length.

Certain he'd died and gone to heaven, Rainer watched her move over him in ardent need. She licked up his length and spun her tongue over his head, as she reached low to cup and massage him.

"Oh fuck, yes," growled from him. He throbbed between her lips. She lapped up everything that leaked from his head. Her body writhed as she worked. She sucked hard.

"More," he demanded. Her unending moans reverberated through his soul.

"Em, I need you to tell me right now if you need me to stop or to slow down, because I'm about to lay you out on this car."

"Take me," she gasped as she sat back up. Her chest rose in rapid, hungry pants. "Don't stop. Just take me now."

With that he grasped her hips and laid her back on the hood. He parted her thighs.

"Show me how wet you are, baby. I want you dripping for me." He positioned himself in front of her soaking wet lips. She cried out for him as he leaned in and licked the slick spicy heat pouring from her.

Another loud moan echoed from her as she writhed on the car. Rainer had never seen anything hotter. Unable to stop himself, he lifted her hips and threw her legs in a V around him. He gave a desperate thrust and plunged her depths.

"Take it, baby. Take it just like that. Just like I want it," he ordered.

She pulsed and bucked as he pounded into her. He watched himself enter her repeatedly. The provocative display was intoxicating.

"Yes," hissed from her as he continued his unrelenting thrusts.

"Tell me you want more," he commanded.

"Oh god, I want more," she pled deliciously as she swelled again. He continued to pound with unrelenting force.

"Do you feel that, baby? I'm gonna explode."

This time, his orgasm drove hers. He couldn't steel himself. He lost control. The display was just too much.

She continued to convulse as he withdrew, still not fully believing that he was awake. She sat up and gave him a lusciously naughty grin.

"So, I take it we're keeping the car," she teased.

Still gasping for breath, Rainer lifted her off the hood.

"I will never, ever deserve you, but that was absolutely the most incredible thing I have ever seen or done."

"Good," she sassed. "Can we go back to bed now?"

"We can do anything in the world you want."

She giggled as he carried her back into the house. He watched her pull off the lingerie and then crawl back into bed with him. He cradled her on his chest.

"By the way, hey there," he chuckled.

"I missed you saying that to me every single day."

With an elated grin, he kissed her forehead. Their rendezvous in the garage continued to occupy most of his brain.

"I texted it to you," he reminded her.

"That's not the same," she sighed. "So, what do you want to do today?"

"Baby," Rainer shook his head, "I just had sex with you on the hood of a Porsche that I now own. I will never, ever need another thing as long as I live." His vow had her laughing hysterically.

"Well, we do actually need to drive it, and we have to go to Sam's and pay him for it."

"You've been gone for weeks. Is there anything *you* want to do?"

She gave him her dazzling smile, the one that made her eyes sparkle as she gazed at him with rapt adoration. Her bottom lip slid through her teeth, and her cheeks colored.

"I want to spend every waking moment with you, and for you not to pay anyone else any attention until you have to go back to work Monday," she giggled.

While laughing at her willingness to admit that to him, Rainer nodded. "Done, and I actually have next week off." He watched her eyes light from his surprise. Glee flowed through her rhythms. "So, how about this, Miss Haydenshire?" he urged. "As sad as I am to say this, why don't we get dressed, and I'll take you out for breakfast? Then I thought maybe we could do something like go for a drive up the ridgeway."

"Really?" she trilled.

"Really." He delighted in her smile.

CHAPTER 20
PART OF HIS SOUL

Rainer's stomach flipped with eager anticipation as Emily handed him the key to the new Boxster.

"Are you ready?" she tittered excitedly.

"I will never, ever deserve you, and this is beyond my wildest dreams. Thank you."

Rainer opened the garage door. The midday sun had vanquished the raging storm. He pressed the button on the key fob and unlocked the doors. Emily giggled as she watched him.

"Now you know, I loved the Mustang," she assured him, "but you couldn't do that in the other car."

Rainer chuckled. He certainly had to allow that. He opened the passenger door for Emily while he stared at his new Porsche with rapt adoration. More ecstatic than a kid on Christmas morning, he moved to the driver's side, opened the door, and studied the dash.

"Well, come on," Emily sassed, "take me for a ride, Mr. Lawson."

"I just did that, baby. Are you ready for another?"

She laughed as her cheeks colored. She'd appeared slightly embarrassed at her own sassy talk and the recollections of her earlier display. The effect made Rainer fall even more in love with her.

He placed the key into the ignition on his left. His heart picked up pace as the raspy, metallic roar of the aspirated engine resonated in his soul.

Though he would never have admitted it to Emily, he was mildly disappointed that Logan had gotten his Boxster's virgin run. He mentally called himself a prick as the words "popped its cherry" formed in his mind.

He felt the low, firm leather seat form around him as he inhaled the heady scents of high-grade leather and new car.

Rainer revved the engine and shuddered in delight as Emily continued to laugh at him outright.

"Sam said you wouldn't like anything turbocharged." She knitted her brow as Rainer engaged the clutch. He considered the fact that, with all of Sam's enhancements, the Porsche would fly at around two hundred miles per hour. He wouldn't really need to summon and cast the engine.

"Yeah, he's right. They started putting turbocharged engines in sports cars because they are very, very slightly more fuel-efficient, but they also mess with the response of the car. It's like this car can read my mind."

A broad grin formed on Emily's features. She seemed delighted over his enthusiasm.

"A naturally aspirated engine is much crisper, more precise. It's essentially perfect," he vowed reverently.

The sheer power of the automobile worked through him as he drove it down the gravel driveway.

"I'm so relieved you love it. I was a little bit scared I would pick wrong."

"This is more perfect than anything I ever would've picked. You know me better than I know me." Sam's advice on letting her help him had been right on. His advice always was.

Occasionally letting the image of her splayed out on the hood sear through his mind, he also thought about Sam's promise that there would be good memories in his new car as well. He chuckled out loud as he decided the memory of taking Emily on the hood of his new Porsche was a hell of a way to add a little of his soul to his new ride.

As he pulled onto the highway, he picked up speed and felt the engine rev as he lightly pressed the accelerator. The feeling was intoxicating. The Porsche moved at the speed of his thoughts. It was the perfect car, picked out by the perfect woman, both for him. How had he gotten so lucky?

"Okay, is it stupid that I really want to go to Waffle House?" Emily's face colored again. "I haven't had an omelet in weeks."

Rainer shook his head. "Why would that be stupid? I was hoping that's where you wanted to eat. I don't guess you'd want to visit a Waffle House maybe in Florida or anything?"

She cracked up. "I'm happy you love your new car, but I'm gonna want to eat before tomorrow sometime."

After parking and casting the Porsche, as he would never leave either his or Emily's automobile uncasted ever again, he wrapped his arm around her and escorted her into the diner.

Rainer allowed the all-encompassing emotion of having her tucked up beside him once again to fill him with utter elation.

"Vindico found out about Ferg and Tilly," he admitted as he gestured for the waitress to refill Emily's coffee mug.

"He's not going to tell Governess Sherman is he?"

"No, but when I tell you what Logan and I have to do because we didn't tell him, you may wish he would." Rainer decided to go ahead with the story. He warded off the guilt before it set in.

"What do you have to do?" Disappointed hesitation became her predominant expression.

"Remember I told you that Vindico has to go to Moscow on Thanksgiving for Pendergrath's trial the next day?"

"That's awful. Won't he miss his family? I bet holidays are really hard for him after what happened to Amelia." Her deep concern pricked Rainer's heart.

"I didn't get that impression. He kind of seemed glad to be leaving. Anyway, he can't really leave the country and leave Bridgette unprotected. He says more and more *guys* are at The Tantra every day. You know what she's doing for us." He glanced around, but no one was near enough to their back booth to have heard him. It still wasn't safe to say too much in a public place. Emily nodded as her brow knitted. She knew he was stalling.

"Just tell me what you have to do." She cocked her jaw to the side and narrowed her eyes.

"Come on, I missed you so much. Just listen."

She softened slightly. "Just tell me. You're freaking me out."

"Your mom told Vindico that Bridgette could stay at the farmhouse Thanksgiving night until he gets back, and Logan and I have to stay there too. I was really hoping you'd stay with me there as well. We have to take her to work and bring her back. Keep an eye on her. I won't be going into The Tantra," he vowed immediately. "I can't. It was different when the only Interfeci guys around here didn't know who was on the Elite team." He shrugged, not certain what else to say.

"You're definitely not staying there with her and not me."

"Baby." Rainer shook his head. "I have the most beautiful, wonderful woman in the entire Realm sitting across from me right now. I don't deserve her, but she's here, and I would never ever do anything to risk the most precious thing in my entire life. So, other than the fact that I don't want to be anywhere that you aren't, whether or not you're there has nothing to do with it."

Emily melted before his eyes. He winked at her and reached across the table to hold her hand.

"You know Dad's probably not gonna let us stay in my room together," she fussed.

Rainer nodded his lament but then gave her a wry smile. "Our house isn't that far from your parents',"—he waggled his eyebrows—"so if you need to be taken care of, I can arrange that."

"I did notice that you didn't tell me this until after I laid out on the Porsche for you."

Rainer cracked up. "I'm not an idiot."

"All right I guess, but only to keep Fergus from getting fired."

He wondered how long Emily's patience with Fergus and his moronic stunts would last. They weren't kids in school anymore, and Fergus was playing with fire.

As they crawled back into the Porsche, a smile formed automatically on Rainer's face as he cranked the engine.

"This is just awesome. Seriously, I don't ever need another present ever."

CHAPTER 21

KILLER CURVES

After breakfast, they headed to Sam's, and Emily signed the check for the Porsche. Sam quickly informed Rainer that he was a lucky, lucky man, to which Rainer adamantly agreed.

"So, will you take your fiancée, who totally just bought you this kick-ass car, on a drive up the ridgeway?"

"Absolutely. Hop in, baby."

They drove in peaceful contentment for several long minutes as the road began to narrow and climb. It was much too cold to put the top down, but Rainer was deliriously happy just to have her with him with nowhere to go.

"Do you know what you're going to have Uncle Tad engrave on my ring?" Emily asked suddenly.

"I think so." Rainer was still considering a few options. He thought about the inscription on his parents' rings, but he didn't want something quite so overdone. That just wasn't them.

"He's bringing down the ring cases with him for Thanksgiving so we can look."

"I'm ready to get this show on the road. I told you that. I'm counting the days 'til April."

Emily beamed. Her rhythms trilled in elation as they drove up the mountain roads.

"I can't wait either." She let her eyes close, and Rainer wondered what she was envisioning.

She'd been planning their wedding since she was barely out of diapers, but all Rainer had ever wanted was to meet her at the end of the aisle. The details were important to her. He understood that, but all that mattered to him was that she was his forever.

They talked about her not wanting to wear a veil, and Mrs. Haydenshire's disapproval of that. He told her about having to sit through sub-freshman sex ed again. He reveled in her infectious giggles. Every stupid, silly detail that wove themselves into every facet of their lives composed the stories of their time apart.

Rainer realized during that drive that it was the little, seemingly insignificant things that he'd missed the most. Those were what made life worth living.

They discussed which soup kitchen they would be working at on Thanksgiving. The Haydenshires always served Thanksgiving dinner to the needy and homeless around DC and Arlington, while Mrs. Haydenshire and Nana worked tirelessly to produce a large meal for them when they finished up their serving duties.

Emily had gotten the Angels in on the act this year, and they were all working at the largest soup kitchen in DC. It was one that served hundreds of people on a daily basis.

Rainer and Emily had always thoroughly enjoyed giving back and were looking forward to the tradition again this year.

Adeline had volunteered to work all day Thanksgiving, so that other medios could eat the meal with their families since the Haydenshires wouldn't be eating until well after eight o'clock.

It was getting late when they headed back down the gravel path to their home. Frustration worked through him as Rainer saw that the Accord had returned to the driveway. They'd had a near perfect day, and he was planning on keeping that going well into the night.

"I thought we got the whole weekend alone," Emily sighed.

"Me too." Rainer was trying not to be irritated.

They entered the kitchen and heard Logan shouting, "Uh, no. I'm sorry, but it will be a cold day in hell when I let some overmuscled, macho thug named Rocco rub hot oil all over your naked body."

Rainer's eyes goggled as he turned to Emily whose mouth was hanging open in shock.

"Logan." Adeline shook her head. "He wasn't an overmuscled, macho thug. He was a massage therapist. That's what they do, and I'm sure I didn't do anything for him. You're being ridiculous. He sees people undressed every day." She was on the brink of tears. "I'm sure he has clients with way better bodies than mine. I'm not even pretty."

Logan's eyes flashed in fury. "Stop it, now!" He spun to Rainer and ordered, "Tell her how gorgeous she is. She never believes me."

While staring at Logan like he'd lost his mind, Rainer shook his head in utter disbelief.

"We will be having a snowball fight in hell before I get involved in this argument. We're going out for dinner." He grabbed Emily's hand and led her back to the car.

"You could have told her how pretty she is. I wouldn't have minded."

"Sweetheart, your brother came completely unglued when I inadvertently saw Adeline in lingerie, and I didn't even really look at her. Me saying something like that would have eventually driven him insane again. When it comes to her, he pretty much overreacts about everything." He pointed out the inherent problem with Logan, not that the same couldn't be said for him when it came to Emily. "His shield takes over his brain. He can't see through it or around it."

She nodded her hesitant agreement. Logan and Adeline argued more often than she and Rainer ever had. They'd argued even before they'd moved in together, but it was almost always about her mother.

It drove Logan crazy that Adeline would give her mother her paychecks and tips from the pizza joint where she used to waitress. Since Candy Parker inevitably used Adeline's money to buy more illegal substances instead of paying their bills, Rainer had typically taken Logan's side.

"There was no good way out of that," Rainer continued his explanation as he steered the Porsche quickly back toward the road.

"Do you think Adeline's pretty?" Emily quizzed once they'd reached the highway.

"Em," Rainer huffed. "Please, baby, don't do this." Which of her friends he found attractive was not a discussion he was interested in having.

"Come on," Emily urged, "I won't get mad. I just want to know."

Rainer wasn't worried that she was going to be jealous. He was worried she would think he was being unkind.

He watched her customary performance. She pushed her long, auburn hair behind her right ear as determination set in her eyes.

"Where do you want to eat?" he tried feebly to distract her.

"Mexican. Now tell me."

Rainer drove toward Los Carenos, the Mexican restaurant that was their favorite.

"You want the truth, and you won't think I'm a jerk?"

"No, of course not, and yes, I want the truth." She looked rather confused by his question.

"Fine," he quipped. "I don't know why you don't believe this, but to me you are the definition of gorgeous, and you and Adeline look nothing alike." He hesitated and felt like a heel. "She's not hard to look at or anything, but to me she just isn't all that attractive." Guilt settled uncomfortably in his stomach.

Emily seemed to consider. "But she's so tall, and thin, and she has beautiful eyes, and she's so sweet, and that gorgeous jet-black hair. She looks like Snow White," she argued.

Rainer smiled at her. "She is very sweet, and she's perfect for Logan, which is all that really matters. She does have pretty eyes," he allowed, "but, baby, to me, when I look into your eyes, I see so much more than how beautiful they are. I see your soul. I've never really even noticed Adeline's hair." He pulled into the parking lot, turned to her, and gazed into the very windows of her soul.

"I want my gorgeous redhead with killer curves. I need my beautiful bombshell, who's not afraid to tell people what she thinks. I want that fiery temper, as long as I'm not the recipient of it," he teased. She laughed.

"I want the girl who lays herself out on my Porsche after telling me to meet her in the garage, and the one who goes to Brazil and cries over the kids there that she doesn't think she's helped enough.

"I want you, baby. To me, you're absolute perfection. You are the most beautiful thing I've ever set eyes on. Wild in my bed when that's what I want, and slow and sweet when that's what I need. I somehow got all of that in the same woman. I don't know how I got so lucky, but if I'd responded to Logan's question truthfully, it wouldn't have done anything to help Adeline's faltering self-esteem. Everyone is different and everyone is beautiful. I don't get why he can't get that."

Emily swooned. "You're so sweet."

"That's you, baby." Rainer opened her door for her. "Now, let's go get my fiery redhead some salsa, because whether they're home or not, I still have three weeks to make up for." He waggled his eyebrows as she beamed at him delightedly.

When they returned home, Rainer assumed Logan and Adeline had made up. They were locked in their bedroom. Rainer and Emily scooted to their room, after hearing the mattress squeak and several rather loud moans. Emily cracked up as soon as Rainer closed their door.

CHAPTER 22

THE GIVING AND THE TAKING

Sunday evening, Rainer escorted Emily into the farmhouse, where she was embraced heartily by all of her family.

However, she only had eyes for the tiny bundle of joy sound asleep in the bassinet in the kitchen. Nana Anderson managed to give her a long embrace before Emily eased over to the cradle.

"Oh, please let me hold her," Emily begged Will. He laughed and did look rather exhausted.

"Of course. She'll probably want Brooke when she's hungry, but go for it," Will encouraged.

"Hi Lily Ana, I'm your Aunt Emily."

Everyone watched with adoration as Lily Ana's eyes blinked open to study Emily.

Will and Brooke had named their little girl after both of their mothers, and Rainer was certain the grandmothers were delighted. Emily kept Lily Ana cradled to her chest while everyone else set the dining room table for dinner.

"Well, baby girl, you certainly look much happier than you did at the airport." The governor grinned at her.

Emily nodded. "Food, sleep, and showers do make me happy." She soothed her father's slight discomfort over what he suspected had made the biggest difference in her mood.

A harsh knock sounded on the front door. Everyone grimaced, save Garrett.

He smirked. "Ah, Grandpa's here."

Rainer would never understand how Garrett managed to put up with the governor's father, but he never seemed to let Grandpa Haydenshire get under his skin. He had Grandpa's number.

"Garrett." Grandpa Haydenshire grinned as he stepped inside the farmhouse. "How's life, son?"

"S'good. Can't complain."

"You got a girl?"

"Got several."

"That's my boy."

Emily rolled her eyes and continued to gaze at Lily Ana as everyone found a seat at the table.

"That yours?" Grandpa pointed to the baby and took his usual seat.

"No, Grandpa. This is Will and Brooke's little girl."

Brooke looked highly annoyed. Lily Ana did resemble Will, but she had her mother's beautiful Brazilian coloring and jet-black hair. She certainly looked nothing like Rainer or Emily.

Governor Haydenshire sighed as he carried a platter of pork chops to the table. Mrs. Haydenshire followed him in from the kitchen. She was carrying two huge bowls of potatoes au gratin. Patrick and Lucy had rolls and Mrs. Haydenshire's delicious coleslaw.

Everyone settled in and began eating. Rainer was impressed with Emily's ability to hold her new niece and eat at the same time. After deciding that he had nothing better to do, he indulged himself in his fantasy of her pregnant.

A slight grin formed on his face as his mind constructed the imagery, Emily swollen full of their baby. His hands and mouth on her bump. His eyes slid to the side as he stole a quick glance at her kissing Lily Ana's tender head.

"Well, son, you've landed in the most powerful seat in the Realm. Now what are you going to do with it?" Grandpa Haydenshire demanded abruptly.

Weary exhaustion etched the lines beside Mrs. Haydenshire's eyes. She rubbed her temples for a long moment.

"I feel certain that however I respond it will not be what you want to hear, Dad, so why don't you just get wherever it is you're going," the governor challenged.

Rainer tried to conceal his grin as he loaded potatoes into his mouth.

"You know perfectly well that you need to instate mandatory military service for every young man in this Realm. Go a long way in fixing this ridiculous idea that teenagers need to express themselves." All of Emily's brothers' heads shot up as did Rainer's.

Paps Anderson studied the table and cleared his throat. As he was certainly a man of few words, everyone listened.

"Now Bill, I don't think that's necessary. It's a different world than the one we grew up in. Stephen's seen to that. These boys know what they want to do with their lives, and they're all giving back to the Realm. Not everyone needs to serve. Everybody has different things they were meant to do."

The governor nodded adamantly.

"Dad, as I explained to you when I was eighteen years old, I do not believe that every young man in this Realm needs to serve in the Gifted military. I understand that you enjoyed your time in the service, but as I am a parent who has lost a son already, I would never enact a law that would bring about that kind of pain to another family. Serving in the military is a personal choice, not one I'll make for anyone else."

The sudden pain over Cal's death gripped the table. Rainer set his fork down with a quiet tink that seemed to roar in the sudden robbery of air from the room.

Emily grasped his hand as tears threatened her eyes. She drew from him, and he tried desperately to soothe her. It seemed the memories of Cal, so fresh in everyone's mind, even deflated Grandpa's incorrigible desire to argue.

"Uh, Em, tell us about your trip." Will rescued his entire family, just as he had always done. The eldest, the guiding force, and the one they all looked to for direction, came through for them again.

She smiled down at Lily Ana who gave an audible grunt. "I missed you all so much. I really missed Mom's cooking." Mrs. Haydenshire grinned at her. "I guess I didn't miss Garrett since he was there with me, which was really great."

It seemed in light of the comparison, all of her disdain over Garrett and Chloe had melted away. Her big brother had been there, looking after her, and in that moment, Emily seemed to realize how often she'd taken that for granted.

Garrett winked at her from across the table, and her entire body relaxed.

"Em was amazing with the kids. They all loved her."

"I really miss them," she confessed. "Especially Aida. I never thought I would say this, but I'm looking forward to going back sometime. Not for a while, but sometime."

"Aida is the little girl you emailed us about?" the governor quizzed.

"Yeah, she's so sweet. I wanted to bring her home with me. Garrett is her absolute favorite—well, maybe Fionna, actually—but she's the sweetest little girl ever."

The governor shared a grin with his wife.

"Oh, good grief!" Grandpa huffed. "Don't tell them that! That's just what they need, to adopt one. Because the current litter isn't enough. Let's just plant some more fairies in the clouds."

"Dad, watch it," Governor Haydenshire commanded.

CHAPTER 23
GIVE THANKS

They day before Thanksgiving was spent helping with the prep work for the Thanksgiving meal and getting Patrick's old room ready for Bridgette.

Mrs. Haydenshire sank down in the kitchen rocking chair. She looked exhausted. Adeline had instructed her to rest more. The baby's scans weren't improving.

Rainer doubted a houseguest was what she needed.

As Logan and Rainer went upstairs to make up their old beds without any enthusiasm at all, Logan sank down on his mattress. "Adeline despises Bridgette."

Rainer threw his old quilt back over his bed. "Yeah, she's not Em's favorite either. Especially since Emily considers her the reason Dan won't ask Fionna Styler out."

"That's how girls are." Logan shook his head. "If you don't like her friend who likes you, then you're evil."

Rainer recalled Logan experiencing this on many occasions growing up. Kristen Rycroft nursed a crush on Logan all through ninth and tenth grade, but he had no interest. All of her friends would glare at him hatefully whenever they were in class with him. They'd even started a rumor that he'd slept with Kristen and then broken her heart when he dumped her immediately following the act. Every girl at Langley High School hated him for several weeks.

Thanksgiving morning, Rainer blinked hesitantly as he switched off the alarm. He and Emily had become rather accustomed to sleeping in late, enjoying lounging around and drinking coffee and occasionally returning to bed, which seemed to annoy Logan.

Logan also had the days off, but Adeline was working. So, he spent his vacation days wandering aimlessly around the house.

The morning before, Rainer was so intoxicated with the looks Emily was giving him and the requests she'd whispered in his ear, he'd thrown Logan the keys to the Porsche and told him to get lost as he'd led Emily back to bed.

Logan hadn't seemed to mind that one as he'd raced out to the new car.

As he forced his mind back to the present, Rainer leaned and brushed a sweet kiss across Emily's cheek. He didn't want to think about sleeping alone in the room with Logan that night as he took in his baby curled up sweetly on his chest, completely naked.

She moaned and whimpered, then furrowed deeper into the covers and his arms. With an adoring grin, he kissed her again.

"Hey there, Miss Haydenshire. We have to get going."

"But I like it here," she fussed.

Rainer chuckled. "I like you there too, but we're supposed to be at the soup kitchen at five."

She yawned and visibly willed herself to get up though it wasn't yet four in the morning.

"You know, in just a few months you won't be able to call me Miss Haydenshire anymore," she informed him with a broad grin.

The thought took Rainer's breath away. "I can't wait to call you Mrs. Lawson," he tried the name out. His heart picked up pace as he said it.

"Me either!"

~

A few hours later, Rainer was positioned between Logan and Chloe Sawyer, serving turkey, dressing, and all of the fixings on tray after tray as they pushed by. They wished everyone a Happy Thanksgiving as they passed.

Adeline had phoned Logan only once since her shift began early that morning. She was swamped at the hospital.

Emily, Fionna, and several of the other Angels were holding babies and toddlers, helping feed and bathe them, and then supplying them with donated clothing, coats, and blankets.

Levi had manned the stoves, and Rainer was certain the meal was absolutely delicious.

Governor Haydenshire, Will, and Garrett were working the ovens, along with dozens of other volunteers, to keep the food supplied to the lines.

Brooke stayed with Lily Ana at the farmhouse to nurse the baby and help make the meal with Mrs. Haydenshire and Nana.

The Gifted press showed, which seemed to irritate the governor, who considered serving the homeless on Thanksgiving his duty, not something the Realm should praise him for.

Just as the lines were winding down, and Rainer had left the serving line to help Patrick, Connor, and Lucy wash dishes, Logan's cell rang.

"Hey, baby, we're just about done here. I'll be by to pick you up," Logan explained without even saying hello. After a moment of silence, his eyes goggled.

"What?!" he demanded. "I'm on my way."

"What's wrong?" Rainer quizzed as all of the Haydenshires stopped what they were doing to study Logan. His expression was furious, and his shield pulsed fiercely.

"Candy just showed up at Georgetown. She's demanding to see Adeline. She's pitching a fit, and Ad's going to get fired if she continues to make a scene." He jerked his apron over his head and tossed it into the laundry bin.

"I'm coming with you," Rainer and Governor Haydenshire offered at the same moment.

"Fine, *we're* going with you," the governor corrected. "Garrett, make certain your sister gets to the house," he commanded.

"Of course." Garrett looked extremely concerned.

~

They flew to Georgetown Hospital.

There was quite a scene in the emergency room waiting area when they entered.

Patients awaiting medical help were everywhere, and Candy Parker was standing at the desk demanding to see Adeline.

"Medio Parker is with a patient, ma'am. She can't talk to you until she goes on break," the extremely addled woman working the admissions area informed Candy. She sounded both exhausted and frustrated.

"Candy, what the hell are you doing here?" Logan snarled. Ms. Parker spun. She looked highly insulted as she took in Logan's fury.

"Why are you here?" she sneered. "Trying to convince Adeline that I'm the bad guy again? Why don't you just go ahead and leave? She'll never be good enough for you or that Pollyanna family of yours anyway. Some idiot here called her your fiancée," she huffed indignantly. "You can't save her from who she is. I don't give a damn who your daddy is. She'll never be anything more than a gutter-trash mistake."

In that horrifying moment, Adeline had appeared behind her mother's back and had heard her hate-fueled proclamations. She dropped every patient file she'd been carrying and ran back into the ward she'd emerged from.

"Dammit!" Logan raced after her.

Rainer had never seen fury pulse in Governor Haydenshire's rhythms with such acridity. He stalked to Adeline's mother and narrowed his eyes. He kept his tone even, but his words were laced with menace.

"You may not be aware of exactly who I am, Ms. Parker, so listen up while I explain it to you. I am the Crown Governor of the American Gifted Realm, and I and others like me fought long and hard to make certain that the Gifted people don't use their powers to negatively impact the rest of the world.

"But let me assure you that if I ever find out that you've had any further contact with Adeline or Logan, or that you've ever shown your face in this hospital again, I will use every ounce of power I wield to make absolutely certain that you spend the rest of your life behind bars.

"You've always either been too wasted or just too stupid to see what a fantastic daughter you gave birth to, but let me assure you she's not a product of the pitiful environment you chose to allow her to live in. She rose so far out of your league you don't even deserve to be called her mother," the governor snarled.

With a huff of challenging defiance, Candy's eyes narrowed haughtily at the governor.

"Well, Mr. Crown Governor, you can just tell Logan's fiancée," she spat the word hatefully, "that my trial was yesterday. I got off, pending her hearing. The jury just ate up the fact that I only used drugs to be closer to my daughter and that using eased the pain of her father abandoning us after she was born." She mocked sorrow and then laughed.

"I don't think I'll be the one behind bars. But when they put Adeline in the orange jumpsuit, you just make sure I get that ring that Logan will want back as soon as they cart her off." She spun and slithered out of the sliding doors of Georgetown Hospital.

Rainer and Governor Haydenshire stared at one another for the length of several heartbeats, neither of them able to believe what they'd just heard.

"I tried to tell her, Crown Governor Haydenshire," the receptionist at the admissions desk pled. "I tried to tell her that Medio Parker is engaged to Logan Haydenshire. I told her that she didn't want to mess with you or Logan. I kept saying that he was Elite Iodex, but she wouldn't listen. She didn't seem to understand who you are."

Governor Haydenshire drew a steadying breath. "Thank you. We'll take care of everything. Is Medio Sawyer here?" Governor Haydenshire sighed his dejected question.

"Yes, sir. Did you want to see him?"

"Yes, please. I think we'd better talk."

CHAPTER 24

EMERGE AND BLOOM
LOGAN HAYDENSHIRE

Too furious to think rationally, Logan raced through the heavy swinging steel doors that declared the area to be for hospital employees only.

"Adeline!" he yelled, but there was no answer. Candy Parker's hate-filled threats reverberated in his soul. They made him sick. After frantically running from closed door to closed door, in a moment of desperation he flung one open to find a woman in active labor with doctors and nurses and her husband surrounding her.

"Excuse me?" the doctor spat.

"So sorry," Logan flinched and pulled the door shut. He continued his sprint, while calling her name repeatedly. *Where could she have gone?* His heart thundered as the terror over the pain her mother's words had certainly caused fissured his soul.

He continued his sprint through another set of doors and came to another corridor of patients' rooms.

"Adeline!" he shouted again.

"Sir, please, the patients need to rest," came a scolding befitting his mother. Logan huffed. Faces entered and exited his consciousness as he ran. None of them was the one he wanted to see.

"Logan." He heard his name and spun. He nearly fell as he halted abruptly.

"I saw her run in there. I didn't know you were already here. I was going to call you." Brad Metzger, Adeline's training medio, pointed to a closet marked Obstetric Supplies. "She's got it locked. Here…" Brad motioned for Logan to follow him.

Brad summoned a hefty dose of magnetizing energy from the air around him, and he waved his hand over a screened magnetic lock on the door and then followed that wave with his hospital badge.

"Thank you." Logan allowed himself to breathe now that he'd located her, but in that same moment he realized he had to think of what to say. How was anyone supposed to take away pain like that? How could he make up for her mother's hate and cruelty?

"No problem. Good luck, man. She looked pretty upset."

"Yeah, well, she should be. Her mother just got out of prison."

Brad grimaced as he slapped Logan on the back. "Like I said, good luck." With that, he turned and stalked to another patient's room.

Quickly deciding that he'd just wing it, Logan eased the door open.

"Baby." He closed the door behind him, and she fell into his arms sobbing. Logan cradled her to his chest. His desperate drive to protect her was all-consuming as he gazed at her, small and frail, against his tall frame and muscled arms.

"I'm so sorry." His shield orbed around her. It moved of its own accord. Protecting her was the only thing he'd been put here to do. Logan rubbed her back and swayed her soothingly.

"I'm…not…that," Adeline convulsed. She shook her head combatively and knotted his shirt in her fists. "I'm not what she said." Her quaking sobs hissed violently from her mouth. The words begged for confirmation as they fell.

"No, you're not, and it's high time you realized that." He suddenly felt hope begin to vanquish the terror in his heart.

Adeline had never disagreed with anything her mother said or did, at least not verbally. She would let her mother yell and scream. Candy would tell her that she had ruined her life, and that she was nothing but a stupid mistake. Adeline had never argued. She'd never stuck up for herself. She'd believed her mother's malignant words.

Her entire body shook in her fear and sadness. Logan held her tightly and refused to let her go.

"I'm, I'm…" she stuttered, and Logan continued to cradle her in the safety of his embrace. "I'm a good person," she finally managed to choke between her convulsive sobs.

Logan leaned down, held her face in his hands, and wiped away her tears. "Yes!" His own tears pricked and stung his eyes. "You are a wonderful person. I wish every single day that I could somehow figure out how to explain to you what you mean to me, what you mean to my family, and to the people you help here. You are an amazing human. You're the *most* amazing human being on this whole stupid planet, and if your mother refuses to see that, then that's a tremendous loss on her part."

He was unable to believe what he was finally hearing, what she'd finally realized.

From the moment he'd finally worked up enough courage to ask her to sit with him at lunch, Logan had vowed to himself to do anything in his power to make her see what a phenomenal person she really was. She'd always been meek and timid. She'd never thought anything of her abilities and never felt she deserved any accolades or recognition.

He could hardly believe, after five years of being together, that she'd finally chosen to listen to him and not to the woman who'd given birth to her.

Finally the realization of the things she'd done, the things she'd learned and accomplished, began to set in. He watched determination swirl in her eyes and in her rhythms.

"I don't want her anywhere near me." She shivered violently in his arms. Her tone rose in accordance with her fervor. "I don't want to be any part of her world anymore. How could she do this to me? I always tried to take care of her to try to prove that I wasn't a mistake, but I never was a mistake! I don't deserve to have to live her trauma. It's not my responsibility! Nothing I ever did was going to make her like me or want me," she exclaimed as the revelations continued to soak through all of the hurt and the torment of her mother's battering abuse. It was all washing away before Logan's very eyes. He had to wipe away his own tears as he nodded fervently.

"Yes, baby, yes," he vowed, "exactly! You have never done anything wrong. You never did anything to ever deserve being treated like that."

"I don't want her to be my mother anymore, and I don't want to be her daughter. She never wanted me, and you know what…?" she declared as renewed confidence and assurance that Logan had never seen before etched her beautiful face.

With a broad, delighted grin though his tears, Logan gazed at her with rapt adoration.

"What?" He was absolutely overwhelmed by what he was finally witnessing from her.

"She doesn't deserve me!" Her eyes were sparkling through her tears. She clenched her jaw in newly formed defiance. Logan stood to full height again and squeezed her to his chest. He chuckled in his own abject disbelief.

"Yes, exactly, and you have no idea how good it feels to hear you finally say that!"

They both continued to wipe away their tears as Logan held her. Still stunned from everything she finally realized while he'd held her in a supply closet, he began to glance around as he blinked back the last of his tears.

"Uh, babe," Logan chuckled, "what is all of this stuff?" He gestured around uncomfortably as he noticed a large box of pregnancy tests.

Her laughter seemed to dry the rest of her tears as she beamed at him and released her grip on his shirt.

"Well," she giggled. "Those are lots of different kinds of speculums, and that's lube for the ultrasound machines and examinations, and those are bed pads and those are maxi pads, and those are forceps, and those are, uh…" She blushed violently as she pointed to a set of very oddly shaped, metal clamp-like tools suspended on a rubber rack. She bit her lip for a moment and then laughed again at his expression. "Those are penis clamps."

"Ugh-hhh-hhhh," Logan shuddered. "Okay, can we please go home now?" His desperate begging made her laugh. She nodded.

They returned to the waiting room, and Logan was momentarily shocked at what he found awaiting them. As he took in his entire family standing, waiting to make certain that Adeline knew where she belonged and who she was, he knew he shouldn't have been shocked at all. His mother wrapped him up in her warm embrace.

It was the soft, sweet embrace of a woman who'd not only given birth to him but had loved him even when he least deserved it. The woman who'd fed him, not just physical meals, but her wisdom, and her love his entire life. She'd always been there, and he knew she always would be. He could never have earned her love. It had always simply existed. She had not only given him life but would, without a second thought, lay down her life for his because she was a mother. The awe-inspiring title was earned. It should never be given.

Rainer rode back to the farmhouse with Emily and Garrett. That left Adeline and Logan the whole ride home to talk. It was quite a discussion.

Before the Haydenshire family all dug into the delectable meal his mother and grandmother had prepared and casted, so that it was perfectly warm, Logan stood and commanded everyone's attention.

"We decided that we don't want to wait to get married, and we don't really want a big, huge Senate thing anyway. Adeline wants to be a Haydenshire, and there is nothing I want more than that." The adamancy in his voice was so strong that none of his brothers even smirked. "So, I guess I was wondering if you all thought we might could put together a small wedding by next Saturday."

"Yes!" Mrs. Haydenshire beamed. She wiped away tears of her own. Emily squealed and threw her arms around Adeline. All of his brothers, their wives, and girlfriends immediately offered their assistance, and Logan was extremely proud of the family he was going to share with Adeline.

Rainer offered Logan his hand and a broad grin. "Well done, man," he complimented.

Logan jerked him forward and pulled him in for a hug. "Hey, you'll be my best man, right?" He already knew the answer.

"Nowhere else I'd ever be," Rainer scoffed.

He and Logan performed the secret handshake they'd made up when they were six. Everyone laughed and shook their heads.

"I don't know how we'll ever have time to do this, but thank you all so much." Adeline blinked back renewed tears. Logan moved to brushed a kiss across her cheek.

Mrs. Haydenshire's delighted smile warmed the room at large. "I happen to have a little brother who has a husband who is rather magical about the events he makes happen, so how about we celebrate how thankful we are that you're going to be a Haydenshire in just over a week and eat all of this food. He'll be here in an hour or so. If you'd like their help, I know Taddy and Nathan can make this all happen."

Adeline nodded excitedly as she drew a steadying breath, but fear played just behind the excitement in her eyes. Logan saw it, even if no one else did.

"What if I have to go to jail?" she whispered as she turned and hid herself away in his chest.

"Baby..." Logan shook his head, but Governor Haydenshire stepped in.

"Adeline, sweetheart, you have no idea how proud Lillian and I are of you, and how proud we are of you, Logan. I am extremely impressed that you didn't let others' opinions form your own," Governor Haydenshire complimented. "And Miss Adeline,"—he turned his adoring gaze back to her—"I knew that you were going to become my daughter from the first night Logan invited you over for dinner and he spilled two full glasses of tea and then dropped the butter dish, knife and all, in your lap when he thought you needed to butter your roll," Governor Haydenshire teased.

Everyone laughed from the memory.

"I was nervous," Logan admitted.

"We noticed," Rainer assured him.

"I don't think I ever got the butter out of that blouse," Mrs. Haydenshire commented as she cut green beans into bite-sized pieces for the twins.

"I thought it was really sweet that you were nervous," Adeline admitted. Her cheeks colored as all of Logan's brothers swooned mockingly and batted their eyelashes at Logan.

"But the point is," Governor Haydenshire quieted the table, "the Realm failed you. We should have stepped in long before Logan did. I should have insisted that you come and live here years before you did."

Adeline shook her head. "I kept telling you no," she reminded him sweetly.

Governor Haydenshire nodded. "And I shouldn't have taken no for an answer. But the Realm will stand behind you now. You're not going to jail if I have to pardon you myself. We're going to put all of this behind us and let you and Logan start your life together, looking ahead to the future and not letting the past be such a burden. I want to apologize on behalf of the entire Realm for what's happened, sweetheart, and we are going to fix all of this somehow."

The hope Logan had seen earlier reappeared in Adeline's beautiful, onyx eyes. She nodded her appreciation to the Crown Governor of the Gifted Realm, and then threw her arms around his neck in a fierce embrace.

Governor Haydenshire chuckled as he cradled her to him. His strength and dignity were palpable to the entire table, as he soothed his newest daughter.

After saying grace, everyone dug in to the delicacies before them.

CHAPTER 25

BABYSITTING

RAINER LAWSON

As pecan and pumpkin pie were being served, a knock sounded on the door.

"Time to babysit," Garrett chanted as he took in Logan and Rainer's grimaces. He stood and answered the door. Everyone turned from the table to greet Dan and Bridgette.

To their surprise, Jack Stariff, the top lawyer in the Realm, asked if he could come in for a few minutes as well. Jack had gone to the academy with the Haydenshires and Rainer's parents. He'd immediately agreed to take on Adeline's case against her mother as soon as Governor Haydenshire had phoned him months before.

Mrs. Haydenshire assured him that he was always welcome and began fixing more dessert plates and coffee.

Vindico introduced Bridgette to Governor and Mrs. Haydenshire, then moved around the table rattling off everyone's name until he came to Sarah.

"Uh," he furrowed his brow.

"This is my girlfriend, Sarah." Levi offered Bridgette an uncomfortable smile. Sarah didn't look any too thrilled with Bridgette's arrival.

Bridgette offered everyone hellos though she looked furious to be there.

"Jack, pecan, pumpkin, or are you like all of my boys who are having both?" Mrs. Haydenshire beamed at her sons, who were indeed devouring pieces of pie like they'd never tasted anything so delicious.

Emily fixed Rainer a third piece of pecan pie, which was his favorite, and added Nana's whiskey cream sauce. Rainer groaned his appreciation as he let the warm, gooey mixture fill his mouth.

"See?" Mrs. Haydenshire laughed as she gestured to Rainer.

Jack chuckled. "Well, he got Miss Emily Anne, and I just saw the new Porsche in the barn, so I'd say Lawson has good taste just like his old man. I'll take a piece of that." He pointed to the pie Rainer was consuming.

Everyone laughed their agreement.

"Dan, Bridgette, pumpkin, pecan, or both?" Mrs. Haydenshire asked as she pulled another of the ten pies, five of each kind, toward her to be cut.

"No, thank you, Mrs. Haydenshire. I just came from Mom and Dad's, and I need to be on my way," Vindico bristled.

Bridgette gave a haughty eye roll. "Uh, sorry, but I have to watch my weight." She gestured to Mrs. Haydenshire's rather round stomach. Rainer clamped his hand down on Emily's shoulder. She was vibrating in her fury.

"She's five months pregnant," Emily informed her with a great deal of disdain. Mrs. Haydenshire gave a polite chuckle and shot Emily a look that said for her to be nice. Uncomfortable silence filled the room momentarily.

"This is phenomenal, Lillian." Jack pointed to the pie with his fork, quickly puncturing the tension in the room.

"Bridgette, can I get you anything else to eat? After that, the girls can get you settled in your room," Mrs. Haydenshire instructed.

"I'm dancing tomorrow, so I don't eat until after my shifts," she informed Mrs. Haydenshire.

"But it's Thanksgiving." Emily's brow furrowed. Rainer rubbed her thigh and wondered where this rather bizarre Thanksgiving meal conversation might go next.

"Right, so the guys tomorrow will be drunk off their asses,

desperate to get away from their families, and I'll get some sweet tips." Bridgette glared hatefully at Emily.

With a concerned nod, Mrs. Haydenshire didn't comment further.

Vindico carried Bridgette's suitcase up to Patrick's old room. He thanked the Haydenshires, then bid everyone farewell without even so much as a goodbye for Bridgette. He seemed single-minded in his purpose. He was focused on nothing but Pendergrath and Moscow.

"I certainly didn't mean to interrupt the Haydenshire Thanksgiving meal, but I need to apologize to you, Adeline," Jack offered sincerely.

"Oh, for what?" Adeline knitted her brow.

"I knew your mother's lawyer was pushing for a trial yesterday. She kept insisting that she wanted nothing more than to spend Thanksgiving with you." He tried hard not to roll his eyes.

"Right," Logan huffed indignantly.

With a shake of his head, Stariff continued. "Anyway, I had no idea the judge would actually agree to it. He wanted to clear his docket. Apparently, his wife's family is celebrating Thanksgiving in New Orleans. They had seats at the Superdome, and he didn't want to miss out. I suppose the fate of the people of Virginia could just be damned," Stariff shot furiously. Everyone exchanged an uncomfortable glance.

"There was nothing you could have done. You don't owe me an apology," Adeline assured him.

"I do, and they've got this entire thing so trumped we've certainly got our work cut out for us. Thank you for the pie, Lillian. Like I've been saying for years, if Stephen hadn't snatched you up in school, I'd get down on my knee right now," he teased. The Haydenshires both laughed heartily.

"Watch it now, Jack," the governor goaded. "That's my ring she's wearing, and I'm responsible for *that* as well," he gestured to Mrs. Haydenshire's swollen midsection. "I may be too old to fight anymore, but that's why I had so many boys." Everyone cracked up.

"Can we talk for a minute in your office, Stephen?" Jack asked after the laughter had died down.

"Of course." Governor Haydenshire stood and gestured to his home office, just off the living room.

After they left the table, Bridgette's eyes narrowed in on Will, who was cradling Lily Ana in his arms. He was kissing her fat little cheeks and talking baby talk to his little girl as if no one else was there. His adoration was very evident. Brooke beamed at them.

"Can I hold her again, Will?" Emily seemed to decide that she was going to enjoy her family even with all of the events of the night.

"Sure." Will managed to retrieve a burp cloth for Emily's shoulder and hand off his daughter in a rather adept move.

Henry was quite certain he did not care for Lily Ana and all of the attention she'd been receiving. He demanded that Rainer hold him if Emily was going to hold Lily Ana.

Rainer scooped Henry up. He proceeded to tell the baby bye-bye repeatedly.

Will draped his hand over Brooke's shoulders and gazed at Lily Ana in Emily's arms. He turned and shared a contented grin with his wife and then brushed kisses on her cheek instead of his daughter's.

"How old is she?" Bridgette quizzed.

Brooke beamed. "She's just over three weeks," she stated proudly.

Bridgette narrowed her eyes at Brooke and glanced up and down her body.

"Yeah, I guess that's the thing about kids. They completely ruin your body," she spat as everyone's mouths hung open in shock.

Will looked thoroughly stunned and uncertain as to how to defend his wife.

"Uh, excuse me," he stammered. "Trust me, she's even more beautiful now than the day I married her," he huffed viciously. Will was not an Ioses Predilect, but when it came to defending Brooke, he would stop at nothing. His Duco bands even tinged green like a shield. The table braced for impact.

Rainer watched in horror as Bridgette sneered.

"Yeah, that's always what they say when they're with their wives, but trust me, we get loads of new dads at the club during those first few months. You know, when you can't keep 'em happy because delivering the baby made you hurt there or whatever." Her eyes lit in defiant victory that no one but she seemed to recognize. "We hear them talking about how fat their wives got, and that they're always too tired. They tip well, so I guess they're pretty hard up. I think that's when they start cheating too. I mean, they're still all gorgeous," she gestured to Will, "and you're not anymore."

The entire table sat in stunned mortification as Will shook his head stupidly, and fire roared from Brooke's eyes. She leapt up and shot her chair back across the hardwood floor into Mrs. Haydenshire's vast china cabinet.

Words in very heated Portuguese flew from Brooke's mouth, and Rainer was certain that none of them were family friendly.

Brooke showed off her fiery temper as she made an extremely rude gesture to Bridgette and then stomped out the front door. Will bolted after her as Emily glared at Bridgette and tried to soothe Lily Ana, who'd responded to her mother's screeching voice by sobbing.

Mrs. Haydenshire appeared shocked and furious. Rainer couldn't recall another time in his life when anyone had done anything that surprised the woman who'd raised him. She drew a deep breath and stood.

"Emily, you and Rainer take Lily Ana into the living room and walk with her. She likes that. Her pacifier is in her portable crib.

"Logan, you and Adeline please show Bridgette to her room. See if there's anything she'll need for the next few nights. Patrick, you and Lucy put the twins to bed for me. Everyone else can help with the dishes," she commanded.

As several rounds of yes ma'ams rang from the table, everyone moved quickly. Rainer handed Henry to Patrick. They shared a dumbfounded glance before they proceeded to follow their orders.

CHAPTER 26
THE WAY IT'S SUPPOSED TO WORK

Rainer handed Emily the pacifier. She tried to walk with a very natural bounce to soothe Lily Ana.

Rainer shuddered to think of how they were all supposed to make it through the next two days. It seemed Emily was too furious to calm the baby. Her moves and her energy were too quick and ragged.

"Here, give her to me." Rainer reached for the baby. She handed her to Rainer with a furious huff.

He tried to remember everything he'd been told to do when the twins had been born. He softly shushed Lily Ana much the way he did Emily when she cried. After a few minutes, the baby fell asleep on his shoulder.

"Do you think that's true?" Emily demanded.

"Do I think what's true?"

"Do you think you won't like me after we have a baby? That I'll be fat or whatever?" Imminent tears threatened her eyes. Not certain if he was more stunned over Bridgette's statements or over Emily's question, Rainer shook his head.

"No, baby, I don't."

"Are you going to cheat on me if my stomach looks like Brooke's after I have a baby?" She became overwrought and quickly lost all sense of reason.

"Emily Anne Haydenshire." Rainer tried not to wake Lily Ana in his offense. He shook his head in disbelief. He laid Lily Ana down in the crib and gently covered her with a blanket. "Come here to me." He took Emily's hand and pulled her onto the couch.

"First of all, how could you ever think something like that of me? Second, right now, Brooke looks like she just had a baby. It was my understanding that's what's supposed to happen. She gave Will a beautiful, healthy little girl." He gestured to Lily Ana sleeping peacefully in her crib. "But you know what? Will doesn't see that she gained weight. He sees his wife, the love of his life, the reason he gets up in the morning, and his little girl.

"What he told Bridgette was true. She *is* more beautiful to him now." He cupped his hand under Emily's chin and refused to let her drop her gaze. "And I'm sure there are a lot of assholes out there. Guys who would go somewhere like The Tantra after their wife gave birth to their baby." He felt sick at the very thought. "But I'm not like that and neither are any of your brothers."

"I heard Will tell Garrett that he misses her, and I know he meant sex." She sounded truly frightened.

"Of course he does," Rainer adamantly defended Will. "He loves her. He wants to be with her. He knows he can't for a few more days. He misses that part of their relationship, but he's not going to try to fill that with some cheap, tawdry thrill. He wants her. He wants his wife, not a lap dance from some woman he doesn't know."

Rainer grinned as he recalled a conversation he'd overheard that morning at the soup kitchen. "He was teasing Levi and Garrett this morning while we were cooking. He kept telling them how good breast milk tastes, and I'm not thinking Brooke poured it into a glass for him. I think your brother and sister-in-law are just fine."

Emily tucked her head onto Rainer's shoulder. He then attempted to kiss her into a better mood.

"You know..." He gave her what he hoped was a sexy grin as he angled his head and brushed her lips again. "When I think about you" —he let his breath mingle with hers—"having my baby..." He dipped his tongue into her mouth before devouring it. "It drives me wild." He pulled away long enough to watch a slow, sultry grin spread across Emily's face.

"Really?"

"Oh yeah." After a few more slow, sensuous kisses, they were interrupted when Lily Ana began to fuss again. Emily scooped her up and brought her back to the couch. She laid the baby in her lap.

Rainer and Emily gazed at Lily Ana as Emily talked to her sweetly. She changed her diaper and then returned to the couch. She placed the pacifier between Lily Ana's rosebud lips and patted her back tenderly.

"Why did she say that? Brooke is still out there. I'm sure she's crying." Emily couldn't keep her mind off the conversation over dessert.

Governor Haydenshire and Jack Stariff were still in his office and Nana and Paps had gone home.

"Because she's jealous and she's afraid, sweetheart," Mrs. Haydenshire answered as she eased in from the kitchen and sank into her chair with a mug of tea.

Logan and Adeline returned to the living room. They looked like they might've made a stop off in Logan's room to celebrate the fact that they were getting married in a week.

After that, everyone else began bidding their goodbyes with promises to be back early the next day for Football Friday. The day after Thanksgiving the Haydenshires spent the morning playing football and the afternoon watching the games they'd recorded while they all worked at the soup kitchen. Football Friday was a long-standing Haydenshire tradition.

"Garrett, are Will and Brooke still outside?" Mrs. Haydenshire asked.

Patrick stepped in. "They're on the side porch. He's swinging with her. It's gonna take some pretty tall talk to undo *that*." He gestured up the stairs, indicating Bridgette.

"Will's never let her down, and he won't now," Garrett vowed. Fury was etched on every tensed muscle inside his well-formed physique. His shield lit in angry pulses.

Mrs. Haydenshire nodded her agreement with both sentiments. She looked rather worn.

"I still can't believe she said that. What a bitch!" Emily spat. She was still holding Lily Ana tenderly.

"Emily Anne." Her mother raised her eyebrow in the look she'd perfected many years before, the one that let her children know they were most definitely in trouble.

"Well, she is," Emily defied.

Rainer tried not to laugh.

CHAPTER 27

YOUR FATHER

As everyone began to trickle out the door, Mrs. Haydenshire turned her attention to Adeline and Logan. "Did you get Bridgette settled?"

"I don't really know or care." Logan shrugged. Mrs. Haydenshire's brow knitted. "She said she doesn't like Patrick's room. She says she needs something with an attached bathroom. She didn't seem to like the hall baths," he offered somewhat confusedly.

Emily and Adeline rolled their eyes. "Well, I suppose she could stay in your room, and you and Rainer could stay in Patrick's, but I'm fairly certain that Connor won't want to share a bathroom with her. What's she doing now?"

"Her nails," Logan informed his mother.

Before anyone could comment, the governor and Jack Stariff emerged from the office. Deep concern tensed in both of their rhythms. The governor walked Jack to the door.

"I'll take it from here," Governor Haydenshire bid him farewell.

"Let me know if you need my help in any way."

"Will do."

With a heavy sigh, Governor Haydenshire took his seat next to Mrs. Haydenshire.

"Where are Will and Brooke?" he quizzed as he noted Emily cradling Lily Ana. Both of them were wrapped up under Rainer's arm.

"I'll tell you later. What did Jack have to say?" Mrs. Haydenshire asked.

The governor turned to Logan and Adeline and swallowed harshly. "I don't know of any other way to do this. Unfortunately, sweetheart, I don't know you quite well enough to know if I should tell Logan this kind of thing first and have him tell you, the way we do with Rainer and Emily."

Rainer chuckled as Emily rolled her eyes.

"So, I'm going to shoot straight with you," Governor Haydenshire began. "There are several obvious problems with your case as well as your mother's. In this situation, our constitution isn't helping you. We have to play by the Non-Gifted rules for the trial, and they can't quite seem to decide how it will occur. Your mother has the jury eating out of her hands with tales of why she used, and that she was in her current line of work because of the cost of raising a child. We know that Paulo, your mother's..." Governor Haydenshire hesitated.

"Employer," Mrs. Haydenshire offered.

The governor gazed at her appreciatively. "Employer," he repeated. "Is actually working with the Interfeci. Dan and Jack seem to think he might be one of Wretchkinsides's top drug suppliers, so we would very much like to see Paulo spend time in prison along with your mother."

Adeline nodded as Logan wrapped his arm around her and pulled her closer.

Pain etched the governor's face as he continued. "If things continue on the way they've been going, your mother may just convince another jury that you are a drug user and that prostitution was the only option she thought she had."

He halted as tears began to pour down Adeline's face. Logan cradled her tenderly and whispered in her ear. Everyone looked away to try to allow him to soothe her without an audience.

"Now, like I said, I would never allow you to serve time," Governor Haydenshire vowed, "so, that isn't the problem. The real problem is that if we don't do something drastic, Georgetown won't allow a medio with a drug charge to be employed, even one that's so obviously trumped-up." The governor's eyes closed as Adeline began to sob in earnest. "There may be something we can do," he offered quickly.

"What?" Logan demanded. "I'll do anything."

"I know, son, but this may be a near impossible task." Governor Haydenshire drew another deep breath. "Adeline…Jack thinks he may have found your father." Governor Haydenshire studied Adeline closely as everyone else in the room gasped.

"What?" Adeline shuddered as she wiped the tears from her eyes. Governor Haydenshire offered her a hesitant smile.

"And as it turns out, he could potentially be a way to make this all go away and for you to go on and be the outstanding medio that you are."

"Well who is he?" Logan urged.

"Is he in England, or is he here?" Adeline sounded nervous. The only thing she knew about her father was that her mother always told her he was English.

Governor Haydenshire hemmed. "Neither really."

"Where is he, and who is he, and how can he help?" Mrs. Haydenshire asked.

"He's, uh…he's one of the Premier of Australia's sons."

"What?!" Logan gasped.

"The Australian Realm's ruling monarchy refers to him as Premier. He would be like the Crown Governor to our Realm. He has four sons, all fairly close in age. Jack had a vial of Adeline's blood tested and searched the Realms all over the world. It's definitely one of his sons."

"But my mom always said my dad was British."

Governor Haydenshire offered her an uncomfortable smile. "I was thinking perhaps she misread his accent in the limited time she spent with him."

"So my grandfather is the Crown Governor of Australia?"

Governor Haydenshire chuckled. "Yes, for all intents and purposes, that's precisely what he is."

"How can he help?" Logan was still focused on Adeline's trial.

"Jack did a little more digging and found out that when Adeline was born there were drugs in her system."

Logan shook his head and cocked his jaw to the side. "Unbelievable."

"Adeline is obviously a Valeduto Predilect. So, once she was out of her mother's womb, her body healed itself. There were no ill effects from the drugs. Clearly, Candy Parker was using when she was pregnant, and Jack believes that if we could somehow convince Adeline's father to testify that Candy was in business when you were conceived, and that he never knew of your existence, that it would most certainly blow her case of abandonment and lack of money right out of the water. All he has to do is create doubt, and your name is free and clear. So, I have a proposal for you," the governor hedged. "For the four of you, actually." He gestured to Rainer and Emily as well. "Let's have a wedding and get you married to my son. Let's make you officially Mrs. Logan Haydenshire."

Logan and Adeline beamed.

Rainer chuckled discreetly. He'd never seen Logan so excited. The governor gave them a wry smile and continued. "Emily's last conference challenge is next Sunday afternoon, so how about Monday morning I send the four of you to Sydney? You can see the sights, honeymoon a little, and have a real vacation. You've all had a pretty rough year. I'd like all of you to get away and relax. Get away from Wretchkinsides," he explained with a slight shudder.

"While you're there, I'll arrange for you to have dinner with the ruling monarchy, as my children representing the American Realm. If you can figure out who your father is, perhaps you could approach him and see how far you get, but this really is our last hope." Governor Haydenshire sounded desperate as he made everyone understand the situation.

"Aside from the obvious annoyance of having my best friend and my kid sister on our honeymoon, what do you think?" Logan asked, as Rainer and Emily laughed. "We do get our own rooms, right?"

"I'll see to it," Governor Haydenshire laughed.

"But,"—Adeline glanced nervously from Logan to his father—"what if he doesn't want me, or what if he *does* know about me? No one wants their illegitimate child to just show up. What if he's married and has his own kids? His wife won't want me around." Her heartbreak was evident in her tone.

Governor Haydenshire looked sorrowful, but he shook his head.

"Only the two oldest of the Premier's sons are married. His oldest son has never traveled outside of the Australian Realm. At my inaugural ball, the Premier and his two middle sons attended."

Logan gasped. "Oh my gosh! That's why I thought I knew him. I've shaken your dad's hand."

"What?" Adeline's eyes goggled.

"Remember?" Logan demanded of Rainer. "I asked you if we knew that guy, and Em said maybe I knew someone he was related to."

"Yeah, but are you sure that's him? Her uncle would also have a similar energy reading to hers," Rainer reminded him.

"His two middle sons, Arlo and Ethan, are both Valeduto Predilects. So, it might be one of them, or it could be his youngest son, Lucas," Governor Haydenshire elaborated.

By this point, Will had come back in the room. He'd already walked Brooke and Lily Ana up to Emily's room for her to nurse. He'd fixed Brooke a glass of water and grabbed a few throw pillows off the couch on his way. After making sure she was taken care of, and that she knew of his undying devotion to her, Will had returned and listened to everything his father was saying.

"Adeline, if I had a child from my past even if it wasn't Brooke's, I'd want to know," Will joined in.

Logan, Rainer, and the governor all nodded their agreement.

"My mom always said she didn't know his name."

"Why don't you go find out, sweetheart?" Mrs. Haydenshire grinned. "I have a good feeling about this, and your father deserves to know what a wonderful daughter he has, even if he doesn't get to know you until now."

Logan drew a deep breath. "Look at me, Ad," he soothed. She turned her terror-filled eyes to his. "All we have to do is have dinner and go on a honeymoon. If we get there and we meet them, and you don't want to do anything more than that dinner, we won't say anything at all, but I will be right there with you the whole time. I think Mom's right. Your dad deserves the opportunity to know you exist."

Adeline stared into the depths of Logan's eyes as everyone else in the room willed her to agree. She drew a steadying breath and nodded hesitantly. "Okay, let's go to Australia." She seemed to draw on deep resolve as the room rejoiced with Logan.

Tad and Nathan finally made their way to the farm, and Brooke returned with Lily Ana. Will hung all over her and then took them home.

Just as everyone was about to retire for the evening, Bridgette appeared, with garish red toenails that were still dripping wet. She walked carefully across the floor.

"Logan, did you tell your parents about my needing my own bathroom?"

"Yeah, but there's not really another room, so..." Logan shrugged. He very obviously did not want to be distracted from Adeline and everything she was going through that evening.

Mrs. Haydenshire introduced Bridgette to Tad and Nathan. They gave her polite hellos but were far more interested in planning the wedding that was only a week away.

With a loud huff, Bridgette let everyone know she didn't like the lack of attention she was receiving.

"Well, you see," she drawled loudly, "I sleep in the buff."

It was abundantly apparent that she was hopeful this bit of information would impress someone in the room. No one cared.

"Yeah man, but you should pick somewhere really cool to stay Sunday night. You can take the Porsche." Rainer was elated for Adeline and Logan and for the opportunity to take Emily to the only populated continent on the planet where Dominic Wretchkinsides had no men and no power.

"Seriously?" Logan trilled. Adeline and Emily laughed at his exuberance.

"So, like I was saying," Bridgette was nearly shouting in her defiance, "unless you want me walking the halls completely naked, then I need my own bathroom."

Mrs. Haydenshire turned her weary eyes on Bridgette. "Since you are a guest in our home—and though you're certainly welcome here, you are here for your own safety—perhaps you could wear a robe or borrow something of Emily's until Dan returns from his trip." Her tone dared Bridgette to argue.

Bridgette turned her glare on Emily, and Rainer narrowed his eyes.

"Uh, I don't think so," she sneered.

"It's your choice, but I don't have any other rooms to offer you," Mrs. Haydenshire concluded.

With a dramatic eye roll, Bridgette spun and stomped up the stairs as everyone continued their excited conversation about the wedding and the impromptu Australian honeymoon.

CHAPTER 28

THE SWAN

Later that evening, Rainer and Logan lay alone in the beds of their youth. Rainer stared out the window at the star-strewn Virginian sky and remembered all the nights he'd slept in that very bed.

Before he'd even come to live with the Haydenshires, he'd spent many nights there with Logan.

"Did you ever wonder about all of that when you were drooling over Adeline for all those years?" he quizzed Logan. It was something he'd always been curious about but had never asked.

"Wonder about what?" Logan sounded peaceful and sleepy.

"You know, all that stuff everybody used to say about her not having a last name, or a crest, or whatever. Did that ever bother you?"

Logan was quiet for a moment. "I don't know. I never thought too much about it. Most of the pricks who were awful to her I couldn't stand anyway, so I sure as hell didn't care what they thought. I guess it's like Dad said after we went out for pizza that night and then I asked her to have dinner here the next week. All I could really think about was making her a Haydenshire. I know that's weird, but it's just always been what I wanted." Logan's confession was riddled with self-doubt. It was almost as if he was afraid Rainer would think he was odd.

"I don't think that's weird at all." Rainer recalled the fact that one of the large glasses of tea that Logan had spilled on the fateful night had landed in his lap. "I think that's the way it was meant to be. If you'd played the field like all of your brothers kept telling you to, or you'd slept around just to do it, even though you knew the girls who flirted with you weren't really who you wanted, I'm not sure Adeline would've had enough confidence to go out with you. Her mom had done a real number on her by the time she got to the academy."

"Yeah," Logan agreed, "but I guess she has a name and a crest now." He sounded almost in awe. Governor Haydenshire had informed Logan and Adeline that her father's last name was Nguyen, and that their crest was of the swan, known for grace, empathy, and power. It was also the symbol of self-transformation. Rainer smiled as he thought that might be exactly what Adeline was doing.

"Hey, Logan, Emily and I were talking, and as soon as we find a place, we'll move out. You and Adeline keep the guesthouse. She loves it there."

Rainer hoped Emily wouldn't mind him going ahead and telling Logan their plan.

"You don't have to do that. We like you and Em living with us. Nothing's gonna change really."

Rainer didn't believe that for a second. As he thought about it, he knew that he and Emily hadn't been ready to live alone when they'd moved in together. Perhaps Logan and Adeline weren't ready just yet either. Everything had changed rather suddenly. Rainer decided not to bring it up again until after their trip to Australia.

There was a slight knock at the door. Logan eased upward and leaned to reach the doorknob.

Adeline appeared, and Rainer started to grab his jeans and leave, but Emily scooted in behind her. Rainer could just see the glisten of Adeline's tears in the slight moonlight as she moved toward Logan.

"What's wrong, baby?" Logan soothed.

Emily grinned at her. "I think it's kind of been a huge day, and apparently she just doesn't like sleeping with me the way she likes sleeping with you, even though I have repeatedly pointed out how much cuter I am than you."

A smile appeared on Adeline's face.

Rainer chuckled. "Why don't we go to Em's room?" he offered.

"No, let's all just have a sleepover," Emily suggested. "I think Bridgette's wearing Mom's nerves kind of thin."

"Come here." Logan guided Adeline into his bed and swathed her in the quilts and blankets and then in him. "And no messing around over there," he commanded Rainer as he threw the quilts back onto his own bed and allowed Emily to curl up with her back to his chest.

"I make you no promises," Rainer goaded.

Adeline's sweet giggle filled the room.

CHAPTER 29

MEMORIES

DAN VINDICO

Utter hatred pulsed through Dan's veins as he paced the corridor of the Russian Senate just outside the overstated courtroom. He downed another espresso shot from the vending machine. It was two in the morning at home.

He'd landed a half hour before. The trial was scheduled at nine, but Pendergrath had delayed the proceedings. He'd feigned illness and requested an appointment with a medio. It was to gall Dan. He was trying to piss him off.

As he continued to let his fury drive him, he began going over all of the crimes he knew that Pendergrath had committed, the crimes Dan didn't have enough evidence on to keep him in prison.

He could still hear his haunting laugh from his trial five months before, the sparring match Dan had finally won. He reminded himself that he'd only gone on with the arrest to save Rainer and Emily, but he'd taken solace in knowing Candor was in Diapoley. It had somewhat sated the demons that ruled Dan's life.

He'd been there that night. He'd been in his house. He'd left a burning cigarette on their leather-inlaid table, the one Amelia had picked out. The cigarette was only half-burned. He'd been there mere minutes before Dan had arrived home. The pages of the photo album Amelia had been constructing since she was eleven were singed on the edges. The pictures of their entire relationship, their entire life together, gone just like she was.

He'd helped Cascavel take her, and then he'd disappeared and never left enough of himself to be caught.

A Shengcao cigarette—expensive, extra-long, Chinese brand, sold heavily on the Russian market that Dan would always associate with evil—kept the vengeance-filled fire fueled in his soul.

He'd lit the smoke and never let it touch his lips. He'd worn gloves. He'd left his mark without leaving his trace. The acrid smell of unfiltered tobacco had hung in Dan's house for weeks.

It would always be the smell of horrifying, unthinkable death. That smell was the reason he'd finally sold the house. It was too much. It held too many memories, too much of her, and it had all been more than he could bear after he'd buried Amelia, his beautiful baby, his everything.

He'd refused to sell it for weeks after. He prayed that since they knew where he lived, they'd make a return visit in an effort to take him out as well. He stalked the halls at night, a loaded Browning nine mil in his hands, eager for a chance to have his say.

They'd never come, and he was unable to walk the halls anymore. He could see her there in the kitchen, or in the bathtub, sitting on the couch with one of her copies of Austen's works that were her favorite and a mug of tea he'd supplied her.

It was too much. He'd left one night and stayed in a hotel. He'd never returned. His parents had cleaned out the house and sold it for him.

Bile rose violently in his throat as he forced the memories that he hated from his mind. He continued his relentless trek to nowhere.

Rainer Lawson

Rainer awoke with a stiff neck from trying to sleep two people to a twin bed, but he was happy to feel Emily's warm, soothing curves against him.

Suddenly Patrick and Connor burst into the room.

"Get up! Dad's making pancakes." They shook the beds. Logan

groaned, and Adeline looked rather taken aback. She pulled the covers up to her neck, though she was fully clothed.

As Rainer, Logan, and Emily were quite accustomed to being awoken like this, they didn't think too much about it.

"I'm sorry," Logan offered. "My brothers are idiots, and they need to get the hell out of my room."

"Dude, it's Football Friday, and it'll be your last one before you get yourself all married up. So, get outta bed, have pancakes, watch football, play football, stop being a bearded clam," Patrick huffed.

"Do you think you could not be such a prick in front of my fiancée? I'd like her to want to be in my family."

"Yeah, yeah, just get up. Dad won't feed us until we're all down there," Connor pled.

"Fine, leave," Logan demanded.

"What is Football Friday?" Adeline still looked mildly bewildered.

"You remember, don't you? I think you were here last year. I know I've told you about it," Logan urged, but Adeline shook her head.

"I always had to work at Pete's the day after Thanksgiving, remember?"

"Right." Logan nodded. "The day after Thanksgiving, Dad won't let Mom cook at all since she cooks so much for the Thanksgiving meal. Dad makes pancakes and bacon and eggs. This afternoon we'll watch all the big games from yesterday. Once everyone is here, we play an epic game of pigskin and then order like thirty pizzas and eat them for dinner. It's a Haydenshire tradition. We even let the twins play for a little while."

Adeline smiled at him. "Do you play, Emily?"

"I tried once, but no one will tackle me because they're afraid of making Dad and Rainer mad, and no one will pass me the ball because they think I can't catch it. I sort of just stood there. It wasn't any fun." Rainer chuckled and kissed her cheek. "But we have wedding work to do today anyway," Emily reminded her.

CHAPTER 30

THE PASSIVE INTERROGATION

Everyone stood around the kitchen in sweatshirts and torn jeans.

Mrs. Haydenshire shook her head at all of her sons devouring the governor's pancakes. She sat at the table with Emily and Adeline. They were all having coffee. Bridgette appeared wearing her customary scowl.

"Bridgette, would you care for some breakfast?" Mrs. Haydenshire offered sweetly as the governor pulled another batch of pancakes off the griddles and casted them to stay warm.

"Uh no, I don't eat before I dance, remember?" Bridgette explained again. Her face held a mixture of embarrassment and incredulity.

Mrs. Haydenshire nodded. "Are you certain that your current line of work is what you want to be doing? If I may, you don't seem very happy or fulfilled, and everyone needs to eat. I know Daniel wouldn't want you starving yourself."

Anger threatened Bridgette's eyes. "I don't really have much choice, do I? I'm not Gifted. I don't have whatever it is that you all can do so that you have tons of money and power."

Silence loomed over the kitchen as everyone stared at their plates uncomfortably. It was true. The Gifted families had long-standing family names that had been around for thousands of years.

Most of them were rather well-off because of hard work and inheritances, but also because energy was all around them and at their infinite disposal.

There was energy in the stock market, and Visium and Duco Predilects could read it like a book. There was very little risk with investments. The energy could be seen, read, and profited upon readily. Receivers could feel the emotions around start-ups and tell you who would succeed.

"Could I offer you a cup of coffee then?" Mrs. Haydenshire's voice shook Rainer from his reverie.

"Yes, thank you," Bridgette accepted as Mrs. Haydenshire rose and fixed her a mug.

Logan's cell phone chirped again. He rolled his eyes and pulled it from his pocket.

Will was eager to get back to the farmhouse for Football Friday, but Brooke adamantly refused to come over until after Bridgette left for work. Will had been texting Logan repeatedly asking when she would be heading to The Tantra so that he and his family could join in the festivities.

As attention seemed to be what made Bridgette happiest, it seemed Mrs. Haydenshire decided to play along. Rainer watched as she placed the coffee mug, along with the cream and sugar bowls, at the place at the table between Emily and Adeline.

"Tell us how you and Daniel met?" Mrs. Haydenshire quizzed with a kind smile.

Bridgette's eyes lit, but everyone else in the kitchen knew an inquisition was at hand. Mrs. Haydenshire was gathering information.

"Iodex did that takedown of a bunch of Nic's boys that day at the club, and I met Dan. I agreed to keep an eye on the rest of Nic's guys. They're in a lot, so I hear a good bit," she informed them as everyone nodded and forced smiles.

"We started dating a few days after that. I told Dan that I'd keep spying if he made it worth my while. I get paid by Iodex or whatever, but Dan's fun."

The governor looked extremely concerned. "Bridgette, do you feel

202

like what you're doing is safe? I'm not certain how I feel about Dan allowing you to spy for us. Dominic Wretchkinsides is an extremely dangerous man."

Bridgette seemed elated with the governor's concern. "Nic's not in all that often. I wish he'd come every day. He's a big old teddy bear, and he tips with fifties. He's the best," she stated with a wistful look in her eyes. "My dad used to be a guard at Felsink, so I knew about The Realm, anyway. Plus, I'm sure if I needed him, Dan would come."

Rainer and Logan shared a quick glance that said they weren't at all certain that was true.

The governor nodded. "What's your father's name, dear? I appreciate all of our Felsink guards. I try to meet with them a few times each year. I'm sure I've met him."

Bridgette's eyes flashed in panic. "Uh…Ted Meyers," she supplied. Rainer and Garrett shared a quick glance of unease.

The governor gave her a concerned nod. "I do know Ted," he stated cryptically. "I'll mention that we met you the next time I see him."

Bridgette drew a quick sip of her coffee.

The twins padded into the kitchen in their footie pajamas just then. They were both carrying their favorite blankets.

"Wainer!" Henry held his arms out. Emily, Adeline, and Mrs. Haydenshire all swooned as Rainer scooped him up.

"Hey, buddy." Rainer smiled as Henry laid his head on his shoulder.

Keaton had the same reaction to Logan being there, and Logan looked extremely honored as he hoisted Keaton upward.

"They've missed you two," Mrs. Haydenshire stated with just a hint of scolding. They needed to come see the twins more often.

"Want some pancakes, and then we'll go play football," Logan enticed the twins.

"Putball!" Keaton's eyes danced as he beamed at his big brother.

The governor and Garrett began making plates for the twins and cutting the pancakes into tiny bites, while Levi filled their juice cups. Mrs. Haydenshire turned her attention back to Bridgette.

"So, have you been out to the Vindicos' manor house to meet

Arthur and Marion?" she quizzed, though Rainer knew perfectly well she already knew the answer.

Governor and Mrs. Vindico had a huge mansion in a quiet, gated subdivision in Great Falls. It was the kind of home that looked very opulent and proper from the outside. A home that couldn't seem to contain the amount of pain their son had lived through or the kind of behavior Lindley Vindico displayed on a regular basis.

"Oh, uh, no. I guess we're not really ready for that yet," Bridgette bristled. "I think Dan's parents are kinda hard on him. He doesn't like them. I think they're always harping on him or whatever. That's why he doesn't talk about them much. Dan's kind of a player. He's in his thirties, and he's never even been in a serious relationship."

Awkward glances flew around the room as Mrs. Haydenshire offered Bridgette a kind smile and a nod.

As Bridgette finished her coffee, she stood. "So, I guess I need to get ready." She stalked toward Logan who was leaned over and seating Keaton in his booster seat at the table.

"You taking me to work, stud?" She let her hand slip from Logan's back over his backside. He jerked upright and looked thoroughly shocked.

Mutinous fury lit Emily's eyes. Logan's reaction had the men in the room trying hard not to laugh as Bridgette sauntered back up the stairs.

While shaking her head, Mrs. Haydenshire shot her husband a look that said something was going to have to be done about Bridgette.

"Garrett, you and Rainer and Emily can drop Bridgette off wherever it is that she works." She gave Logan an out, and if Emily were with them, it was unlikely that she would be concerned.

"Don't you think you should say something to her?" Emily demanded of Logan.

"If he makes a big deal about it, she'll just do it more." Rainer caught Henry's juice cup before it hit the floor.

"He's right, baby girl. She needs attention. She wants one of us to reprimand her for acting like that or the way she did last night. She's a very sad woman, and I don't know how to help her." Governor

Haydenshire shook his head. "But I can tell you this, Ted Meyers has two sons and no daughters."

Garrett sighed. "So what's her game? Is Bridgette even her name?"

"Someone gave her the backstory. Someone provided her the name of a guard. Ted might've told her. I don't know."

"Gifted prison guards are well paid for their secrecy. I doubt he's running his mouth," Garrett pointed out.

"I think Daniel and I are going to have a long talk when he gets back from Moscow."

Garrett nodded. "Well, I think Nic set the whole thing up. I thought it was all too convenient from the beginning. I think he's been playing Dan all along just like he always is."

Logan stared at Adeline to see how she was going to handle this particular turn of events. "You know I didn't want her to do that." Adeline drew a deep breath and nodded.

"Trust me," Connor chimed in, "you're the only girl he wants grabbing his ass."

"Connor," Governor Haydenshire scolded, "why don't you let your brother and his fiancée work this out on their own?"

"I really don't like her," Adeline stated in a pained whisper as Logan pulled her to him.

"Me either." He cradled her into his chest and kissed the top of her head.

Governor Haydenshire shook his head. "Whatever her game is, she will not be allowed to cause this much discord between my sons and their spouses. I assume that's why my granddaughter hasn't yet made an appearance on her first Haydenshire Football Friday?"

Logan nodded.

Garrett rolled his eyes. "Come on, Dad. You know she's furious Dan left her here, and"—he leaned a long way back over the vast kitchen island to make certain Bridgette was still upstairs, then he dropped his voice to a whisper—"Dan doesn't give a shit about her at all. If she doesn't know anything about Amelia, then she doesn't know anything about Dan Vindico. So, even if Nic set this up, she doesn't know anything. The worst part of that is if she's supposed to be giving

Nic information, eventually he'll get tired of her not being able to. And when Nic gets sick of your shit, he puts a bullet in you."

The governor gave a morose nod. "However, I think Mr. Wretchkinsides would be only too thrilled to know that she was staying at the home of the Crown Governor."

CHAPTER 31

LESSONS OFF THE FIELD

Rainer opened Emily's door for her, then moved to the driver's seat of the Hummer while Garrett and Bridgette crawled into the back.

"Hurry. I want to play a little before I head to the station. I told Sorenson I'd run a shift for him later. He's taking a bunch of Non-Gifted out on some kind of sting," Garrett urged Rainer.

Rainer picked up speed as Garrett's phone rang.

"Hey man, you okay?" He sighed as Bridgette let her hand fall across his leg. A moment later, he shifted away from her. Concern etched his face. "Why don't I catch a flight? You don't have to do this alone." There was a long pause. "Uh yeah, sure, I'll tell her. You sure you're all right? Okay," he conceded quickly. "Yeah, we'll see you tomorrow." Garrett ended the call and turned to Bridgette. "That was Dan." The conversation was playing heavily on his features. "Pendergrath got the trial delayed, so Dan won't be home until late tomorrow night. He said he'd pick you up after he landed or that you could go stay with Tuttle."

"He couldn't call me himself?" Bridgette spat.

"You know Dan. He's really focused on the trial. No messing around. No distractions."

Certain that Garrett had just given Bridgette more information about the guy she was sleeping with than Dan ever had, Rainer glanced in the rearview mirror. "How'd he get the trial delayed?"

"He's just fucking with Dan. Told the arzio he thought he had the flu. They detained him, and he was taken to Nasoova. They didn't find anything wrong with him, of course,"—Garrett rolled his eyes—"but he still burned a day of Dan's time."

"What's the arzio?" Emily asked.

"Russian Gifted doctors. They're like medios here," Garrett supplied.

"What's his deal with Nic anyway?" Bridgette crossed her arms over her chest. "His guys are kind of pricks, but Nic's the greatest."

Garrett shook his head. "Dominic Wretchkinsides is a murderer. He runs numerous drug rings, illegal arms deals, and human trafficking details, all by way of an extremely powerful criminal organization that has committed heinous crimes all over the world, all in the name of getting richer. He considers himself vastly better than Non-Gifted people, and is fully of the opinion that you should serve us, namely by turning over all of your money to him and by becoming our sex slaves." He willed Bridgette to understand what he was saying. "Just please don't ever forget that. Wretchkinsides would just as soon kill you as look at you. In fact, he's killed his own men because they got on his nerves. He's fixed sporting events, elections, anything he can get his mitts on and make fall his way."

Bridgette rolled her eyes. "Okay, so he's a bad guy," she drawled flippantly. "What's Dan so hung up with him for? He works all the time, and it's always something stupid about Nic's guys or his case. Aren't there any other bad guys?"

"Right now, he has all of our attention because of his cruelty and his vast reaching power."

"Whatever," Bridgette fumed. "Dan needs to get over it."

"I've been friends with Dan since we were toddlers, and I guarantee you he's not going to get over it."

"What time will he be back?"

"Depends on how long the trial lasts. It'll be sometime tomorrow, but probably be pretty late. The only flight tonight from Moscow to

DC is in a few hours. He had a ticket, which he'll now have to change because obviously he won't be making that one."

"I'm working a double shift tomorrow," Bridgette complained.

"We told Dan we'd take care of you, and we will," Garrett assured her.

Garrett, Rainer, and Emily returned to the farmhouse kitchen after dropping Bridgette at The Tantra. Mrs. Haydenshire, Tad, Nathan, Adeline, and Brooke were seated at the kitchen table discussing the wedding. Emily joined in excitedly.

Mrs. Haydenshire smiled at Rainer. "I know you're excited to get in the game, sweetheart, but would you go get Logan and Will? I think we need to have a little talk."

"Yes, ma'am." Rainer suddenly felt like he was ten years old again and had done something he was about to be punished for.

"Taddy, you and Nathan run along and either join the game or pick up those dress samples, bring them back, and see about the lilies," she continued her orders.

Tad chuckled as he stood with the sketches he'd been making of rings.

"She's still just as bossy as when she was a kid," he teased as he and Nathan headed out the back door to start the games.

Rainer returned with Logan and Will. They each looked equally guilty, though none of them knew what they'd done wrong. They all took seats beside their significant others and waited on Mrs. Haydenshire to begin.

"Now, I'm certain that none of the women seated at my table feel that they are better than Bridgette, either because she isn't Gifted or because she takes her clothes off for a living."

"Mom, I don't think I'm better than Bridgette. She's just a mean person." Emily's contradictory statement made Rainer stifle a chuckle.

"Did you hear what she said to Brooke last night? That was just cruel, not to mention completely untrue," Will fired back.

"It was cruel, and it was untrue in your case, William," Mrs.

Haydenshire edged. "All I'm asking is for you to consider what made her say those things."

"Okay, why *does* she say stuff like that, and do stuff like she did to Logan?" Emily demanded.

Rainer laced his fingers through hers as he considered. Emily was at a loss because Bridgette wasn't Gifted. Emily Haydenshire went through life interacting, for the most part, with the emotions of the Gifted Realm.

She was a Receiver. She had become quite accustomed to being able to discern other people's energies and intentions by reading their energy.

Bridgette had no external forces of ambient energy in her body, therefore, Emily had nothing to read.

"You and Brooke grew up fortunate enough to be raised by parents who love and respect you. We taught you to respect yourself. You both have fathers who adore you and taught you how you should expect a man to act toward you. Bridgette never had any of that, and what drove her to say the things she said last night and to do what she did this morning,"—she gestured her head to Logan—"is that she is so very jealous that you three have the all-encompassing admiration and love of the men seated beside each of you.

"She has none of that. As sorry as I am to say this, the truth is that she's nothing more than a distraction from Daniel's pain. He's never going to take her to meet his parents. I doubt his parents even know he's dating anyone. He's certainly never going to marry her, which is what she so desperately wants for him to do. You three have everything she's ever wanted. Everyone needs to feel like someone is on their side, that someone will be there for them.

"When Dan introduced you"—she squeezed Will's hand—"as one of his best friends, and there you two sat, with your arm around Brooke, the love between the two of you was evident in the way you exist together. You were both gazing adoringly at the result of your deep, abiding love." She gestured to Lily Ana. "It was more than she could quite handle. She reacted thusly. Hurt people hurt other people."

The entire table was quiet for a long moment.

Rainer saw Emily's jaw clench, and he waited for the fallout.

"Okay, fine, but she flirts all the time. And what if Garrett's right and she's spying for Wretchkinsides or something?"

"She may well be. She does seem largely motivated by money, and nothing good will ever come of that. But there's nothing we can do but treat her with the same decency and respect I would want my daughter treated with if you should ever find yourself somewhere you didn't want to be with people you didn't know.

"As for her flirting, do you three have so little faith in the men seated at this table, who I would like to point out I raised, or in your relationships, that you're concerned that if she flirted just enough or just the right way that she would turn their heads?" She gestured to Logan and Will.

"Believe me, I understand that it's difficult to watch her flirt with them, but you all seem to me to be in the extremely lucky position of having the loves of your lives wrapped around your fingers." Rainer smiled and took Emily's hand. He nodded at her as Logan did the same for Adeline. "I don't really think you have anything to worry about. She acts that way because that's how she's always gotten attention. Instead of being furious with her, why don't you try a little sympathy? I have a feeling Bridgette doesn't have many female friends outside of work, and I'm certain she could use a few." Mrs. Haydenshire's wishes were met with varying degrees of disdain.

"I'll try," Emily agreed begrudgingly.

"That's all I'm asking for." Mrs. Haydenshire winked at Emily and then leaned and kissed her cheek. "Okay, now all the boys outside for the game, and please watch your language while the twins are playing with you." She gave Logan a look that said she was primarily referring to him.

"And the girls are going to plan out the reception and try to find a place where Logan and Adeline can get married a week from tomorrow." She beamed at Adeline as a broad smile formed on her face.

Logan brushed a kiss across her cheek. "I don't care where. I just want to marry her."

Will and Rainer chuckled at his exuberance.

. . .

After a hard-fought game, Governor Haydenshire's team, which consisted of him, Nathan, Will, Patrick, Connor, and Keaton, when he wasn't napping, emerged victorious.

"How did we lose to the senior citizen team?" Garrett goaded his father and Will.

"Hey, watch it." Governor Haydenshire shoved the football hard into Garrett's gut. "I can have you assigned to parking deck security. Don't forget that."

They fell into the kitchen laughing as Emily and Lucy began supplying them with large cups of water.

"Come here, sweetheart. Give me a hug," Patrick teased Lucy. After inhaling quickly, wrinkling her nose, and laughing, Lucy shook her head. "I think I'll just let you shower first."

Patrick shot Lucy a look that told the entire room he wouldn't mind her helping him with his shower.

While pretending he hadn't noticed the lascivious look Patrick was still giving his wife, the governor called, "Okay, who's staying for pizza?"

"Can't, Dad. Gonna run a shift for Sorenson. He's taking a bunch of guys out tonight for some big sting," Garrett lamented.

"Where?" the governor quizzed.

"Don't know. Not a Gifted thing. That's why we're running everything else tonight."

"Be careful," Mrs. Haydenshire called from the living room. They were discussing a dress for Emily as she would be serving as Adeline's maid of honor.

Garrett grinned with a slight eye roll. "Will do, Mom. I'll try not to get run over by the hordes of shoppers trying to get their hands on a flat-screen TV, for twenty bucks, that was gone at six o'clock this morning."

Everyone understood that Garrett probably wouldn't be in any real danger that evening. He checked his cell.

"Dan still hasn't called," he commented concernedly, but then a broad grin lit his face. He touched the screen of his phone and brought it to his ear as he downed more water.

"Hey, honey, d'you call?" His voice was suddenly low and thrumming. "Yeah, I missed you too, baby."

All of his brothers and Rainer rolled their eyes.

"Everything okay?" He looked momentarily concerned. "Hey, it's all right. Just get rid of him, and then I'll come over. I'll take care of everything else." He glanced at his watch.

"Yeah, I need to take a quick shower then I have to pull a quick shift, but I can come by now or after I get off. Oh yeah," Garrett drawled as a broad grin spread across his face. Whatever the girl on the other end of the phone had promised, Rainer assumed it had to do with the shower Garrett needed as he looked extremely pleased. "I'm always down for that." He gave everyone a wave as he headed out the door.

Governor Haydenshire shook his head. "I knew we were in trouble when I got a call one day asking me to come pick him up from school because he informed his third grade teacher that she was a hottie." Everyone cracked up.

"Who's Serenity?" Patrick, who must've seen the screen name when Garrett had answered the call, quizzed Will.

"New girl. Let's just say she's definitely Garrett's type."

Emily chimed in, "Tall, blonde, big boobs, lacking morals and clothing?" She hit the nail on the head.

Everyone guffawed as Will nodded. "Yeah, pretty much."

With a shudder, Governor Haydenshire picked up the phone to order the pizzas as everyone dispersed to the farmhouse's many bathrooms to shower.

CHAPTER 32

VINDICO VS. THE RUSSIAN BOARD

DAN VINDICO

Pendergrath shot Dan an arrogant sneer of certainty as they waited. Forcefully resisting the deep desire to sink his fist into those perfectly capped teeth, Dan turned his head defiantly. The governing board had been gone almost an hour.

They want to make it look good. Dan's stomach twisted in derisive repulse. Wretchkinsides had paid off at least two of the governors that Dan knew of.

When it came right down to it, there really hadn't been enough evidence to put Pendergrath away for more than tax evasion, which the Russian board of governors didn't deem worthy of a stay in Diapoley.

He was going to get out, and he knew it. Fury began to course through Dan's weary veins. He was going to walk again. He was going to get away with all of the heinous crimes he'd committed.

Dan reminded himself that he'd waited ten long years to end Cascavel and that he would take out Pendergrath as well. He continued to make this vow to himself as he let his hatred fill his soul.

If it was the last thing he did, he would take down Candor Pendergrath, and Alexi Pravus, and Dominic Wretchkinsides. He would end them just like he'd ended Cascavel. He'd bury them so deep no one could ever dig them out. Amelia would finally rest in peace.

Amelia. His stomach clenched as his jaw tightened in fury. How could these six men, who'd never known what a beautiful smile she had, how sweet she tasted, how kind she was, how her ocean-blue eyes lit when he walked in the room, the way she felt in his arms, or how much he'd loved her, how could they look him in the eye and tell him that the man before them wasn't guilty? The man who'd taken her from their home and had done what they'd done to her, how could they let him walk? It was too much. He couldn't stand it. He wouldn't allow it.

The governors returned. They walked callously in their robes, to sit on their raised platform in pious judgment just before enjoying the hefty compensation they would receive for delivering a not guilty verdict.

They were right about one thing, Dan decided as he narrowed his eyes at the Russian Crown—Diapoley wasn't worthy of Pendergrath. That was too kind. Hell was the only fitting place.

The translator called, "Please rise for the verdict." Dan stood. The translator was only necessary for the spectators. The governors, Pendergrath, and the top lawyer for the Interfeci all spoke perfect English.

Dan's heart gave sluggish, heavy beats. It struggled under the weight of the bitter malice that filled his blood. He never moved his hateful scowl off the Crown.

The man glanced around nervously. His eyes drifted once again to the woman throwing him salacious gazes. She was seated in one of the spectator seats.

She winked at him, and the Crown couldn't quite hide his grin. He'd checked on her constantly during the trial.

His mistress. Dan's suspicions were confirmed.

The Crown hadn't just been baited. He'd been blackmailed. The woman winking at him was most definitely not the Russian First Lady. The first governor's name was called.

"Not guilty," he drawled in Russian. Pendergrath sneered in delight. Tension hung in the air of the courtroom. It pulsed with trepidation as the next governor's vote was called for.

"Not guilty," was repeated by the Crown and then four of the other governors. The final governor was called.

He held Dan's eyes with his own, as he stated, "Guilty." He must've wanted Dan to know what his vote might cost him.

With calm clarity, Pendergrath narrowed his beady eyes.

It didn't matter. It was all for naught. The rest of the board had either been purchased or terrified, and that was the only vote of guilt.

Pendergrath laughed derisively. He shot Dan a goading grin, and it was simply more than he could bear. His muscles flexed and tensed of their own accord as he stalked past the security guard in front of the governors. With the very little effort that it required, he threw the guard to the ground.

"You are nothing but a pathetic group of useless cowards," Dan snarled with his voice full of menace. "How much did he pay for your votes? I sure as hell hope you asked for the fucking moon, because you just let a murdering, mother-fucking asshole walk, so you can buy your cum-bunnies a fur coat. And you know what else? I don't need you. I'll take him down myself without any of your help. So, enjoy your payoff, gentlemen, and you can suck my fat cock on your way to hell. At least then you'll know what one looks like," Dan spat the vengeance that spewed from his body.

The governors, in utter shock, ordered him detained, but he threw his shield out on either side of himself and knocked four guards into the walls of the courtroom. Concrete dust filled the stale air.

"Nice try. Maybe you should actually train your Iodex," he sneered as he grabbed his laptop case, threw open the doors, and flew from the chamber.

Russian Iodex guards descended, and Dan began to sprint. He threw his fist out and caught one in the face. He knocked the guard backward, and felt the satisfying crunch of the man's teeth under the blow of his fist.

He reached the doors, threw them open, and shot a cast backward that knocked two more onto their backs.

His mind raced as he breathed in the freezing air. He welcomed the pain as the icy wind pierced his lungs. They were going to keep coming. He'd just told the Crown Governor of the Russian Realm to suck… He shut the thought down quickly and kept running.

There were no more flights out that night, not that he'd be allowed on a plane. The airport would be the first place they'd look.

Then as a goading grin spread across his face, he ducked into an alleyway and pulled out his phone.

CHAPTER 33

ON OPPOSITE SIDES

While keeping his head down, Dan sprinted through the streets of Moscow. Onion dome spires bloomed ahead of him, but he doubted he'd find sanctuary in the churches. He tried to blend into the crowds as Russian Iodex officers spilled out of the courthouse.

"Shit," slipped through his teeth as he debated his lack of options.

He checked his back constantly. His breathing came in shallow gasps. He snatched a baseball cap and a sweatshirt from a vendor gouging tourists in Red Square.

He ducked into another alley and pulled the shirt over his dress shirt. He donned the cap before slinking along the sidewalks and staying out of the light of the streetlamps and the endless number of cameras.

Heading away from the square, he stuck to the alleyways and debated. The enemy of his enemy was his friend, and Nic's shit governing board had likely infuriated an endless number of Russian people who were all being taken advantage of.

He ducked behind an overflowing dumpster as the footfalls of officers echoed nearer. A door behind him opened. *Fuck. Fuck. Fuck.*

A nun stepped out of the door. Her knowing eyes glanced from

Dan to the Iodex officers. Dan's heart pounded out an SOS. He used his eyes to plead with the woman.

She raced to the end of the alleyway and called to the officers. Dan turned to sprint away, but then she pointed the opposite direction and ordered the officers down another corridor. Once they'd turned and gone the other way, she eased back to Dan.

"Thank you," he choked. He didn't know how to speak as much Russian as he understood.

She gave him a kind smile. "I don't know l'anglais as much," she explained. She did appear to know some French, and he could make that work. "Come." She guided him inside the back door of a convent. For all of the opulence of its cold exterior, the inside was simple and warm.

"I need to get to the metro."

She looked confused. Two other nuns joined her. They both gave him wary smiles. She explained something to them in rapid Russian. Dan only made out the words police and good. He didn't understand what she'd said, but the other sisters' expressions eased.

He tried again. "I need to get to the metro. A friend of mine has a ticket waiting for me. I have to get out of the country."

"Yes." His rescuer nodded adamantly. "But they will see there."

"We'll go with him," one of the other nuns spoke this directly to Dan. She seemed to speak much better English than his savior.

He shook his head. "I don't want you to get into trouble on my account."

The woman who spoke English smiled. "When the laws serve only their makers, trouble loses its meaning. Come eat." They led him to a kitchen area and seated him at a wooden table and prepared him a bowl of borscht.

"Thank you, but I've got to get to the train station."

"Not now. Tonight," she instructed. He saw her magenta energy glow in her hand as she turned it orange to heat his soup. She was a Receiver. Despite everything he'd done and said, she must've felt that he was trying with all of his exhausted might to do good. That's why they trusted him.

As dusk fell, the sisters let him exchange his clothes for some in the donation box. They gave him a large coat with a hood.

"There will be border stop. Belarus," one of them worried.

Dan gave her a reassuring nod. "I know. I'll get off the train before that and cross the border on foot."

"Miles many to Belarus train station," she worried.

"I'll be okay. Thank you so much for your help."

An hour later as darkness consumed the city, they headed toward a train station on the outskirts of Moscow. Dan thanked them again and slipped inside. He watched every single person surrounding him, but no one seemed to be looking for him.

He headed to an available ticket teller. "A friend of mine phoned in a ticket for me on the enhanced express to Poland leaving in five minutes," he informed the clerk in a decidedly French accent.

"You from France, but you learn zee English and no Russian?" the woman scolded in an obvious attempt to flirt. Dan gave her his signature cocky smirk and winked at her.

"No, je suis désolé. Je parle français et un peu l'anglais." He raised his eyebrows expectantly before continuing. "I should learn Russian. Perhaps, when I return to the city, you could teach me."

She smiled. "That would be an honor." She batted her eyelashes.

"I just need my ticket, mademoiselle," he kept his French accent flowing heavily and tried not to laugh at the fact that the woman was several years too old to be referred to as mademoiselle.

She asked his name.

After quickly supplying the agreed-upon alias, she slid him the reserved ticket, along with a small piece of paper where she'd written her phone number and address.

Dan chuckled, held up the paper, gave her an approving nod, winked at her again, and slipped it into his pocket as he moved toward the enhanced train boarding for Warsaw.

As soon as he was out of her sight, he threw the paper away. If he got caught, he didn't want her implicated in any way.

He entered the train and moved to the back corner. He studied every other passenger on board. No one seemed interested in him, and he relaxed slightly as the enhanced train roared to life. It flew down the tracks. He would be off Russian soil soon, but that was only the beginning of his escape.

After he pulled the fur hood low over his eyes, Dan waved several rubles at the woman who was pushing the cart down the aisle.

He pointed to a copy of Moscow's primary newspaper and ordered three cans of Coke in order to stay awake. He paid the woman and watched her move to the next train car. She paid him virtually no attention.

A minute later, two men in trench coats entered his car. They were speaking rapidly in Russian as they scanned the passengers.

His heart sped. His chest vibrated. There was no way out of that car. Dan's blood raced through his veins in chilling spikes.

He sank down in his seat, sending up a futile prayer to a God he refused to believe in. He pulled the cap lower over his face and picked up the newspaper he'd just purchased. He kept a close watch on the men as they glanced around the car. One shook his head as the other shrugged, and then they moved on.

He exited the train at the stop closest to the Belarusian border and checked the enhanced map on his phone. He began his sprint toward what may well be his doom.

He reminded himself it was far easier to get into Belarus than it was to get into Russia as he breathed another prayer to any deity willing to listen.

Several hours and two rounds of hitch-hiking later, he finally slipped into the train station in Minsk. He purchased another ticket on an enhanced express in a different name and slipped the teller two hundred American dollars to keep his mouth shut, which he seemed willing to do.

Every mile farther away from Moscow eased the tense set of his shoulders, but he still had miles to go before he could afford to breathe.

Rainer Lawson

Rainer held Emily in his lap on the couch as they devoured several pieces of pizza. He paid no attention to the football game on TV. He reveled in her energy, now flowing in smooth, languid waves as she laid her head on his shoulder and let him feed her bites of pizza.

At nine, the phone in the governor's office rang.

"Oh, honey," Mrs. Haydenshire lamented, "your phone rang several times this afternoon. I meant to tell you. I'm sorry." Her hand was rubbing over her bump. Weary exhaustion plagued her eyes.

Governor Haydenshire placed a gentle kiss on her cheek. "Don't worry about it. The Senate is closed today, and everyone knew I planned to spend the day with the kids." He headed to his office and answered the phone. He didn't bother to close the door.

After a few moments of silence, "He said what?!" roared from the governor, and everyone abruptly stopped what they were doing. "Where is he now?"

Everyone in the living room moved to stand outside the glass-paned French doors of the governor's office.

"Da-yee is mad!" Henry announced. He shook his head back and forth and clasped his hands over his ears.

A knock sounded at the front door. Mrs. Haydenshire furrowed her brow as she scooted to answer it. Emily scooped Henry up.

Rainer followed Mrs. Haydenshire. He was concerned over who might be calling at such a late hour.

"I've got it," he assured her. She beamed at him as he positioned himself between her and the door.

"Oh, uh, hi," Rainer welcomed Governor and Mrs. Vindico. They both looked terrified.

"Marion, Arthur, come in." Mrs. Haydenshire smiled. "What a nice surprise. We were just watching the game." She gestured to the living room.

Mrs. Vindico's face was pulled into a terse pout. She awkwardly patted Henry in Emily's arms as if she felt she must.

"Can one of the boys make you some coffee or tea?" Mrs. Haydenshire offered.

"No, thank you, Lillian," Governor Vindico lamented. "I'm sorry, but this isn't a social call."

Mrs. Haydenshire nodded. Confusion colored her soft features.

"Arthur!" roared Governor Haydenshire.

"I'm right here." Governor Vindico sighed as he headed into the governor's office. He closed the door behind him.

"Well, uh,"—Mrs. Haydenshire forced a smile—"why don't you come sit down, Marion, while they sort out whatever it is that's happened." She guided Mrs. Vindico into the living room.

"Daniel just wasn't thinking. He doesn't understand that people have opinions about our family because of him," Mrs. Vindico stuttered as everyone nodded their complete lack of understanding.

Mrs. Haydenshire looked bewildered as she hugged and patted Mrs. Vindico who'd begun sobbing on her shoulder.

"Hey, Em..." Rainer gestured to Mrs. Vindico and took Henry from Emily's arms. Emily moved to the other side of her mother and Mrs. Vindico. She patted Mrs. Vindico's forearm and began pushing her soothing Receiver's cast into the woman weeping on her mother's shoulder.

"Logan, you and Rainer please go put the twins to bed for me," Mrs. Haydenshire urged as Henry rubbed his eyes and laid his head on Rainer's shoulder. He'd just started to suck his thumb.

While they were in the nursery changing the boys' diapers and putting on their pajamas, Logan's cell rang. He propped the phone between his face and shoulder.

"Haydenshire," he answered as he zipped Keaton into his pajamas. Rainer sat in the rocking chair with Henry as Keaton raced away from Logan and grabbed the book *Cars and Trucks and Things that Go*. He handed the book to Rainer, and both of the twins settled in his lap.

Rainer tried not to whimper when he got to the page *the fast red car goes vroom vroom vroom*.

He stopped reading as Logan cursed under his breath. "Tell me this is some kind of horrible joke," Logan begged. "What are we going to do?" He paused for a moment. "Fine. Let us finish putting the twins to bed for Mom, and we'll come get her. Yeah, yeah, I got it." He ended the call.

"What?" Rainer urged as the twins began filling in the story that they'd heard dozens of times for him.

Logan shook his head in disbelief.

"You know the Non-Gifted police sting Garrett was talking about?"

"Yeah?"

"It was at The Tantra, and one of the undercover cops propositioned Bridgette. She offered him a whole lot more than a lap dance, and she got herself arrested."

Rainer's mouth fell open in horror.

"Wait, it gets better," Logan shook his head. "Garrett got her out, but she's under house arrest. Guess whose house she has to stay at until Vindico comes home? Garrett says Dan has more pull than he does, so he can probably get the charges dropped. We have to keep her here under constant surveillance until he gets back. We have to make sure she doesn't skip town or anything."

CHAPTER 34

NO GOOD DEED

DAN VINDICO

The following afternoon, Dan exited the final train with a broad, goading smirk. While laughing hysterically and shaking his head, Fitzroy stalked toward him.

"You told the Russian Crown to suck your fat cock. Man, I have always loved you, but you are now officially my hero."

Dan joined in his hearty laughter.

"Come on, Maddie's got your room ready. She made all of your favorites. You must be starved." Fitzroy continued to chuckle as they walked out into the busy, soothing streets of Paris.

"You don't think they knew I was coming here?" Dan couldn't fight it anymore. His nerves were getting to him.

"Doesn't matter if they did. You're on French soil now, and you know none of the French Parliament give a damn what you called the Russian Crown. He's a crook, and everybody knows it. Besides, it was a crime de passionnel," he teased as they both laughed.

Dan's lungs and muscles began to unknot. They allowed him to breathe, a sensation he hadn't felt in quite some time.

Sitting at the Fitzroys' table and forcing all thoughts of just never turning his phone back on from his mind, Dan casted the phone and brought it back to life. He thanked Maddie for the coffee she poured for him.

"Great," he moaned.

Fitz chuckled. "How many?"

"Oh, let's see here… eleven missed calls from my old man, seven from Crown Governor Haydenshire, and nineteen from Governor Willow, who is actually my boss."

Fitz continued his laughter. "I don't know why they're so upset. The Prime Minister here wants to shake your hand."

Before he could choose who to call back first, his phone rang. He decided he might as well go ahead and face the music. "Vindico."

Dan held the phone away from his ear as his father began shouting. With a roll of his eyes, he waited on his father to stop screeching.

"I'm at Fitz's, Dad. I'm fine. I'll be home in a few hours. You can yell at me when I land," he promised. "Yeah, yeah, I'll issue a formal apology when I invite them to share a table in hell with me."

"Dammit, son. You've done it this time," his father growled.

"I'm heading to the airport in an hour. Bye." He hung up the phone.

Fitz was still laughing heartily. "Tell the governors to go play a round of golf. The Russian board got what was coming to them."

Maddie shook her head at the antics. "Perhaps we won't retell this particular story to the boys."

"Oh, come on. It's important that they learn to stand up to…wait, what was it you called them?" Fitz teased.

"Uh, I believe it was a pathetic group of useless cowards," Dan supplied. He was not sorry he'd said it. If given the choice, he'd do it again.

"See?" Fitz threw his arms out in praise. "Those are the kinds of idiots the boys need to call out."

Maddie met his exaltation with a withering glare.

"Maybe we could tell them about it when they're older," Dan negotiated with a wry grin.

"Yeah, okay," Fitz agreed.

An hour later, Dan's nerves spun into apathy as he boarded a 747 due to land at the Senate in four hours' time.

The roar of the engines had his stomach churning.

Pendergrath got out, and he's going to America. Dan let that horrific information cement in his mind.

Fitz had been a soothing reprieve. He'd gotten him out of a sticky situation, just as he always had. He'd allowed him a moment to not think, not recall what he'd done or, more importantly, why he'd done it.

Dan despised flying. There was too much time to think. He grabbed his laptop and popped it open as the plane leveled off.

Rainer Lawson

After an hour of paperwork and still unable to believe what had happened either with Dan or Bridgette, Rainer pulled the Hummer into the barn.

"I didn't do that," Bridgette insisted for the hundredth time.

"Uh-huh, the undercover cop who has a service record so clean you could eat off it seemed to think you did." Logan dragged Bridgette out of the Hummer, and they guided her into the house.

The evening's events had Emily extremely concerned, and she'd taken her mother's wishes to heart.

Rainer smiled at her when they walked in the kitchen. The lights were out in the house, but Emily had a lamp glowing on the counter, along with the light over the stove.

Rainer inhaled deeply of the aroma of her and of the food she'd just heated as it mixed with the warmth of the farmhouse kitchen. Peace settled in his soul.

"I made you dinner." Emily set a plate full of some of her mother's leftover Thanksgiving turkey, dressing, sweet potatoes, green beans from the garden, cranberry sauce, and Waldorf salad in front of Bridgette. "I mean, you know…you can't go to work tomorrow," Emily choked before going on. "So, I thought you could eat now."

"Yeah, thanks." Bridgette seated herself at the table. "That was really nice of you."

Emily smiled as she poured Bridgette a glass of water. Bridgette hesitantly cut a piece of the turkey and brought it to her lips. A moment later, she seemed to relax before Rainer's very eyes.

"This is delicious."

"Yeah, Mom's a great cook," Emily assured her. "She's a Double-Prec..." Emily began, but then abruptly stopped talking. With an awkward smile, she shook her head slightly. "Never mind. Just eat."

Bridgette didn't have to be told twice. She devoured the food Emily supplied her. After Bridgette finished seconds, which she seemed woefully unable to turn down, Emily washed her plate and silverware. "I'm gonna go on to bed."

Rainer pulled her into his chest. "Thank you," he whispered in her ear and squeezed her to him. "Sleep well, baby."

"Okay." Emily looked momentarily hesitant to leave Rainer and Logan alone with Bridgette, but she drew a deep breath, blew Rainer a kiss, and scooted up the stairs.

The fact that Bridgette was on house arrest under their care until Dan arrived back in the country meant that Logan and Rainer wouldn't be sleeping. They would either be seated outside her bedroom or stalking the upstairs hallway.

"If you want to go with her, we can do this in shifts," Logan offered. Rainer smiled. He assumed that him staring longingly after Emily had given him away.

"Nah, I want to be awake in case we hear from Vindico anyway."

Bridgette thanked them begrudgingly for picking her up.

"Yeah," Logan huffed. "Just do me a favor and don't try to leave. I don't want to arrest you again."

"I didn't really do anything to get arrested the first time."

Rainer gestured up the stairs and waited on Bridgette to go ahead of him. The lights were still on in Governor Haydenshire's office. Governor Willow had joined Governor Vindico and Governor Haydenshire just a little while ago.

Kara, one of Dan's sisters, had arrived before Rainer and Logan departed for the Non-Gifted precinct to take her mother home.

Bridgette's adamancy about her innocence had Rainer wondering. They led her upstairs, sealed and casted the windows in Patrick's old bedroom, and then locked her in.

He sank down onto the hallway floor. Logan handed Rainer one of the chilled Dr Peppers he'd brought up from the kitchen. They could hear the murmurs from the governor's office.

"What exactly do you think he said to the Russian Board?" Logan whispered.

The story had unfolded, and Governor Haydenshire and Governor Vindico had refused to repeat whatever Vindico had shouted at the Russian Crown and governing board.

"It's Dan, so I'm sure it was particularly nasty." Rainer cringed.

"He does have an awful temper."

Rainer took a long, restorative sip of the Dr Pepper.

"It must've been pretty bad." Logan gestured his head toward his father's office.

"Yeah, I think now they're just trying to figure out where he is."

"You don't think they've got him cornered somewhere in Russia, do you? Maybe they're not telling Dad." Logan sounded deeply concerned about their boss.

"No, you know him. If he's anywhere he doesn't want to be, he'll find a way out."

Logan nodded his agreement. He rubbed his eyes as he downed more Dr Pepper.

"Do you think he's all right?" Logan stared down at the worn hardwood floor they were seated on, and Rainer knew he didn't mean physically.

Rainer glanced at Emily's door. He momentarily thought about how peaceful and beautiful she was when she slept. He shook his head.

"No," he whispered, "I think he's coming unglued. I think it's all finally getting to him."

"Yeah, me too." Logan's tone was rough and tired. "But you know what?" Rainer stared at him with his eyebrows raised. "If it was me and that had happened to Adeline, I don't think I'd be any different." He laid his soul on the hardwood floor for his best friend.

Rainer offered him a comforting smile. "Yeah, me either."

CHAPTER 35

ROCK BOTTOM

Logan's elbow rammed into Rainer's bicep.

"Dan, where the hell are you?" they heard Governor Vindico demand furiously. Logan and Rainer edged to the top of the stairs. They listened intently.

Governor Vindico began shouting that his son would issue formal apologies to the entire Russian governing board, asking him just what he thought he was doing and why he hadn't called.

"How the hell did you get to Fitzroy's?" Governor Vindico bellowed.

The air that had been trapped in Rainer's lungs escaped in utter relief. Logan smiled as the tension eased from his features as well.

"I told you," Rainer whispered. They were both extremely impressed.

"Dammit, son! You've done it this time. Dan, no…wait!" Governor Vindico spat, but then silence loomed. "He hung up."

"Is he okay, Arthur?" Governor Haydenshire asked calmly. His words were laced with deep concern.

"He told the Russian Crown to suck his cock on his way to hell. No, he's not all right, Stephen. He's damn lucky he's not in Diapoley," Governor Willow huffed.

Rainer and Logan's mouths fell open in shock as they stared at one another in an endless moment of stunning realization.

"If I never have to hear that statement again, it would be fine with me," Governor Haydenshire reprimanded.

"Sorry."

"He said he was leaving for the airport." Governor Vindico's voice resumed its normal timbre.

"Go on home and get some sleep. We're meeting his plane with Elite Iodex. He's either going to listen, or I'm going to have to fire him," Governor Haydenshire explained.

"Please," Governor Vindico pled. "We've been friends for almost forty years, and I've never asked you for any favors. I'm begging you. Don't fire him. Think about what he went through and what he has to live with every single day."

"Fine, but he's about to get a big reality check, and he's going to have to agree to a few stipulations that I have."

"Anything. I'll see to it myself," Governor Vindico pledged.

"I'll go along with whatever you want, Stephen. You're Crown now, but let's not forget that Iodex falls under my rule. I want to help him," Governor Willow insisted. "And I say this with all of the respect I have for Joseph, God rest his soul, but he appointed Dan because of Maggie. He wanted vengeance as much as Daniel thirsts for it. He chose this way to focus all of that anger Dan has. Joseph let him act this way and do the things he's done.

"I don't think he's ever let his wounds even begin to heal, and you and I both know Joseph never did either. He let Dan get away with far too much. He never reined him in, and he'd never let me do it either. We've got to bring him back down to earth."

Rainer was stunned. He'd never heard anyone say out loud that his father had ever done anything wrong. He was always hailed a hero. The weight of admission that his own father wasn't perfect severed like a knife through his soul.

"That's my plan," Governor Haydenshire decreed. "And as much as he's going to balk at what I'm about to demand of him, I think it will do him some good. He can't go on like this. He's hit rock bottom."

Rainer and Logan barely drew breath. They watched from the top of the stairs as Governor Willow and Governor Vindico left the farmhouse.

"Are you okay?" Logan whispered.

Rainer shut his eyes and shook his head. He didn't want to think anymore.

Governor Haydenshire returned to his office, turned off the light, and closed the door quietly.

Logan and Rainer scooted away from the landing. Rainer felt like he was ten years old again. He recalled all the times they'd snuck to the top of the stairs to watch Will, Garrett, and Levi end their dates for the evening, or to overhear them being yelled at by Governor and Mrs. Haydenshire for something.

They made it back to Patrick's door before Governor Haydenshire crested the stairs.

"We're meeting Dan's plane. You both need to be at the Senate, in uniform, at five thirty. You can keep Bridgette in the holding cells until Dan figures out how to handle that situation as well."

"Yes, sir." They watched as the governor eased the door to his bedroom open. An adoring grin cast his weary face as he took in Mrs. Haydenshire sleeping soundly in their bed.

"Good night, boys," the governor whispered as Rainer and Logan returned the sentiment.

Dan Vindico

"Well, you must've done something big this time, son." Pete Namphis approached and took the empty seat beside Dan.

Dan certainly couldn't disagree with that.

"Just got off the phone with our new Crown Governor. He informed me that I wasn't to let you leave the plane." Pete's brow knitted tightly. "I asked him how exactly I was supposed to keep Dan Vindico anywhere Dan Vindico didn't want to be. He said, 'ask him.' So, I'm asking. I'm only a few years from retiring. I'd like to keep my job if it's all right with you."

"Governor Haydenshire wouldn't fire you, but I won't leave. I won't get you into trouble on my account. You flying the Paris route now?" Dan hoped to change the subject.

Pete smiled. "Back and forth almost every day. Took a sideline to Rio a few weeks ago for our friend, Mr. Lawson."

Dan chuckled and nodded his understanding.

"But mostly it's Paris," Pete concluded.

After studying Pete briefly, a genuine smile formed on Dan's face. "What's her name?"

While laughing and shaking his head, Pete grinned. "Guess that's the risk of having a drink with the Chief of Iodex." He skirted the question.

"Haven't started drinking yet, but that'll come, I'm sure."

Pete glanced around and seemed to note that there were very few people on the flight to the Senate, and no one was in their general vicinity.

"Her name's Sophia. Those French girls, let me tell you, they got something special."

"So I've been told."

"What'd you do, son?"

"I didn't realize this was quid pro quo," Dan sighed and went on with it. "I might've gotten in a little over my head with the Russian board of governors. Probably said several things I shouldn't have. I might've told the Crown just exactly what I thought of him and what he could do with himself. I do seem to recall letting my fists talk to a few of the guards on the way out of the Senate building." Dan examined the knuckles of his right fist. After deciding to get Garrett to heal them for him, he moved his hand from Pete's gaze.

A low whistle slid between Pete's teeth as a grin spread across his kind face. He shook his head. "I take it they did something you didn't care for?"

"Setting a murderer free tends to piss me off."

"This guy the one?" Pete's voice turned low and soothing.

"No." Dan shook his head. His gut clenched of its own accord. "It's, uh…his right-hand man."

"Seems your thoughts turned themselves into words, and then your words turned into actions."

"Yeah, you could say that."

"You can't keep it bottled up forever. It'll make its way out eventually, and maybe not in the way you'd prefer." Pete stood and offered a slight wave as he headed back to the cockpit.

CHAPTER 36

THE END OF THE LINE

RAINER LAWSON

Garrett rushed to join the entire Elite Iodex team on the tarmac just moments before the plane was due to land.

"When I said five thirty, son, that's what I meant," Governor Haydenshire scolded.

"Sorry, Dad." Garrett made no attempt to explain his tardiness.

"So, we'll go over it once again for our late arrival." Rainer couldn't recall a time he'd seen the governor so furious. "Chief Vindico is being detained on the plane. If he attempts to leave or refuses to follow my orders precisely, you are to arrest him," the governor bellowed.

"Yes, sir," the entire team responded.

Terror swirled in the pit of Rainer's stomach as he tried to envision himself arresting Dan Vindico.

The plane landed at seven o'clock on the dot, and Rainer's pulse raced as he watched passengers begin to descend the airstairs. The engines quieted and the pilots and coolant officers made their exits. Captain Namphis gave Rainer a kind smile that he returned.

"Let's go." Governor Haydenshire headed up the stairs, followed by Governors Willow and Vindico.

Rainer and Logan followed Portwood and Ericcson in a somber march. Vindico remained in his seat. He watched the new arrivals enter. His face held a mix of bemused curiosity and exhaustion.

"Gentlemen." He nodded his head to the governors and Iodex. "Surely you aren't all here for my benefit."

"You know what, Daniel? I think you've done quite enough talking, so shut your mouth and listen up," Governor Haydenshire snarled.

It thoroughly shocked everyone, save his sons, who'd heard him speak this way on many occasions growing up.

Vindico threw a glance at Rainer who was in his direct line of sight. "We're here to arrest you, man. Just please do what he says." Rainer's tone was pleading.

"Arrest me for what?" Vindico demanded.

"Oh, let's see here. How about behavior unbecoming an officer of the American Realm on foreign soil, disorderly conduct, contempt of court, and multiple felony counts of assault." Governor Haydenshire narrowed his eyes. "One of the officers you hit is in the hospital. So, last chance, do you think you can keep your mouth shut, or do I need to send the Chief of Iodex to Felsink for a night out?"

Vindico held up his hands just before crossing them over his chest with a defiant huff.

Governor Haydenshire began to pace as everyone moved away from him to allow him room to complete his trek.

"I do understand, Dan. I understand that they let a murderer go free, and that there wasn't anything you could do about it. I understand that you're angry and that you've been angry since that horrible night ten years ago."

All of the blood drained from Vindico's face as he glared hatefully at the governor.

"Don't you dare!" Governor Haydenshire lunged across the seats and into Vindico's face. "Don't you dare sit there and glare at me because you think I don't know what hell you've been through, because I do.

"I buried my son a week before his twenty-third birthday because of Dominic Wretchkinsides, so don't you sit there like a pompous ass and tell yourself that you're the only one he's ever hurt, because you aren't. Every single day, every time I sit down at my dining room table, and there's an empty chair. Every time I walk past his old room. Every time I look into Lillian's eyes and I see the loss, and the pain, and the agony, that I can't ever make better for her. So, don't you dare sit there and act like I don't know how badly you hurt," Governor Haydenshire roared.

Vindico swallowed harshly. He held the governor's eyes with his own. Silence filled the plane for the length of one heartbeat.

"We've sat back and let you drown in your own misery for long enough. You never wanted any help. You never wanted anything at all as far as I can see except to dismantle Wretchkinsides and the Interfeci with your bare hands.

"Here's what's going to happen, and let me go ahead and assure you that if you fail to follow any of my demands to the letter, you can find yourself employment not only outside of Iodex, but outside of law enforcement of any kind."

Vindico bristled. His jaw clenched. "Fine," he snapped.

"First of all, I am not firing you because your father asked me not to, so when we're finished here you might want to take a moment to tell him how much you appreciate what he's been through on your account. As far as I can see, you've had about as much time and respect for him as you've had for any of the rest of us since we buried Amelia all those years ago.

"Next, you will phone the Russian Crown Governor and apologize for your horrendous outburst, and you will beg his forgiveness just before you phone every other member of the governing board of the Russian Realm." Governor Haydenshire halted. He seemed to be waiting on Vindico to argue, but he didn't.

"You will make these phone calls from my office in front of me." He concluded his first demand.

Vindico's eyes narrowed in disdain, but he said nothing.

"Then we're going to have a nice long talk about your decision-making skills. You've put me in a very difficult spot, Daniel. Not only have you embarrassed the American Realm on foreign soil, but you've made me greatly question your reasoning. And that's a problem, as I'm the one who signed the papers allowing two of my sons to join Elite Iodex, at only twenty-one years of age. I'm also the man who signed those same papers when Cal had been invited to join the Elite team right out of the academy.

"So, you sit and think about what goes through my head each and every time I hear Logan or Rainer's or Garrett's cell phone ring, or I watch them leave for yet another extremely dangerous mission. I need to know that you can keep your head screwed on straight. Trust me, you calling the governing board of Russia a pathetic group of useless cowards doesn't do a lot to restore my confidence," Governor Haydenshire growled.

"A situation arose while you were cussing out the Russian governors. The woman you brought into my home to keep safe, was not only extremely rude to two of my daughters-in-law, but to several of my sons as well, not to mention my wife. Then, if that weren't enough, she was arrested last night on a solicitation charge."

"What?" Vindico gasped.

This appeared to be the first thing Governor Haydenshire said that had truly shocked him. He glanced toward Logan and Rainer, who nodded solemnly.

"Yes, and I can also tell you that she lied to you about her parentage. Her father is not a Felsink guard. I'll let you draw whatever conclusions you're going to draw from that, and I certainly can't tell you whom to date, but might I suggest that you find a woman who actually does something for your heart, and your mind, and other parts of your body? Someone who you have some actual interest in outside of the information she can provide on Dominic Wrechkinsides. Let me tell you the cold, hard truth, Dan. We didn't bury you in that graveyard when we buried Amelia. You're still alive, and she wouldn't want you going on this way. You know it, and so do I.

"So, if Bridgette really makes you feel something that you just don't think you can live without, then go for it, but I think...no," Governor Haydenshire retracted slightly, "I *know* the only thing Bridgette does for you is make you feel like you're just a little bit closer to bringing down Wretchkinsides. You're using her, and if you keep this insanity going with her, eventually that's going to blow up in your face as well.

"She's in the holding cells inside. You can handle her charges as you see fit, but be very, very aware, son, that I will be watching your every move for the next several months like a hawk," Governor Haydenshire warned. "If I find out that you did not do something to make certain she is not in the sights of the Interfeci because of your asinine decision-making skills, I will end your career.

"As for the rest of my requirements, they go something like this. I went back this morning and read over the parking deck security logs. I wanted to see how many days a week you were coming in and how long you were staying. You've either been in that office or on location for work somewhere almost every single day for the past nine and a half years. No weekends, no vacations, nothing but work, nothing but Wretchkinsides, and it's eating you alive." Governor Haydenshire's expression morphed from fury to concern.

"You're suspended without pay for the next two weeks," Governor Haydenshire stated firmly. "And yes, I'm well aware that you have copies of every single piece of evidence or material that you've collected on Wretchkinsides and the Interfeci for the past twelve years at your home. So, work on it if you must," Governor Haydenshire offered, "but there are a few other things you're going to do. Please remember that any variation from these decrees will land you in the unemployment office.

"You will come over to my home for dinner with my family at least two nights this week. I'll make certain Will and Brooke are there, along with Garrett, Rainer, and Logan. You're going to sit and eat, and be filled, and have a few beers, and laugh, and just generally be a human again. You used to eat with us two or three times a week. We haven't seen you at our table since we buried her. You're going to go out with people who love and care about you a few nights this week. Have a drink, play pool, go bowling, I don't give a damn what you do as long as it isn't work.

"Then you are to happily have dinner with your parents, and perhaps your sisters one night this week as well. Saturday afternoon, you and the rest of Elite Iodex are going to attend Logan and Adeline's wedding and reception."

Vindico's brow furrowed as he glanced at Logan who mouthed, "Long story."

"Sunday, Chloe Sawyer has graciously provided me with a ticket for you to the Angels' last conference challenge which you will attend. Chloe has also extended you a personal invitation to the end of the season party for the Angels, which you will also be attending. Bright and early Monday morning, you, along with Logan and Adeline, and Rainer and Emily, will be making the long flight to Sydney, Australia."

Dan looked like Governor Haydenshire had just informed him that he was to remove a limb without anesthesia.

"While you're there, you will vacation. You will sleep in, stay out late, eat too much, hell, even drink too much, but do something that isn't obsessing about Wretchkinsides and revenge. Help Logan and Adeline celebrate their nuptials, give Rainer a little time to heal, have a good time. I'm not sure you've gotten your own head out of your ass long enough to realize that Rainer's had a hell of a time since becoming an Elite Iodex officer.

"While you're in Australia, you will also help them discover which of the Australian Premier's sons is Adeline's father."

Vindico's eyes goggled momentarily, but he said nothing.

"You will also help convince her father to come back to the States to testify against Candy Parker. I know this may be a shock to your system, so to make this just a little more palatable, I'll point out that if Adeline's father can get Candy Parker to turn on Paulo Ramirez, you can add his feather to your collection of Wretchkinsides's top dogs that you've either put behind bars or killed.

"When you return from your vacation, you may return to work, assuming you can keep your tongue and your temper in check." Governor Haydenshire held Vindico's eyes with his own as he awaited a response.

Vindico choked out the words, "Yes, sir."

Rainer noted that the acceptance of his reprimands appeared to taste very bitter.

With a single nod, Governor Haydenshire accepted the terms of his agreement.

"Bridgette was signed over to Rainer and Logan last night from the precinct, so they'll need to sign the release papers if that's what you decide," Governor Haydenshire instructed. "After you've dealt with that, you can come to my office. You have several phone calls to make."

With a heavy breath, Vindico nodded.

"Everyone else, go enjoy the rest of your holiday weekend. Thank you for your help." Governor Haydenshire dismissed the rest of the Elite team.

Everyone disembarked from the plane as Dan and his father followed Logan and Rainer outside.

"Thanks, Dad," Vindico choked.

"Anytime, son, but you should know that by now," Governor Vindico scolded softly.

"Yeah, I should," Vindico agreed. Humility didn't seem to set well with his body or his shield. He joined Logan and Rainer as they strolled into the Senate building. "I take it you and Ms. Parker are expecting?" He didn't look any too pleased with his assumption.

Logan shook his head. "Nope. She needs a last name, and I need her."

Dan smiled. He looked deeply impressed with Logan.

"Do you think maybe at some point on our Australian vacation, after a few beers, we might could hear what exactly you said to the Russian Crown and how the hell you got to Paris without getting caught?" Logan asked hopefully.

Vindico laughed outright. "I think I probably owe you two that much," he begrudgingly agreed. "I'm sorry about Bridgette."

"Yeah, actually," Logan hemmed but then continued on with his sentiment, "I think of all the stuff Dad just yelled at you, what he said about her might be the most important."

Vindico appeared to consider that. "Maybe," he sighed, as they made their way to release Bridgette from the holding cells.

Dan Vindico

Dan bit holes in his tongue to keep from scowling at Governor Haydenshire. Maybe in a few days' time he'd manage some kind of appreciation that he hadn't been fired, but at the moment he felt nothing but disgust and fury.

He grabbed the keys to the holding cells from the locker. Since he never had any real idea what to say to Bridgette anyway, it wasn't shocking that he had nothing to say now. He leaned into the disgust he felt. If he gave in to the fury, the entire governing board was likely to be the next recipient of his temper.

He stalked down the corridor and released Bridgette from the cell. "Look, I don't know what the hell you were thinking, but I'm the Chief of Iodex. Prostitution is illegal in Virginia. We're through."

She rolled her eyes. "I didn't do anything."

"Tell it to the judge. I'm out. I'll get you a job at another club. You need to stay the hell away from Nic Wretchkinsides."

"You're not getting me a job at a different club, and we are *not* breaking up."

That was the first time Dan had laughed in days. "You can either lose my number or I can block you, but we're done. Do you want me to check into other clubs or not?"

Bridgette narrowed her eyes in disdain. "I assure you breaking up with me will be the biggest mistake of your life."

"Oh, honey, trust me, you would not make that bet if you had any idea what I've been doing for the last forty-eight hours."

"I'm serious, Dan. I'll make certain you regret this."

Dan stared her down and rolled his eyes. "Not nearly as much as I regret agreeing to this in the first place, and that regret doesn't even make it on the first page of my lengthy list." He fished his wallet out of his back pocket. "Here." He handed her a twenty. "Get an Uber and never call me again. If you want to keep working at The Tantra with Iodex as your side hustle, you can send your reports to Tuttle."

"I could tell Nic," she sneered.

"Tell Nic what?"

"What I've been doing."

Dan wasn't playing this game. "You do whatever the hell you want, but hear me say this—Nic would just as soon shoot you as look at you. So, unless you're fucking suicidal, walk away quietly and keep your mouth shut."

Rainer Lawson

By Friday evening, Emily had quizzed Rainer a dozen times over whether or not Vindico had dumped Bridgette. As he ran a brush through his hair, just before heading to the farmhouse for Logan and Adeline's rehearsal dinner, she asked yet again

"Baby, I told you I don't know. This week, I've eaten dinner with him twice at the farmhouse, been to a bar with him and your brothers, not to mention him texting me a dozen times about what we're doing at work, so I think he probably would've mentioned it if he'd dumped her, but I have no idea."

"I thought Dad forbid him to work?" She rolled the ends of her hair around her curling iron.

"Yeah, well, old habits die hard, especially when Clarence was suspended from the academy, and his old man was released back into the country."

Logan Haydenshire

As no other place had become available, Logan and Adeline had decided to hold the wedding at the farmhouse.

When everyone arrived for dinner, they were immediately assigned a task for the wedding the next day. Dinner wasn't served until after eight, and it came from Lesco's.

Logan grabbed his and Adeline's burgers and fries and pulled her out onto the side porch. He seated her on the swing and sealed heat into the fibers of the quilts his mother left out there as he covered them up. He cradled her to his chest. Their breaths mingled visibly in the cool evening air.

She'd been busy all week, either working or planning their wedding, and he'd hardly seen her. He just needed a moment with her out of the fray.

"I missed you." Logan kissed the top of her head and felt her smile against him.

"I know. I'm sorry I've been so busy," she apologized.

With a sigh, Logan kissed her again.

"You didn't do anything wrong. I just missed you," he reprimanded. She blushed in the glow of the porch light.

"I am kind of looking forward to the wedding part being over with and just being in the hotel room with you tomorrow night."

"Oh, trust me, I'm looking forward to that as well."

She giggled. The sound made everything in Logan's entire world fall into perfect balance.

"I wish you would tell me where we're staying," she requested again, as she began to nibble her cheeseburger.

"Hey, Dad sort of took over our honeymoon. At least let me surprise you with our wedding night."

Adeline drew a deep, steadying breath. Logan could feel her energy spinning in nervous, jagged arcs.

"Actually," she hesitated, "I kind of think my father took over our honeymoon."

Logan smiled and shrugged. He couldn't argue that, so he let his fierce shield surround her and began pushing soothing waves into her.

"Tomorrow night you'll be Adeline Marie Haydenshire," he whispered just to feel the joy flow through her energy.

"I can't believe how lucky I am." She was giddy in her excitement. It overwhelmed him.

"No, baby. I'm the lucky one. You're just incredible, and I can't believe I'm the guy lucky enough to get to be your husband."

"I can't wait." She set her food beside her and turned to cuddle up in his warm embrace.

"Me either." Logan brushed sweet, tender kisses into her hair.

Rainer Lawson

Thankful, once again, that Adeline had a change of heart the night before, Rainer kissed Emily awake. She wriggled beside him and tucked her face into his chest.

"Hey there, baby. We have to get up. We have a wedding to throw."

"I'm so glad Adeline finally told Mom she didn't want us to stay at the farmhouse last night." Emily kissed Rainer's chest before snuggling beside him.

Mrs. Haydenshire had repeatedly suggested that Emily and Adeline spend the night at the farmhouse and let Logan and Rainer stay at the guesthouse. Everyone knew it meant a great deal to Mrs. Haydenshire.

Around eleven the night before, just as Logan and Rainer were getting ready to leave, Adeline had managed to choke out a plea to her future mother-in-law that she be able to stay with Logan that night.

Mrs. Haydenshire had started to object, but Logan stated firmly that if Adeline wanted to come home and stay with him, that was exactly what she was doing. That had effectively ended the protest.

"Rainer?" Emily whispered nervously.

"What, sweetheart?"

There was an abrupt change in her tone. "Do you think we'll beat the Phenoms tomorrow?" The Phenoms and the Angels had both only lost one challenge in conference play. As they'd both lost to different teams, and the teams they'd lost to had lost more than one challenge, the match tomorrow would determine who won the Northeastern conference title.

Rainer hesitated. He wasn't certain the Angels would win. This hadn't been their best season by a long shot.

"You'll be amazing, Em. You always are, and I already picked up a grape ring pop for good luck."

She giggled sweetly. "Aww, you're the best." Emily sat up and stretched her hands over her head. "Okay, I'd better take the bride to the farmhouse and get her ready, and you better make sure her groom is standing at the altar at two."

"This is Logan and Adeline we're talking about. She's probably already in her gown, standing outside of our door, patiently waiting on you to get up so she can drive you very carefully to the farmhouse herself. Logan is probably already positioned at the altar in front of your parents' hearth. He will stand there all day."

Emily laughed, but then she shook her head.

"He's really nervous," she explained.

"I'll get him there."

A devilish grin formed on Emily's face. "And Adeline's dress has about a thousand pearl buttons all the way up the back. She can't get into i without me and Mom."

Rainer chuckled as he followed Emily out of bed. "Is she trying to torture Logan or something?"

"Trust me," she sassed, "I took her lingerie shopping Thursday night when you and Logan were out with Vindico. Logan is most definitely not being tortured."

Rainer chuckled and kissed the top of her head. "You go get Adeline all taken care of and get all dolled up yourself, and tonight I'll let you torture me." Rainer waggled his eyebrows.

With a naughty glint in her eye, she grinned. "I *have* been looking for a sex slave."

Rainer growled, "Where do I sign up, Miss Haydenshire?"

Emily shook her hips for him as she grabbed her makeup bags and curlers that she'd set out the evening before.

Rainer swatted her backside as she scooted by him.

"Behave, Mr. Lawson," she commanded.

"Only until I get you back in here, baby."

CHAPTER 37

DR PEPPER GETS MARRIED

Rainer was seated between Logan and Patrick among all of Logan's brothers and his father at Lesco's. Les had insisted they use the pub for Logan before it opened for a breakfast, and he'd had the chef serve up a delicious meal for them all.

"So," Garrett teased, "you're getting married, and I think it's time you and I had the talk." He bit back laughter.

Logan rolled his eyes. "Thanks, but I think I've got it," he assured Garrett with a great deal of pompousness.

"No, now, we're your older brothers, so before you introduce Adeline to Dr Pepper, we need to go over a few things," Levi chimed in.

"I was thirteen. Why will I never live that down?" Logan laughed.

Everyone joined in the teasing as Connor quipped, "If you're good, maybe she'll let you mount-n-do her."

Logan shuddered and shook his head.

Patrick grinned. "Well, just until you Squirt."

"Okay, that was bad," Logan scoffed.

Upping the ante, Garrett goaded, "Hey, does Adeline like your cream soda, Lo?"

"Dad, come on. Help me out," Logan pled.

"Sorry, son, I have to give them free rein until she walks down the aisle. Consider it a rite of passage."

"This is why I eloped." Patrick's confession made everyone laugh.

"Come on now, Logan and Adeline have been together for a long time," Will snickered, and Rainer knew he wasn't coming to Logan's defense. "He's already had some cherry pop," he drawled, to the groans of his brothers.

After several more rounds of rather dirty puns and general harassment of Logan, the Haydenshire men went to their homes to get ready for the wedding.

Governor Haydenshire returned to the guesthouse with Logan and Rainer. They were all getting ready together.

"Hey, Rainer," Logan called as he was retying the tie on his tux for the fifth time.

"Yeah, man, what's wrong?" Rainer quizzed as soon as he saw Logan's face. His shield was pulsing with terrorized, nervous fear. He dragged Rainer into the bedroom and shut the door behind him.

"Will you do me a favor and not make fun of me for asking?"

"I'm the best man. That's my job." Rainer didn't point out that he was the only guy seated at the table at Lesco's who hadn't teased Logan.

"Will you just go up to the house and check on her, please? Just make sure Mom and Em aren't getting to her and that she really wants to do this."

"Of course, but trust me, she really wants to do this."

"I know she doesn't want me to see her before, so would you just give her this?" Logan held up a note, folded tightly, before he continued. "And just make certain she really wants to do this today."

Logan Haydenshire was beginning to unravel before Rainer's very eyes. Rainer didn't point out that Logan could text her and ask if she was okay and tell her whatever was in the note.

"Sure." Rainer took the note. "Are you sure you're okay?"

"Yeah," Logan hesitated. "I just don't want her to do anything she doesn't want to do, you know? I don't want her to feel forced into this because of her mom."

"Why don't you grab a beer? I'll be right back."

With a slight nod, Logan drew another deep breath. "If she's not dressed yet, get Emily to give it to her," he commanded.

Rainer couldn't quite hide his slight eye roll. He chuckled. "I'm not gonna walk in on your bride without her gown on, okay?" He willed Logan to think rationally.

As he pulled on his shoes and tossed the jacket onto the couch, he caught Governor Haydenshire's eye and gestured to Logan who'd begun to pace nervously.

Governor Haydenshire smiled as he nodded to Rainer.

"Logan," the governor moved to his son. "I know it's a little chilly out, but grab your coat and we'll take one last walk around the lake for old times' sake. What do ya say?"

"Okay." Logan looked relieved.

Rainer tried to hide his smirk as he held up the note to show Logan what he was going to do.

A short while later, Rainer returned but found Logan more nervous than when he'd left.

"Is she okay?" Logan panicked. "Em's not putting tons of that crap on her face, is she? She's beautiful just the way she is. I don't like it when she wears tons of makeup."

After sharing a concerned expression with the governor, Rainer nodded. "She's great. She didn't have her gown on, but she was wearing some of your sweats, so I gave her the note. She...uh...cried, but like in a good way. You know, I could tell she thought it was sweet," Rainer explained quickly.

"And she gave me this for you." He handed Logan the note from Adeline. He felt a little like he was in fourth grade again only this time he was delivering notes to girls via his Porsche instead of his bike. "Em's doing her hair and makeup, but it's not weird or anything. She looks beautiful."

"Of course she's beautiful. Wait, what do you mean she's beautiful? I'm marrying her," Logan pounced. He was furious all of a sudden.

"Okay." Rainer shook his head. "You need to chill. Here,"—he handed Logan a beer from the refrigerator and guided him to the couch—"read the note."

Logan seemed to realize he was being slightly insane.

Whatever Adeline had written caused Logan to choke up, though he tried very hard not to let his father or Rainer see him blink back tears.

An hour later, Rainer helped Logan shrug into his tux jacket and pinned on his boutonniere.

"Are you ready?"

"Yeah." Logan's nerves seemed to have been replaced with excitement. Something caught Rainer's eye as Logan turned toward the door.

"Hey, there's something on your tie." Rainer wondered if Mrs. Haydenshire could get whatever it was out before Adeline walked down the aisle on the Crown Governor's arm.

"Huh?" Logan panicked. He lifted his tie to inspect it, but then they both saw it. Something was written on the underside of the tie. Rainer tried not to read it, but he was standing right beside Logan when he'd revealed the words.

Don't be nervous. I can't wait to be Mrs. Haydenshire, so come kiss me because I love you! Adeline.

Logan grinned. His breathing steadied. "She's kind of amazing, you know?"

"I know." In that moment, Rainer did know that Adeline was amazing, and he tried not to lament the fact that maybe she knew Logan even better than he did.

All of the furniture had been moved out of the living room and replaced with white folding chairs in just enough rows to form a very short aisle.

Governor Haydenshire was upstairs awaiting his cue to walk Adeline down. Mrs. Haydenshire was seated beside Tad and Nathan, close to Nana and Paps.

Grandpa Haydenshire had refused to come. He wasn't all that pleased that Logan was marrying Adeline. Logan had informed him that he wouldn't be missed.

Rainer suspected Grandpa was smarting over the fact that Adeline had turned out to be an Australian Realm Princess instead of the stray cat he'd insisted she was for so long.

All of Logan's brothers and their dates filled the rest of the rows behind Mrs. Haydenshire. Elite Iodex and friends of Adeline's from Georgetown filled the other side. Rainer and Logan made their entrance from the kitchen to stand beside the minister.

Music played softly, and Emily made her way down the stairs. She was beaming at Rainer. His heart raced. He suddenly found himself wishing that it was his wedding day. He was tired of waiting.

She was dressed in a simple, jade sleeveless dress that cinched at her waist and fell to her ankles. She was stunningly beautiful, and he wanted to make her his wife.

Rainer winked at her as she took her place. He put the wistfulness away for the moment. Their turn would come.

Logan shot Rainer a terrified glance, and Rainer smiled. "This is all you've wanted since orientation night. Remember?"

Logan nodded and turned back to look at the stairwell in his parents' home. The music swelled from an enhanced speaker system under Nathan's casting, and everyone stood.

A moment later, Adeline appeared, holding the governor's arm, and Logan choked back tears. She was exquisitely beautiful, dressed in a sleeveless, mermaid gown with pearl and lace detailing over the satin.

Her hair was gathered loosely on her head, with several tendrils falling to her shoulders. There were dozens of pearl buttons up the back of the dress that Rainer was certain Logan would waste no time working through.

He chuckled softly as he took in his best friend. Logan looked like he would love nothing more than for everyone else to just leave him alone with his bride.

Governor Haydenshire kissed Adeline's cheek and placed her hands in Logan's. He took his spot next to his wife as everyone watched Logan vow to love and adore her, to be there for her, and to take care of her for the rest of their lives. She pledged the same to him.

Tad had designed beautiful wedding bands for both of them, and sweet tender tears leaked down Adeline's face as Logan slipped the ring onto her finger.

Wolf whistles filled the room as the minister gave Logan permission to kiss his bride. She threw her arms around his neck as he leaned her back and kissed her heatedly to the applause of the small crowd.

Rainer was absolutely certain he'd never seen Logan Haydenshire so pleased as he appeared when he turned, and the minister announced that they were now Mr. and Mrs. Logan Theodore Haydenshire.

CHAPTER 38

THE RIGHT COMBINATION

Rainer walked Emily into Angels Arena the next afternoon. They waited outside the locker room until Chloe and Fionna approached a moment later with the keys.

"So, you're sure he's coming today?" Fionna looked more determined than Rainer had ever seen her, and that included her fierce expression during Summation challenges.

Chloe nodded. "And to the party tonight. Crown Governor's orders. You should wear that leather skirt you bought. I oddly have a really good feeling about tonight."

"Uh, obviously." Fionna beamed. "I look so freaking hot in that skirt." She and Chloe promptly cracked up. "I have a good feeling too," Fionna admitted. Her tone changed. "And no offense, but my feelings carry more weight than yours."

Chloe grinned. "I know."

Rainer watched a faraway stare steal Fionna away. He wondered what she was seeing. Emily tried to hide her frown as she turned back to Rainer.

He took her engagement ring, dropped the chain necklace through it, and fixed it around his neck. He hid it behind the Angels shirt he was wearing.

After quickly switching it for the duplicate ring, Rainer supplied her with her customary ring pop, and Emily glowed.

"Good luck, baby. I know you'll be amazing."

"I hope."

Rainer kissed her again and then went to join the rest of the Haydenshires and the Vindicos in the Angels box.

He'd gone all out for the final challenge and worn the *My Girl's an Angel and I keep her Tank Full* T-shirt with Emily's number on it. He grimaced when several photographers snapped his picture as he made his way to his seat.

"Rainer, can you tell us if it's true that Logan married Adeline Parker yesterday?" rang from every reporter within earshot.

The marriage license had been filed, but they wanted a comment. He said nothing and picked up his pace. He sprinted into the Angels VIP box. Vindico gestured to a seat beside him. Rainer nodded, grabbed a Dr Pepper, and took the seat.

He had a sneaking suspicion that Dan wanted to sit beside him because he was already annoyed with his mother and sisters who were to his left. Rainer decided not to be offended.

Garrett appeared a few minutes later sporting one of Chloe's numbered T-shirts.

"I thought Serenity wanted you full-time." Will chuckled.

Garrett scoffed. "I don't do full-time. You know that."

"Okay, so I've been doing some research on which of the Australian Premier's sons might be Ms. Parker's father," Vindico began as soon as he had Rainer's attention.

With a slight chuckle, Rainer understood that Dan was desperate to work on something even if it wasn't Wretchkinsides.

"Great, but I'm pretty sure she never wants to be called Ms. Parker ever again."

He grimaced. "Right, I forgot."

Rainer wondered what exactly had been on his mind when he'd sat in the Haydenshires' living room and watched Logan and Adeline get married the day before.

Patrick and Lucy appeared just then, and Dan turned back to Rainer. "Do you think she would mind me calling her Adeline?

There's too many Mrs. Haydenshires now." He chuckled as he gestured from Emily's mother, to Brooke, and then to Lucy.

"Adeline is fine, I'm sure."

With that, Dan began going over all of the research he'd done. He produced the blueprints of the Premier's massive castle home and the names of his servants.

Rainer shook his head. "You know you're supposed to be relaxing."

"Yeah," he huffed, "I don't relax. I don't think it's in me, but I'm trying." He turned to glance back at Governor and Mrs. Haydenshire, who were seated two rows behind him, each holding one of the twins. The governor nodded to Vindico who returned the gesture.

"This isn't what I'm not supposed to be working on," he justified.

Just two minutes before the challenge course was revealed, Logan and Adeline rushed into the box. They were being followed by dozens of reporters.

"Nice of you to join us," Rainer chided.

With a wry grin, Logan nodded. "I was busy." He waggled his eyebrows and effectively cracked Rainer up.

The press was frantically buzzing outside the doors to the box seats, and security was having trouble keeping them at bay.

"They got a shot of her ring when I parked. Now, they're like vultures."

"I forgot to cover my hand," Adeline lamented.

Logan shook his head. "You're not supposed to cover it up. I want everyone to know you're mine. I just don't want them bombarding you everywhere we go." The buzzers sounded, and the course was revealed. "These are always tough. It could be anybody's challenge."

Dan and Rainer nodded their agreement.

It was a Tesslometer course. Four supersized, semiconductor diodes were positioned on each side of the field in a square.

Along the sides of the course were different forms of energy that could be harnessed and pushed into the diodes. Screens on the opposing walls of the arena would show when the teams had the correct form of energy in play and then in the correct diode. A team could burn up a great deal of time figuring out the pattern of energy to make each diode convert to electricity.

Either Emily or Fionna would have to force the electricity to travel along the square course and free their iode. Each Receiver would also only be allowed to convert the energy once in a turn. If the conversion was incorrect, they would have to return to the energy provided for them on the sides of the field.

Rainer studied the energy sources—a windmill, fire, and a combustion engine, but the mechanical heat energy from that wouldn't convert to electric energy without either Emily or Fionna's assistance. There was a generator, a microphone, speaker system, and a large piezoelectric disk that would have to be forced to change shape in order for it to remit voltage.

"Should be a good challenge." Vindico looked genuinely interested in what was to come.

With another sound of the buzzer, the announcer welcomed the Providence Phenoms to Angels Arena. A relatively small group of fans on the other side of the field, dressed in green and gold, went wild.

After the Phenom players were introduced, the announcer drawled loudly as a drum roll boomed, "Arlington, Virginia, is proud to announce its very own sweethearts of Summation, the Arlington Angels!" The Angels box lit up. It shook as everyone stood. They whistled and applauded loudly.

The announcer elaborated on the Angels' mission trip to Brazil, and what they'd done while they were abroad. Then he gave a quick bio as each of the players' names was called.

Rainer let out his customary wolf whistle when Emily ran onto the field. The announcer gave Emily's stats for the season and then asked over the microphone, "Now, Miss Haydenshire, are we to understand that this will be your last conference game with the name Haydenshire on your jersey?"

Emily beamed and nodded.

"That's right, folks, our new Crown Governor has relented and is going to allow Rainer Lawson to marry one of our favorite Receivers," he stirred the crowd who was cheering raucously.

Rainer laughed and blew Emily a kiss.

"And finally, please welcome the most beautiful captain in Summation, our Angels' captain returning for her eighth season, Miss

Chloe Sawyer!" The crowd bellowed again as Chloe waved to her fans.

The announcer welcomed Governor Vindico and Governor Sapman, and then the crowd cheered for Governor Haydenshire, who stood and let Keaton wave to the crowds.

After everyone returned to their seats, the buzzer sounded and the challenge began.

"They should start with the generator. That's easy," Logan urged.

Dan shook his head. "It won't be the generator. That's *too* easy."

Rainer was surprised to see his boss really getting into the challenge. He was even smiling.

Chloe moved in first and pulled the heat from the fire. She lost only a small amount as she moved it from the side of the field to the diode in play. Everyone turned to see the screen.

0 and 1 displayed.

Heat from the fire was one of the sources, but it didn't belong in the first diode. While using straightforward logic, Chloe ran back to the side of the field and sent Sasha in to move the heat to the next diode.

1-1 read the screen, and the Angels' fans cheered. It was in the right spot. The Phenoms were trying a completely different tactic. They used four players at once. They each put a different form of energy into the diodes.

The Phenoms' screen read 1-2 instantly. They had one in the correct location and two of the correct forms of energy. By cycling their players four at a time, their Duco predilect guided the sequencing carefully, and they were ahead.

Chloe sent Katie onto the field. She pulled from the generator, but the screen remained at 1-1. Vindico was right. The generated electricity wasn't going to be used.

Quickly making the same assumption, Chloe sent Dana onto the field to force the piezoelectric disk to contort and produce voltage.

It took Dana quite a while, and the Phenoms' board read 2-3.

Rainer's jaw clenched. He still hadn't fully forgiven Dana for harassing Emily about only ever being with him. Dana pulled the voltage and forced it into the first diode. The board lit at 1-2. The crowd cheered Dana on, and Sasha took the field. She moved the voltage to the third diode. 2-2 flashed, and Rainer joined in the applause.

Emily entered the field, and Rainer whistled again. She summoned and forced the engine to fire. Her joule meter dropped a bar. She gathered the heat energy and converted it to electricity. She worked it quickly to the first diode. 2-3 flashed onto the board.

With a delighted grin, Emily moved off the field, and Chloe returned. She transferred the energy from the first diode to the last and turned to watch the board light up 3-3. Rainer jerked his head back to the Phenoms.

He panicked when he saw that the Phenoms' board read 3-3 as well, and their lead Receiver was already turning the windmill and moving the energy to the last iode.

Fionna was sent on to pull the sound energy from the microphone and convert it to electricity. She threw the energy into the remaining iode, but the board still read 3-3. Fionna looked devastated as she ran off the field.

"The battery, the battery!" Logan yelled.

Carys entered the field and pulled the energy from the battery. She transferred it quickly to the last diode. Both boards lit 4-4 at the same moment.

Fionna raced back onto the field, harnessed the electricity from the first diode, and created an arc to the second as the Phenoms' Receiver did the same.

Everyone in the stadium was on their feet screaming. Fionna moved the next arc to the third diode, but the Phenoms' Receiver had more energy, because they hadn't used him to convert the sound energy from the microphone. With a fervent push, he lit the fourth diode a split second before Fionna completed the last arc. The Phenoms' iode released.

Fionna's head dropped in defeat. Tears formed in her eyes, and with a quick glance to his left, Rainer noted that Vindico looked extremely concerned.

The Angels crowded around Fionna with exuberant hugs.

"She really is an amazing Receiver," Dan commented. He was still staring at Fionna who was being hugged rather vigorously by Chloe.

"She is, and she's also an amazing woman." Rainer wasn't certain if Dan would catch on, but he couldn't think of one of Emily's friends who he liked or respected more than Fionna.

Rainer and Garrett waited outside the locker rooms for the Angels to be released.

"You know they're all in there crying." Garrett rolled his eyes.

"They did lose." Rainer thought Garrett was being rather callous.

"Yeah, but it was still a winning season. There's always next year."

As the arena emptied, Emily, Fionna, and Chloe exited the locker room together.

Emily and Fionna had indeed been crying. They were Receivers, after all. They'd had to feel everyone's devastation, not just their own.

Rainer pulled Emily to him. "Are you okay?"

She nodded and forced a steadying breath.

"Okay, no more tears. We have to go home, look fab, come back, and party," Chloe commanded.

"So, the leather skirt with what top?" Emily quizzed.

Fionna considered as Rainer attempted to guide Emily out of the arena.

"I'm thinking that flowy, white silk top that cuts down low and shows off my girls," Fionna strategized.

Emily nodded excitedly. "Yeah, and your black, crisscross strap Louboutins."

"Oh, that's perfect." Fionna grinned. Her tears were drying quickly.

Garrett shook his head. He seemed to be considering something. "All right, fine. If you're hell-bent on doing this, then I'll help you. But I'm agreeing to this only if you promise me that you understand he's going to break your heart. But I know Dan Vindico better than just about anyone. I know what he likes."

Fionna looked like Garrett had just named her Queen of the Realm.

"Really?" she buzzed. "Oh my gosh, Garrett, you are the best!" She threw her arms around Garrett's neck while jumping up and down.

Laughing at her outright, Garrett shook his head. "He's gonna break your heart," he warned again.

"I don't think so. Something is changing. I can feel it even here."

No one seemed to have any idea how to explain her cryptic statement, but Rainer sincerely hoped she was correct.

"Will you really help me?" Fionna gestured to her shapely figure. She seemed to have lost some of her confidence in the space of a few seconds.

"Fi," Garrett scoffed, "do you ever look in a mirror? You're gorgeous, and he knows it. Believe me. I'd say now is probably the perfect time. You've waited long enough. So, come on. I'll tell you how to work this, but if he's with you tonight and then leaves tomorrow morning, don't say I didn't warn you."

"Okay, you warned me. Just please," Fionna begged. "You don't know what I know."

"I'll be over at your house tomorrow morning to let you lie in my lap and cry all day. Then you're going to wish you'd listened." Garrett appeared to be rethinking his offer.

"Garrett, please, please, please!"

"Fine," he agreed as he held the driver's side door of Fionna's bright-yellow MR2 open for her and then moved to the passenger side.

"Good luck!" Chloe waved to them as she unlocked her Corvette.

"My Porsche!" Rainer swooned and pretended to hug his car. Emily laughed. He'd driven the Accord to the challenge for Logan to take home after he returned Rainer's Boxster.

As they drove, Emily sighed dejectedly.

"What's wrong, baby?"

"I just wish Fi wouldn't do this to herself. She's hell-bent on Dan going home with her tonight, and she's going to be a mess when he either turns her down again or takes her up on her offer, then walks out when he's finished with her."

Rainer tried to think of some other outcome for Fionna's plans but didn't really see any other options.

"I'm sure she thinks she can get him out of her system." Emily rolled her eyes. "Sleeping with him is only going to make it so much worse."

"Maybe he'll be really bad in bed."

Emily chuckled. "I somehow doubt that."

"What about Bridgette?"

"Chloe told me that Garrett said that's between Bridgette and Vindico, and this is between Fionna and Vindico, whatever that means. Garrett also said he thinks he broke it off with her after he signed her release papers. He offered to get her a job at a different club apparently."

"How does Fionna plan on getting him to her house?" Rainer wasn't really certain how people did the whole meet a person at a bar and end up in their bed thing. It was certainly not something he'd ever done or ever wanted to do.

Emily gave him an extremely confused look. "Uh, you've seen Fionna, right?"

"Yeah, I've seen her," Rainer agreed cautiously.

Fionna Styler was an absolute knockout, but she didn't do anything for Rainer. He never wanted Emily to think that she did. She'd been propositioned to model in numerous magazines, Playboy included, but she'd never agreed. In Rainer's opinion, her humility made her even prettier. Fionna truly didn't seem to think that she was anything more than average.

"But is that her only plan, a short skirt and a low-cut top?" Rainer thought it would take more than that to get Dan Vindico to agree to sleep with a Receiver.

"No, that's why Garrett's over there now. I think he's going to tell her everything to say and do tonight to get him interested."

CHAPTER 39

THE ENTRANCE AND THE EXIT

Emily and Rainer were in their room, getting ready for the party. Emily had decided to stop worrying about Fionna, at least for the moment, after Rainer had pointed out that there wasn't anything she could do to save Fionna from herself.

They packed for Australia right up until time to leave. Emily was elated that it would be warm and sunny on the beach for their trip.

Since their flight was at nine o'clock the next morning, they'd all decided to forgo anything more than beer at the party that evening.

A little after seven, Rainer climbed into the driver's seat of the Hummer and drove everyone to Anglington's Bar. He tried desperately not to think of everything that had happened at the Angels' season-opening party.

The party was picking up pace when Emily flashed the badges to get Rainer, Logan, and Adeline in. Thrumming music blared from the band as they sang the rather dirty lyrics to the song.

Chloe, Sasha, and Dana were passing around trays of food, and the alcohol was free-flowing.

"Where's Fionna?" Emily had to scream for Chloe to hear her.

"Garrett's bringing her in a little while."

Emily shot Rainer a concerned glance. Apparently, Fionna wanted to make an entrance.

Vindico arrived fifteen minutes later. He sank down at the table between Rainer and Logan.

"I am too damn old to be at an Angels' after-party." He waved a waitress over and rather rudely asked if they had any Scotch that wouldn't be embarrassing to drink.

"Come on, man. Garrett will be here in a few minutes. You're not old yet," Logan scoffed.

Vindico took a sip of the Scotch he'd been provided. He looked pleased as he set it on the napkin in front of him.

"Listen, I don't want to intrude on your honeymoon or your and Emily's week in Australia. You don't have to hang out with me while we're there. Just do whatever you want, and I'll meet you at the palace." Vindico looked like he was truly concerned about going with them to Australia.

"Nope." Logan shook his head. "First of all, we like hanging out with you. Second, you promised us a few stories, and third, the girls are gonna want to go do stuff that girls do and then the three of us can hang out."

Rainer smiled. Logan Haydenshire was incapable of making someone feel unwanted. He couldn't stand the popular scene and crowds the entire time they'd been in school together. It was why he and Rainer were friends with guys like Fergus. Truthfully, Rainer considered, it was the way he'd landed a girl like Adeline.

Vindico shrugged. He appeared genuinely touched. "Fine, but if you four want to go do some couple thing, don't worry about me."

"The only thing I'm worried about is finding Adeline's dad and convincing him to help us." Logan leaned to the side to make certain that Adeline was still in the restroom with Emily. "Adeline loves being a medic. It makes her so freaking happy. I cannot let her mother ruin that for her."

Dan and Rainer nodded their understanding and their agreement.

Another fast song started to play as Emily and Adeline made their way back to the table. Several of the Angels started dancing in a group and pulled Emily onto the dance floor with them. Emily grabbed Adeline's hand and dragged her along.

When the song neared its last verse, the door to the bar flung open, and in walked Fionna Styler hanging off Garrett's arm.

Not only did Dan sit up and take notice, but every heterosexual male in the room turned to watch her make her entrance.

She was wearing a leather miniskirt that hugged her curves perfectly and had a zipper that ran from the top of her skirt, which sat low on her hips, all the way to the bottom. With one quick move, the skirt would be on the floor. She'd added a soft, creamy silk blouse that cut down low to show off the matching set of curves on top. Her hair was fixed in loose waves that draped down her back.

As Vindico was staring at her, thoroughly enamored, Logan chuckled and whispered in Rainer's ear, "Uh, I am an extremely happily married man, but he might as well grab his jacket and get in her car, because he's going down tonight."

Rainer laughed. "Yeah, and I'm pretty sure she'll let him."

"Fi-onnnn-na!" rang out from all of the Angels on the dance floor as they cheered her name. While smiling and laughing, she let Garrett lead her to the floor.

Almost as if on cue, which Rainer was fairly certain Chloe had something to do with, an extremely lurid rap song blared from the speakers. It encouraged the girls to shake it all. The Angels spread out and began performing the dance.

Adeline returned to the table, and Logan pulled her onto his lap. Rainer watched Vindico's eyes. They were glued to Fionna as she shook it for him. She showed off several rather sexy moves.

Unfortunately, it wasn't only Dan who noticed Fionna's dancing. After the song was over, she followed Chloe toward the bar and was approached by several men.

She laughed and flirted and appeared to order a drink which several of them offered to pay for. One guy, who'd already had a little too much, moved in.

Fionna's face went from smiling to deep concern in a second flat. She looked frightened, and she took a step back from the man. He advanced.

Fionna shook her head and glanced around nervously. Garrett was attempting to get to her through the crowds of people who were dancing and talking, but he was having a difficult time.

Fionna fended the guy off again, and then Rainer watched in horror as the guy dragged his finger along the low-cut line of Fionna's blouse.

"Stop it!" she demanded loudly. "Don't touch me."

Rainer and Logan stood immediately, but Dan was already on his feet and standing beside her in three long strides. He narrowed his eyes.

"You got a problem, kid? I'm certain I could help you work that out." His massive biceps bulged, and his shield flared.

The guy held up his hands, shook his head, and backed away after he took in Vindico's infuriated scowl.

"Sorry, I didn't know she was with anybody," he stammered.

"Well, she is, and I happen to have a real problem with assholes who think they can touch whatever they damn well please." Vindico bared his teeth as the guy's eyes goggled. "Get the fuck out of my face."

The guy managed a nod as he walked backward from Vindico, afraid to turn his back on him. He not only got out of Dan's face he left the bar.

"Thank you," Rainer heard Fionna offer. She looked thoroughly embarrassed. The bartender set the wine she'd ordered on the bar, and Vindico very smoothly pulled his wallet from his back pocket and paid for the drink.

"Well, that worked faster than I'd planned." Garrett chuckled as he took the seat Dan had been occupying.

"Did you tell that guy to hit on her?" Emily was furious.

"Hell no," Garrett scoffed, "but it appears to have worked." He gestured back to Dan and Fionna.

"Since I'm afraid I might've just scared off every guy in the bar, would you like to grab a table?" A definite hunger formed in Vindico's eyes.

Fionna played it well. She didn't look quite as elated as Rainer assumed she must've been. Dan pulled a chair out for her at a table for two that was situated in a dark corner in the very back of the bar.

"Garrett, he's going to break her heart," Emily fussed.

270

"She's been sick over him since the academy. She's determined to do this. There's no stopping her. She's well aware of his reputation."

"But he's never going to love anyone but Amelia," Emily whispered.

Garrett drew a deep breath and glanced around the bar. He leaned in toward Emily's ear. It appeared he only wanted Emily to hear him, but Rainer couldn't help but overhear.

"You know what I told you to do after the wreck?" Emily nodded. "I told her how to do the same thing. She's significantly more powerful than you. You never know. He may fall head over heels," Garrett stated hopefully. "You're wrong about him never loving anyone else. He's capable. He just doesn't think he deserves that."

Rainer started to ask, but then realized that Garrett had given Emily instructions on how to take all of the terrifying energy of him killing his uncle away from him while he was inside her.

Only a powerful Receiver could have performed such a hefty task. She'd absorbed his horror and fear. She'd drained his shield of shame, hatred, and terrorizing panic. She'd given him back love and peace as she'd tended to Rainer during those horrifying hours. She'd given him back his life.

A little while later, Emily pulled Rainer onto the dance floor after whispering in his ear that if he'd dance with her as much as she wanted, he could have his way with her when they got home.

Rainer had chuckled and stood immediately. "I would've danced with you anyway, but I'll take what I can get."

As they danced, Rainer slid his hands down Emily's sides as she ground against him. "You know, we could go home, and I could do this to you without all of these clothes in my way."

Emily shook her head with a delighted grin. "You have to earn it, Mr. Lawson."

A slower song with sultry island undertones began, and Rainer wrapped Emily up in his arms.

Fionna and Dan had been tucked in the corner of the bar for almost two hours talking without end. They both seemed completely entranced by the other according to Emily who'd been spying on them and reporting back to Rainer and Garrett.

As the song began, Fionna stood and gave Vindico a look that could've set the entire bar ablaze as she led him to the dance floor and proceeded to lace her arms around his neck.

By the second verse, they'd melted together. She was cradled in his arms with her head on his shoulder facing his neck.

One of his hands was still on her back. The other had slipped to her backside, and he didn't seem willing to move it anytime soon.

Dan was whispering softly in her ear, and Fionna looked like she'd died and gone to heaven.

"How hard do you think he'd hit me if I cut in?" Garrett teased as he danced Chloe next to Emily and Rainer.

"Are you proud of yourself?" Emily looked devastated.

"Come on, Em," Garrett urged, "you're a Receiver. When you think about them, what do you feel?" Rainer could feel Emily concentrate as he swayed her. Her energy spun as she considered.

A minute later, she looked shocked. "Maybe you're right. Maybe it will work."

"He'll call her when you get back from Sydney. I'd bet my badge on it." Garrett gestured back toward Dan and Fionna.

Vindico had her face cradled tenderly in his hand and was priming her lips with his own. The hand he'd positioned on her ass massaged and groped her as he guided her hips in rhythm around what Rainer assumed, from the low moan he heard Fionna gasp, must have been his pronounced erection. She clearly liked what she felt.

In a deft move that appeared well-rehearsed, Vindico slipped his hand from her face, over her delicate neck, and down her rib cage. It was apparent to the entire bar that she trembled in his arms as his thumb caressed the side of her breast. He traced her lips with his tongue, and she opened her mouth as he devoured her.

"Well, okay, then." Emily turned away from the display.

The song ended, and Dan leaned and whispered in her ear what was almost certainly a request to take the show somewhere more private. She gave him a sultry nod.

With a quick turn, he led her out of the bar.

Rainer braced. He wasn't certain how Emily was going to take it when he heard the Agusta roar to life and saw the taillights of

Fionna's MR2 as she sped away from the bar with Vindico following closely behind.

Emily was on the verge of tears, still terrified that he was going to leave Fionna a heartbroken disaster.

"You wanna go on home, sweetheart?"

"Yeah, I guess so. We need to finish packing anyway," Emily commented without any real emotion to her words. She continued to stare out the door where Fionna and Dan had just exited.

CHAPTER 40

NO OUTLET
DAN VINDICO

The thrumming roar of the powerful machine between his legs only slightly drowned out the savage war in his head.

She's a Receiver, you idiot, pulsed through his mind again for what felt like the hundredth time. He fought the thoughts valiantly. With ardent force he insisted to himself, *I'm the Chief of Elite Iodex. I'm the fucking most powerful Shield there's ever been or ever will be. I can suppress anything I don't want her to feel. I just want to feel her.* His libido won out easily. He wanted to unzip that skirt. He wanted to touch her, to taste her, and bury himself inside her.

She wasn't only stunningly beautiful. He reminded himself of just a few of the conversations they'd had over the past several hours. She was smart, and kind, and sweet, and vastly different from any of the dozens of women he'd been with over the past decade. *I won't ever fall in love again,* he vowed to himself. He wouldn't allow it, so he pushed that fear aside as well.

No reason we can't hang out and give each other something we both clearly want for a little while, the head below his belt argued vehemently.

You're leaving for Sydney in just a few hours. His mind, that he was finding to be extremely annoying at that moment, continued its plaguing reminders. He followed her taillights into the dark night as the highway turned into a two-lane road in Alexandria.

If this is half as good as I know it's gonna be, I'll call her when I get back. Hooking up with Fionna Styler for a few months, whenever one of us needs a little bit of sweet release we could so easily provide one another, sounds perfectly reasonable.

He followed her down a street marked no outlet, and she pulled into the driveway of what appeared to be a recently renovated bungalow.

He shut down his motorcycle and made it to the door of her car to open it for her before she could extricate herself.

She looked momentarily startled that he was standing at her car and opening the door for her. He offered his hand and pulled her from the car. Her rhythms pulsed with nervous energy. She stared at the ground and bit her lip hesitantly as she fumbled with her keys and purse.

With a clench of his jaw, he forced himself to be a gentleman, but what he desperately wanted at that moment was to spin her around, lean her over her car, and take her hard from behind like a savage.

Dan swallowed the desire as he forced himself to make his offer.

"Hey, uh, I can go, or we can just have a drink. We don't have to do anything you're uncomfortable with." His hands moved of their own accord. He brushed her cheek tenderly as he cradled her beautiful face in his hands. He raised her head so he could gaze into the most beautiful sienna eyes he'd ever seen.

She stared up at him for a long moment. It was almost as if she could see into his soul.

"I'm not uncomfortable, and I don't want you to go."

He watched her hot breath form sensuous spirals in the cold night air. She shivered slightly as she forced herself to move her eyes away from his. She headed toward the front porch.

He slid out of his leather jacket and hooked it over her shoulders as she walked. A sexy, half-grin splayed across her lush lips as she unlocked the door.

An odd sensation moved through Dan as he stepped into her house. It was warm, soothing, and welcoming. Something stirred inside of him. Though he couldn't recall the exact emotion, he'd felt it before somewhere in the very distant past.

The furniture was a mix of antiques and newer pieces with sleek modern touches. There were quilts folded on the sofa, and everything about the home eased him. Soothing muted neutrals were accented with tropical pops of color in the living room.

"I bought it a couple of years ago." She hesitantly gestured around her house while she hung up his coat. "I've been slowly remodeling it. I'm not quite finished, but I've learned a lot."

Dan watched her every move. She appeared pleased with her work. She'd left the original, wide-planked hardwood floors, with rubbed, battered markings in several places in the cozy living room. It seemed to fit her. She could see the beauty in the imperfect. She sensed the stories behind the blemishes.

"So…uh…do you want something to drink?" she offered nervously. It seemed she just remembered that she should ask. He couldn't take his eyes off her gorgeous curves on luscious display in that leather skirt.

"There are a whole lot of things I want, Fionna." His voice was low and reverent in his need. He watched her abdomen clench tightly from his admission. "But, honey, before I let you make me a drink or we take this any further, I need you to know I'm not looking for anything serious. I'm the guy your parents always warned you about, and I don't want to hurt you. So, if you want me to go, I'll understand." He forced the words from his mouth.

He'd made that same speech to dozens of women. This was the first time he'd ever had to force himself to say them, and somewhere in the recesses of his mind he knew that this time, he didn't really mean them.

She gave him a sultry chuckle. Her eyes were dark and hungry. They made him ache.

"I'll be fine, Dan. I'm a big girl, and I'm not looking for anything other than maybe a good time. I'm not the kind of woman who expects a ring and a commitment just because I take you up to my room."

She made his pulse race. His breaths came in rapid, voracious pants.

"The only thing I expect…" She moved until they were only centimeters apart and let her thumb slide up his length. He groaned. "…is for you to make me feel good and make sure I'm taken care of before I do the same for you." Her wishes were penned in the breathy air between them.

"Oh, baby doll, trust me. You'll be taken care of. I'm about to carry you up those stairs and make you feel better than you've ever felt before."

She shot him a look that said for him to come and take what he wanted. He wrapped his arms around her and devoured her mouth again.

She pulled away just as he dipped his tongue into her mouth. He could feel her energy when he kissed her, and it startled him momentarily. It was somehow intoxicating and soothing all at the same moment. He wanted more. It spun in heated arcs all around him. He wanted to drown himself in it, and that scared him to death. But my god, he needed more.

"I always figured if I let Dan Vindico take me to bed, he'd promise to make me see God," she drawled in heated challenge.

With a deliberate chuckle, he leaned and lifted her into his arms. "Trust me, honey, tonight I'll be your god."

Her body tensed deliciously against his.

"It's the room at the end of the hall." She tucked herself into his embrace and let him cradle her tenderly as he began climbing her stairs.

CHAPTER 41

THE SHIELD AND THE RECEIVER

He kicked her bedroom door shut with his boot. His mind and his pulse raced in ardent need. He wanted to feel it again, feel what he felt when he'd kissed her on the dance floor and in her living room.

The desire conquered the fear with one quick glance at her luscious ass caught up in a tight skirt.

The first time he slept with someone new, *often the only time*, his mind chanted, was never as good as when he'd learned how she liked it and could show the woman he was with exactly how he wanted it.

If kissing her was any indication, her bed was likely to catch fire once he laid her out and showed her a good time.

He stood her up in front of the wall nearest her door. Dan took a split second to take in their new surroundings. The room was entirely her. Photos of places she'd traveled—he assumed, as several of them appeared to be on stunning beaches—were placed around the room and situated among an antique vanity that held a tray of perfumes and jewelry.

An old dress form stood in one corner where she'd stowed numerous scarves and long necklaces.

Her bed was queen-sized, with a cushioned headboard and a

purple, pin-tucked covering. It even held the scent of her, vanilla musk and coconut, mixed with her perfume and shampoo.

Dan inhaled deeply as he gazed into her eyes.

"I'm gonna take your clothes off, baby doll, and then I'm gonna run my hands all over that gorgeous body." His promise made a low moan escape her lungs. The sound set him on fire.

Amelia had finally given in to his begging when they were seventeen. She wasn't Gifted, so he'd never been too concerned about the energy transfer or the commitment level that happened when two Gifted people had sex.

She'd died when he was twenty-two, and he'd drowned his sorrows in plenty of women. He certainly wasn't a novice in bed, and he planned on showing Fionna just what he could do.

He kept his kisses deep and drawing. He traced his hands down to the first button on the extremely low-cut blouse. He had no trouble working her out of the shirt, and with every button he loosened, she came undone.

"You are so fucking beautiful," he groaned and felt himself throb tight as he watched her breasts spill out of the bra he'd removed in a second flat.

Her deep olive complexion glowed enticingly as her body swayed between his and the wall.

He traced his hands up the sides of her waist and drew patterns with his thumbs over her nipples. He watched them tighten and pucker as he slowly ripened her for him.

Her back arched. He knew what she wanted, but he was going to make her beg, drive her wild, until she wanted nothing as much as she wanted him to set her free.

He left her breasts aching and tender. They needed to be sucked and tended to thoroughly, which he planned to do when he was good and ready.

He dropped to his knees, and her breath caught. He traced his index finger just along the perfect line of skin above the waistline of the skirt she was wearing. He could see the very edge of a tattoo from his vantage point, and he was instantly intrigued.

"Let's just see how naughty you can be, sweetheart," he urged as her eyes flashed intently. He slowly edged the zipper that ran the entire length of the leather miniskirt down.

A low, luscious groan spilled from his mouth as he took in Fionna Styler wearing nothing but a pair of lacy, black G-string panties and stiletto heels.

He'd never seen anything so tempting in all his life. Lurid thoughts of what he planned to do to her seared through his mind.

His muscles throbbed in anticipation as he stared at her recently waxed lips, swollen and aching behind the scrap of black lace. In his vast experience, he'd always found that you could tell a great deal about how a woman liked it by the undergarments she wore. A black lace G-string meant she wasn't afraid to be adventurous, and that she also wasn't afraid to tell him what she wanted and how she wanted it.

"I like it dirty too, baby doll, and I'm about to show you what that gorgeous body was really made for."

A moan quaked from her. The sound took up residence in his groin.

With that, he spread her legs slightly with his hands. "Lean back against the wall, honey. I'm hungry. Let me taste how sweet you are."

She did as she was told. He let his tongue swirl over the fabric between her legs. He occasionally pulled away and huffed hot air over her swollen lips. They were dripping with need. He caught a tiny taste of the essence of her energy as he licked. It was even more intoxicating here than in her saliva, and he became frantic for more as he dragged his tongue over the lace.

He rapidly lost all traces of rational thought trying to warn him off as he pulled the scrap of fabric to the side and dipped his tongue inside her. He moaned in starvation. The sensation made her writhe. She tasted like heaven.

"Oh yes," panted from her as he slipped one finger deep inside her and traced until he found the spot that made her breath catch. He kept his finger coaxing her as he licked her again.

She laced her fingers through his hair and pushed his tongue deeper. It made him ache to take her hard and fast.

She was tight. It had been a while. *Good, she's mine,* he thought vengefully. He had no time to consider his own thoughts and desires. She came a second later, and her energy flooded his mouth.

He'd never felt anything like it before. He felt whole. He felt alive. He felt complete. He wanted more. It was indescribable. The permanent pain that existed in his shield slipped away. He'd never felt anything so astoundingly freeing or exhilarating.

"Take me to bed," she demanded in a heated pant as he kissed back up her abdomen and lowered her panties all at the same moment.

She had a beautiful tattoo of pink and violet flowers on a vine that curved delicately from her hipbone to the very heart of her. It was certainly not something many people would get to see. It was almost always obscured by her panties.

It was a tattoo she'd gotten for herself, one that meant something only to her. There was a story there, and Dan wanted desperately to hear it, but not just then.

He dragged his fingertips along the vining of the flowers. He wanted to touch her in the places that she'd marked. He wanted to feel the energy behind the tattoos and the pain they represented.

"I'm gonna take you to bed, baby doll, but I'm not finished yet." He stood fully and turned her around so she was facing the wall. He stared unabashedly at her ass. It was even more lush and gorgeous naked than it was in the tight jeans and skirts she liked to wear.

His desire grew with each hammered beat of his heart. He could see the Angels logo tattoo at the top of her ass as he ran his hands tenderly from her shoulder blades in slow scrolling patterns over her flesh all the way to her backside.

He let the tips of his fingers move over the most stunning ass he'd ever laid eyes on. In a quick, hunger-driven move, he pulled off his pants and boxers and leaned into her back. He caged her between the wall and his body and let her feel his stiff, swollen length nestle between those lush cheeks.

She gasped and shook her backside for him. It brushed his strain and drove him wild. Everything she did threatened to end him. He felt like he'd somehow taken her before. She knew exactly what to say and how to move her beautiful body against his like she could read his mind.

"You feel that, baby doll?" he growled in her ear as he grasped her breasts in his hands. He groped and massaged. Her nipples rose into stiff beads between his fingers. "You make me so damn hard."

With another moan, she continued to let her backside glide against his erection. His need leaked across her back in a hungry claim of ownership. He'd never in all his life seen anything sexier.

He slipped his hands from her breasts, down her waist, and then he traced his thumbs over her mound as his fingers circled her lips. He pulled her apart and allowed the air to caress and agitate the nerve endings he had on high alert.

"You're so wet for me, baby doll," he growled. "I need you dripping like a good girl before I lay you out and let you really feel it deep inside. You're gonna drown my cock in that sweet, sweet pussy."

With a quick move, he slipped two fingers inside of her, and he had it again. Her delicious, soothing energy seared through his body. He'd never get enough. It was incredible, like a drug that washed away all the pain that was engrained in his soul.

"I'm gonna make it feel so good," he promised, and she called out his name as he forced himself to keep going, relying on his signature moves, while he reveled in what he was drawing from her.

He was unable to help himself. He took with greed, and she gave with ample generosity.

She trembled against him. Her muscles clenched tight around his fingers. Though he'd just informed her how good he was going to make her feel once he took her, he knew she was going to feel astounding when he pushed his length deep inside of her.

"I want it. Give it to me," she demanded, and he very nearly lost it all, a problem he hadn't had since he was a teenager. "I want all of you."

"Mmm, you are greedy, aren't you, baby doll?" he challenged. "It's okay. I'm awfully greedy myself. And I'm about to take everything I want. I can feel it. I know what you need, and I'm gonna give it to you. Just relax. Let it build for me. My good girl's needed it for a while, haven't you? So damn tight. I'm gonna open you wide," he groaned in her ear while watching her backside sway as he pushed his fingers deeper into the silken heat between her legs. "I'll fucking ruin you."

A needy moan was her answer, letting him know that he'd been correct in his assumption.

"It's all right, baby doll." He felt her tremble and pant as her temperature rose.

He was shocked once again as he felt her energy spiral in twisted arcs. He'd never slept with a Gifted woman, and once he understood what he was seeing, he knew exactly how to give her what she wanted. Her arc peaked highest when he talked, so he continued his dirty commentaries.

He pounded into her with his fingers. "Swollen so nice and tight just how I want you to be when I fill you full of me," he said forcefully, and he had her.

He could see it. Her orgasm rose in waves from her body. She came undone. Her energy unfurled around him as stunning shock washed over him.

Her energy surrounded him. It permeated his body and his soul, and he'd never felt anything so incredible.

For a moment, he didn't know what to do. He backed away from her. His heart raced, but it was too good, too intoxicating. He had to have more. She spun around and unbuttoned his shirt.

He watched as her eyes traced over his chiseled chest and the six-pack he'd worked so hard to define.

"Mmm, you're so big," her pleasure gasped from her in genuine shock as her eyes landed on his throbbing erection.

Before he could quite hide his cocky grin, she dropped to her knees and spun her tongue up his length.

A low, shuddering growl echoed from deep within him. She lightly traced circles over his sac with her fingers as she drowned him deep in her mouth.

He clenched his entire body to keep from exploding in her mouth. He laced his fingers in her hair and wrapped it around his fist, desperate for her to take more.

As she engulfed him, she cupped his sac and made him feel incredible. She began doing something he'd never felt before.

He didn't know who'd taught her to give a blowjob, but she sure as hell knew what she was doing. His head fell back, and he let her bathe him with her tongue.

There it was again, the intoxicating sensation. He tried to focus, but it just felt too damn good. She was drawing and pulling something from him. He brushed his hand over her face to stop her, lest he lose it all before he'd even begun.

When she slipped her mouth away, he understood she'd been taking his energy, but he didn't feel drained in any way. He felt more incredible than he'd ever felt in his entire life, and he wanted to feel more.

"Fionna, I need to be inside of you, honey, right fucking now. I can't wait anymore. I want to make you feel me." He lifted her into his arms again and laid her out on her bed. He left her lying there for a split second, while he grabbed his pants and pulled a condom out of his wallet.

With a sultry smirk, Fionna shook her head. "You don't need that, Dan. I already did the cast before I left tonight." A sudden and deep sadness etched her beautiful face. "I mean, unless you don't believe me." She moved her eyes away from his.

He could feel the sudden absence. It was painful. His shield shook and begged for her energy to return. The absence was horrifying. He needed her warmth. He needed her trust. He needed her.

"Right," Dan stammered. "I believe you." He forced his head back into the game. He'd promised her the best sex she'd ever had, and her thinking that he doubted her wasn't going to get her where he wanted her to be.

He joined her on the bed, and she reached and traced her fingertips up his cock. He shuddered and pulsed hot and heavy in her hand. His body continued to plead for hers.

"You ready to feel it, baby? You ready for me, my sweet, greedy girl?"

She gave a heavy nod. A desperate whimper shook from her lungs. Her body rolled in yearning hunger.

"Please," she begged. "I need it, please."

"I know what you need, baby doll. I know right where that needy little ache is, and I'll make it feel better. Spread your legs, and let me give it to you. Let's see just how greedy you can be. You're gonna take it all for me," he commanded as he moved over her and separated her lips with his hands.

He lowered his body until he was hovering over her. He kept all of his weight braced against the mattress, so all she could feel was his length pressing against her mound.

He began sliding his cock against her clit. He listened to her intoxicating moans echoing around him. Her arousal rose in her heat. He inhaled it as if his life depended on him breathing the flavors of her.

As she began to writhe in desperation, he dropped low and thrust hard into her. She gasped. Her eyes flashed wildly as she took him in.

He halted abruptly. He didn't know what to do. He felt like an inexperienced, uneducated virgin. Her body tugged him deeper. It shook him from his reverie, and he began to thrust rhythmically. It was unlike anything he'd ever felt. He couldn't even describe the all-encompassing, overwhelming feeling of her drawing the pain, the terror, the harrowing fear, and the hatred out of his body like a baptismal fount that washed away everything that had ever hurt him.

She took it all and, somehow, replaced it with her warmth, and her caring, and her sweet being. The essence of her, a drug he knew he could no longer live without, filled him.

"Give it to me, Dan," she began urging him on. "Fill me up."

It wasn't his release she was after. He could feel what she wanted. She was begging to take everything that had ever hurt him and everything that had ever terrified him. She was willing to take it all away.

He was woefully unable to stop her from draining him of the excruciating grief that choked out everything good in his life.

Then, as if that weren't enough, she refilled him with feelings and emotions he couldn't even describe, but he knew he hadn't felt so alive in over a decade. Their rhythms fused in one arc from where they were joined. They pulsed in heavenly rhythms of perfection.

His heart thundered in his chest. His release tightened in his groin. Blood rushed through his body. The parts of him that had been choked and tainted, the parts of him he'd thought were long dead and gone came roaring back to life as he pumped her full of him.

Her body flushed, and her back arched deeply as he lowered his head to suck her breasts. He was desperate to pull more of the delicious life force she offered him. Her body nursed his rhythmically.

He sucked hard as she called out his name. The heavenly trembles of her intense climax drew his orgasm from him. He couldn't fight it. Her body seemed to control his own. He felt their releases and their rhythms mix in heady ecstasy from which he would never recover.

CHAPTER 42

PLANS, DISCOVERIES, AND DESIRES

With a gruff curse as he heard the alarm on his cell phone chirp, Dan raised his head. He shut the alarm down and blinked several times.

He was still just as unable to believe where he was as he'd been the night before when he'd asked Fionna Styler if she'd mind if he stayed over. He'd never spent the entire night with anyone but Amelia, and he'd never slept so well.

He turned slightly so that he could cradle her luscious curves closer. He never wanted to leave.

She was too good. After he'd had sex with her, he just couldn't go. She'd pulled back the coverings on her bed, curled her naked body up on his chest, and he'd clung to her. He could still feel her intoxicating energy soothing and healing him even while she slept. She was astounding.

Fionna's eyes blinked open hesitantly. He stared at her. The dust of her deep sleep was settled in the corners of the most beautiful eyes he'd ever awoken to.

Her soul seemed to be right there just out of reach. He realized, in his in-depth study, she was on the verge of tears. It broke his heart. He had to fix the problem immediately. Somehow, he knew she didn't want him to leave.

Dan caressed her back and brushed a kiss on her forehead. He allowed himself one brief moment to inhale that heavenly scent of her —vanilla and coconut mixed with orange blossoms, and that sexy musk that was all her own. She smelled like his own personal island paradise.

"Honey, I have to be in Sydney for the next week, and I don't know if what I'm about to say scares the hell out of you like it does me, but..." He halted but was woefully unable to talk himself out of asking her. "I'll completely understand if this is way more than you're ready for, but if you want to come with me, I'd really, really like that.

"Governor Haydenshire is forcing me to vacation, and I'm helping Logan and Adeline out with something while we're there. He's got us booked at The Kingsford Wellborn. It should be really nice." He couldn't shut himself up. He was unable to halt the pleading words as they formed on his lips.

"I need to be at the Senate in two hours. You don't even have to pack anything. I'll buy you anything you want once we get there. Just please." He let his eyes close. He couldn't believe the words coming out of his own mouth and the terror in his soul that she wasn't going to agree. "Please just say you'll come with me."

His heart ached as he prepared himself to hear her say no, that this was moving entirely too fast and that he needed to go and maybe call her later.

She studied him for a long, drawn minute.

"Please," fell from his mouth again. He clenched his jaw and called himself an idiot.

"Emily told me you were going to find Adeline's father."

She was still studying him. Her hair was mussed. Her voice was rough from her sleep. Her eyes were clear and beautiful, and her lips still held the slight swell of his forceful kisses from the night before.

"Yeah." Dan willed her to answer him. She gave him her intoxicating grin, leaned upward, and kissed his jaw. As he tried to prepare for her to decline his request, his heart ached and stuttered out of rhythm. His shield shuddered disconcertingly.

"Are you sure you want to spend the week with me?"

Hope sprung from his soul, and his chest vibrated as his heart thundered back to life.

"If we get down there and you hate it or you hate me, I'll fly you home. You just say the word, and uh…" he choked. "We can talk more about all of this when we get there." Putting off the inevitable conversation seemed the best plan.

She giggled sweetly. "Why would I hate it? And I would never hate you." Sadness colored her features. He didn't understand.

"So…you'll go?" He was unable to believe it could be true. It was too much to hope for.

"Sure, I'll go. I would like to pack a few things." She blushed slightly. The heat moved up her neck and settled in her delicate cheeks. It made him want to lay her down and take her again. "I may take you up on the shopping though," she teased as she let her fingertips trace timid loops over his bare chest.

"Anything you want, it's yours." He reveled in the sensations she was bringing him.

"Okay," she agreed, though she was hesitant.

"Really? You'll come?"

"Yeah, it'll be fun. I hope you don't get sick of me or that I don't get on your last nerve by tonight, and you're regretting that you asked. I really think we should try this out. Last night was pretty incredible. At least, *I* thought it was." The fear and uncertainty in her voice fractured his very recently mended heart.

She'd put him back together, and he had done nothing but take more of her. She looked terrified and unsure.

"Baby." He choked slightly before forcing himself to go on. He pushed away all thoughts of Amelia and prayed that as he told the woman lying beside him in bed the truth, it wouldn't hurt her in any way. "Last night was the most incredible night of my entire life."

Her energy soared. He could feel it as long as she was beside him, and he felt his own energy begin to do the same. The sensation overwhelmed him each time he felt it again.

"Do I have time to have coffee first?" She suddenly felt lighter than air.

"I wish I could stay here and let you teach me how you like your coffee because there's so much I want to learn about you. I'd like to make your morning coffee as often as you'll let me, but I have to go home, shower, and get my stuff. Do you want me to come back and pick you up or do you want to meet me at the Senate? I just need you to know that we don't have to talk about this until the end of the week, but being with me is complicated." He squeezed his eyes closed and braced.

"I know." When he opened his eyes, he found her smiling, but he saw the fear swirl in the depths of her eyes. It was there behind the excitement.

She was worried he'd leave and change his mind. Worried the complications might be an excuse to leave her and hurt her. He'd prove her wrong. He was determined. He had no idea how he seemed able to read her thoughts but assumed it had to do with the sheer amount of energy they'd shared the night before.

He stood and pulled his jeans on. She followed him out of the bed, and he stared at her luscious body, naked and smooth.

Her hair hung in a tangled mass on her shoulders, and her mascara was smeared slightly. She hadn't left his arms long enough the night before to take off her makeup.

Hunger tensed in his rhythms. Long languid mornings, where he spent his time worshipping her body and awakening her with all of him, formed in his mind. He wanted it all. With a pang of regret, he shrugged back into his shirt.

"I'll be back as quick as I can." He pulled her body to his and kissed her sweetly. Unable to refuse the intoxication of her, he added to the intensity. He wanted to feel her again. He pushed his tongue into her mouth until a fresh dose of her energy permeated his own.

"You promise?" she asked in a pained whisper as she turned her gaze to the floor after the intense kiss. He could feel her fear in the saliva that was on his tongue. He lifted her head tenderly with his hand until he was staring into her deep sienna eyes.

"I promise."

"Okay." She seemed to have to will herself to believe what he was telling her. "Just let me run to the bathroom. Then I'll walk you out." She glanced around nervously.

"Okay baby," Dan soothed.

She smiled and then scooted into the master bathroom. She closed and locked the door behind her.

Dan called himself a prick as he moved to her bedside table. *I shouldn't,* he told himself, but his curiosity to know more about her, to know everything about her, won out over his conscience.

He wanted all of her. He wanted every secret she kept. He wanted to guard them all inside his fierce shield. He eased the top drawer open silently.

With a quick, cautious glance back toward the bathroom door, he pulled the drawer all the way open. A broad grin spread across his face as he revealed numerous phallic-shaped electronic devices, all made to hit different hot spots. They were lying among several well-worn erotic novels. There was some kind of lube in there as well, but it wasn't a manufacturer he recognized.

He quickly casted the vibrators to determine which ones had the lowest amount of battery power, and her favorites were easily revealed. He was elated with the knowledge he'd acquired. The fantasies his mind offered of her in bed, vibe in hand, made him ache to learn more.

While he sincerely hoped she wouldn't need any of those for a long time, unless she used them with him, he eased the drawer closed as he heard the commode flush.

As she walked him back to her front door, he noted the kitchen. The lights had been out the evening before, and he'd been far too captivated by her to have noticed anything in the first place.

She'd spent a fair amount of money renovating the kitchen, far more than any other room. She clearly loved to cook. The cookware that hung from the pot rack over the central island was well-worn.

He noted the copper teakettle on the eight-burner range. It looked rather old, though it was well polished. It had several dings in the side. It was something she appeared to take excellent care of, but it seemed she could use a new one.

The negotiations began in his mind again. If he could talk her into a relationship... *Don't be stupid. You'll get her killed.*

After shutting down those horrifying reminders, he made a mental note of the teapot and pulled her back to his body. He slipped his hand under the short silk robe she'd pulled on. He let himself thoroughly enjoy grabbing another handful of her ass as he kissed her and promised he'd be back in less than an hour.

He climbed onto his bike. His mind was so heavy with desperation and fear, he wasn't certain he could contain the agony.

I have one week. I can have one fucking week, can't I? Australia was one of the very few places on earth where Dominic Wretchkinsides had no interest. It was far too remote to import either drugs or guns. The Gifted ruling family had proven to be solid and above the corruption Wretchkinsides wanted to plunder. Australia wasn't worth his time and assets.

It was worlds away from Wretchkinsides, and crime, and Cascavel, and death. It was worlds away from Amelia's grave and all of the haunting memories. No one on the whole continent would know who he was or who he was with. That was all Dan wanted.

She's so damn beautiful and perfect. His mind continued its badgering reminders. *You'll never want this week to end.*

He knew that was true, but maybe by the end of the week he could either get her out of his system or come up with some way they could actually be together.

I'm so much better now than I was ten years ago. I'm the best fucking Shield that ever was or there ever will be. Back then, I was a pompous, egotistical prick. I had no clue how to keep her safe. I can keep Fionna safe. She just has to let me.

His ego rescued him once again.

Then you better show her the whole fucking world this week. If you think a woman like Fionna Styler is going to be willing to be all yours when no one can know you're together, you better be every single thing she could ever dream of having. You better pave every street she walks in gold.

His helmet shifted forward slightly as his body gave a nod of acceptance of his own plan.

~

"Dammit, Dan." Garrett grabbed his cell phone from the bedside table. He knew what was coming. He should never have agreed to help her. He'd just had a hand in hurting his best friend. "Hey baby. I'll go get you some coffee and head over. I'm at Chloe's. I won't be long."

"He asked me to go to Sydney with him." Fionna sounded as astonished as Garrett felt.

He rubbed his hands over his eyes and then down Chloe's ass. He didn't seem to be dreaming. "Are you fucking with me?"

"No! I called to thank you and to mildly freak out before I pack."

"Fi," he warned, "what are you gonna do if you get to the other side of the world and he freaks?"

"It's sweet how you worry about me, but I'm telling you the tides are changing."

Fionna said shit like that all the time. Garrett just wasn't certain what that meant exactly. "Okay, but Dan's still fucked up."

"I know, but he's ready to be saved now. He hasn't been since Amelia died."

If anyone could save Dan, it was Fionna. He just didn't want her to get killed in the process. "Just be careful for me. If he loses it out there, you call me and I'll come out."

"It's going to be okay. I promise. Thank you for everything you taught me. Thank you for everything. You're the *best* best friend in the world."

"Yeah, I just hope you're still thanking me at the end of the week."

About the Author

J.E. Neal (aka Jillian) vastly prefers coffee to tea, guac to salsa, the beach over anywhere else, and the world inside her head over the one outside her front door. She also loves not having to choose.

Driven by the question 'what if,' J.E. Neal's world began to manifest. What if there were people with powers the rest of us couldn't see? What if the energy of our world could be summoned and used at their will? Characters with these amazing abilities took shape in her mind. She created—and continues to create—an endless number of stories full of delicious escape from our reality where emotions are visible, desire is palpable, and danger is universal.

Learn more about J.E. Neal at JillianNeal.com

facebook.com/jilliannealauthor
twitter.com/JillianNeal_
instagram.com/jilliannealauthor

Also by J.E. Neal

ENERGY OF MAGIC

Shield and Shattered Cages (Book 1)

Shield and Faltered Steps (Book 2)

Shield and Splintered Oaths (Book 3)

Shield and Humbled Crown (Book 4)

Shield and Vile Serpents (Book 5)

Shield and Coveted Splendor (Book 6)

Shield and Guarded Shadow (Book 7)

Shield and Worthy Sinner (Book 8)

Shield and Sacrificial Heirs (Book 9)